DEADLY GAMES

SALLY RIGBY

TOP
DRAWER
PRESS

CRIME FICTION BOOKS

Edited by Emma Mitchell of @ Creating Perfection.

Cover Design by Stuart Bache of Books Covered

GET ANOTHER BOOK FOR FREE!

To instantly receive the free novella, **The Night Shift**, featuring Whitney when she was a Detective Sergeant, ten years ago, sign up for Sally Rigby's free author newsletter at www.sallyrigby.com

Chapter One

Dr Georgina Cavendish sat at the old oak table in her kitchen, her hands wrapped around a steaming mug of coffee, mentally preparing for the day ahead. Monday was her heaviest day, with back-to-back lectures and tutorials. If she were lucky, she'd manage to grab a sandwich in the fifteen minutes she had spare at lunchtime.

'Penny for them.' Her partner, Stephen, walked into the kitchen and headed over to the coffee machine. He poured himself a mug and leant against the worktop, smiling at her.

'Just bracing myself for today's onslaught.'

She loved lecturing, apart from having to mould the new first-year students into her way of working. They seemed to have no concept of good timekeeping, thinking they could wander into lectures or tutorials whenever they liked. Sloppiness in punctuality invariably meant sloppiness in their academic work, and that was unacceptable in forensic psychology. However, the current first years were almost house trained, making her life much easier.

'Only a few more weeks and it's the end of term. Then you can relax and look forward to Christmas in the Alps.'

She hadn't yet told her parents she wouldn't be around for their traditional family Christmas. She was waiting for the right time. Telling them she was going with Stephen might soften the blow. They thought he was wonderful. Came from the right family. Went to the right school. His parents were distantly related to Princess Diana's family from Althorp, Northamptonshire. The last time she'd spoken to her parents, her mother had hinted at how much she'd love a wedding to look forward to. Even her father had nothing bad to say about Stephen; a miracle in itself.

'True. I'm looking forward to having a rest.'

'It depends on what you mean by "rest".' His eyes glinted.

'You know what I mean,' she replied, laughing.

'I do indeed. Do you fancy going to the pub later? It'll save cooking. I have a funding meeting all afternoon with our illustrious Head of Department. I'll be wanting to murder a beer or two after.'

'Sorry, not tonight. I've too much to do.'

She had a stack of marking, as well as wanting to work on her latest research project. An Associate Professorship was coming up later in the year, and she wanted to be the front runner. After all the publicity she'd brought the department following her research into familial depression and the development of anti-social behavioural traits, she deserved the promotion. University funding was directly linked to research, and applicants for the post would be judged on their contribution. She wouldn't let the opportunity slip out of her hands.

When Stephen moved in six months ago, she'd worried working and living together would put a strain on their relationship. But they didn't actually see much of each other during the day. They were both in the psychology department but taught on different programmes.

'I'll only steal you for an hour. It won't interfere with the master plan.' He flashed a disarming smile.

George almost gave in, being a sucker for his dimples, until she remembered the second years were submitting an assignment on mental health disorders the following day.

'I've another set of assignments due in tomorrow, and I can't get behind so early in the academic year. What about later in the week?'

'When you'll come up with another excuse.' He placed his mug on the worktop. 'I saw more of you before we started living together.'

He was right. They used to go out at least two or three times a week, either for meals or to the theatre or cinema. She'd had time for him then, even though she'd felt her work had suffered.

They'd only been seeing each other for eight months before he'd suggested they live together. George had agreed because it made sense on paper. They were similar in many ways. Both fiercely independent, due to being at boarding school from an early age. Workwise it was a lot easier. If they saw each other every day, she wouldn't be distracted so much by having to go out in the evenings.

Because career came first. She loved being with Stephen but had no desire to move beyond living together. It worked for him, too. He was divorced with two children, who he didn't see often because they lived overseas with their mother. Early on in their relationship, he'd told George he'd had a vasectomy, so having more children was out of the question. That suited her fine as she had no desire to be a mother.

On the surface, theirs seemed a perfect match. Even if some of his habits drove her crazy.

A few noses were put out of joint when they'd got together. Stephen always had a trail of students and staff vying for his attention. He was the archetypal tall, dark, handsome man. He was good company and had a great sense of humour. Until he didn't get his own way.

'I won't. Promise. You go. I'm sure there'll be someone you know in the pub. There usually is.'

Her suggestion wasn't exactly unselfish. It would be much easier to get on with her work in silence, rather than having the TV or music blaring.

'Suit yourself. Expect me when you see me, then.' He marched out of the kitchen. His footsteps thumped up the stairs.

Even when Stephen was the one being unreasonable, he had the knack of making her feel guilty. She couldn't live her life from moment to moment, like he did. Planning and being methodical was how she was wired. Those traits contributed to her success. She'd make it up to him when he got home later.

Her calm mood now shattered, she decided to walk to work rather than wait for a lift from him. She'd sneak a cigarette. It was her secret vice, something she indulged in only occasionally, and never when he was around.

She slipped on her calf-length, deep blue wool coat, knitted hat and scarf, and headed out of her eighteenth-century terraced cottage, which she'd bought with some of the money inherited from her grandma. She loved its intimacy. It was the perfect size for one. Well, now two. But there was still enough space for them both. She walked down the path and onto the pavement.

A typical chilly November morning, the sun was just beginning to rise behind leafless trees. Her cheeks tingled from the wind. She walked down the road until she came to another path, beside the winding river which divided Lenchester in two, and led to the university.

She followed the river, entering a tall wrought-iron gate onto the university grounds, and then lit up. Inhaling deeply, she allowed the smoke to permeate her body. Instant relaxation. As she blew the smoke out into the air, she noticed one of her colleagues coming along the path. Shit.

She cut behind a large oak tree, making sure to stay out of sight. Something caught her eye, and she turned her head. A pair of jean-clad legs poked out from the other side of the trunk. But that would be ridiculous. Who'd sit on the ground in this weather so early in the morning?

She went to investigate further.

A girl sat on the grass leaning against the tree. Her head was bowed, her hands clasped together, held up to her chest in a pleading pose.

Was she meditating?

'Hello?' George shivered as a gust of wind swept past.

The girl's head tilted, and a pair of lifeless eyes stared up into the overcast sky.

The cigarette fell from her hand. Was she? No—not possible. She stepped closer. The girl's dead gaze stared back at her, unflinching.

George's hands trembled as she reached for her mobile phone and pressed 999.

'There's a body. I think she's dead.'

Chapter Two

Detective Chief Inspector Whitney Walker parked her car and headed towards the imposing Victorian police station. She loved the building, despite the ineffective heating system and it being overcrowded. She'd be sorry to move once the fancy purpose-built station, situated on the edge of the city centre, was finished.

Before she even had time to grab a coffee, she was summoned to the office of her new boss, Detective Superintendent Tom Jamieson, by his personal assistant. She'd messed up on a case which meant the shit was going to hit the fan. Knowing what he was like, she expected he'd be wiping the floor with her.

She tapped on his open office door and walked straight in.

'You wanted to see me, sir?'

He held up his finger, indicating she should wait a moment until he'd finished whatever it was he was doing. It looked to her like he was just shuffling papers. It was probably all for her benefit, but he needn't have wasted his time.

She took the opportunity to glance around his office. In pride of place on the wall behind him was his degree certificate from Oxford University. He always made sure everyone knew he'd gone there. Wore it like a badge of honour. It didn't impress her. Well, it did. But not in respect of his job on the force. He'd only been there a short while and had already managed to piss her off big time.

He'd come into policing via the Superintendents' Fast Track scheme, which meant he had no experience in the field. Unlike her. She'd joined at eighteen and had worked her arse off for her promotion to Detective Chief Inspector. It had been a challenge, especially with her daughter Tiffany to look after and the negative views some of her superiors held, that being a mum and an effective officer was mutually exclusive.

But she was determined to be a success and make a difference. Ever since her brother, Rob, had been attacked by a gang of lads twenty years ago and ended up with brain damage, she'd known what she wanted to do with her life. She remembered the attack as if it was yesterday. The police did hardly anything about it. And never found the boys responsible. She'd move mountains to ensure that wouldn't happen on her watch.

The trouble with people like Jamieson was they thought their superior position meant they knew better than everyone else. She'd like to see what he'd do when confronted with a drugged up, knife wielding thug. He'd shit himself. As far as she was concerned, he was a high-flying paper pusher.

But he was her immediate boss, and she had to answer to him for everything. Usually he left her alone as senior investigating officer to work cases as she saw fit. Except when she screwed up.

He glanced up at her, took off his gold-rimmed glasses, and set them on the desk in front of him.

'Take a seat, Walker. I've called you in to discuss the Hodgson debacle.'

Calling it a debacle was an understatement. Two days ago, she'd orchestrated an early morning raid on a large house in Lewiston, one of the poshest areas of the city. She'd taken fifteen armed officers with her, and a dog handler, as they'd been informed there was a German shepherd on the premises. The dog turned out to be a poodle. And the only drugs in the house were prescribed medication and several bottles of vitamin pills. The fact they'd got the wrong house was bad enough. What was even worse, the house they'd raided belonged to close friends of the Chief Constable.

'Yes, sir.' She sat on one of the chairs in front of his mahogany, reproduction antique desk.

'What happened?' He leaned forward, resting his arms on the desk.

'We were misinformed about the location of the drugs.' From a little shit who was history once she got her hands on him.

'Didn't you check the validity of the information?'

Of course not. We picked an address from Google maps and decided to raid it, just in case.

'Yes, I did. It came from a reliable source, sir.' Maybe not the best thing to say.

'Clearly, not reliable enough. Have you spoken to this informant of yours?'

She'd used her informant on several cases, and he'd always come up with the goods. Someone must have got to him. Knowing if all police efforts were directed in a certain place, they could receive the drugs in a different location.

How much had they paid her informant to do the dirty on her?

'Not yet. He's disappeared.'

They'd tried all his usual haunts. It was like he'd vanished off the face of the earth.

'It gets better by the minute. I will not tolerate fuck ups of this nature. The Chief Constable's breathing down my neck wanting answers. What am I to tell him?'

'My team are on it. We'll find the informant.'

'You'd better, because if you don't, you can forget being SIO on any case for the foreseeable future. Traffic duty will be your remit. And that's on a good day.'

Whitney bit back a retort. Okay, she accepted she'd fucked up, but that was the first time. As her boss, he should have her back. She knew his game. He didn't want to be tarnished by the fallout; it could jeopardise his promotion prospects. Well, she had news for him. They'd all been tarnished by it. The operation had cost the department thousands of pounds to set up. Not to mention the damage it had caused her reputation and the jokes she'd had to endure.

'Yes, sir.'

He had his sights set on being a Detective Chief Superintendent as soon as possible. The trouble with fast track entrants into the force was they lacked the knowledge of real police work and thought everything should be done via the textbook. She'd like to know where in the texts you learn how to deal with double crossing informants who disappeared without a trace?

Her mobile rang, and Jamieson nodded for her to answer.

'Walker.'

'I'm at the university campus. A body's been found by the river,' Matt Price, her Detective Sergeant, said.

'Okay. I'll be there shortly.' She ended the call.

'Problem?' Jamieson asked.

'We have a body at the university.' She stood up to leave.

'Walker.'

'Sir?' she replied, turning back to face him.

'This is your last chance. Don't fuck it up.'

Chapter Three

Whitney seethed as she drove to the crime scene. However hard she tried to be objective about Jamieson, he rubbed her up the wrong way. Even the way he breathed loudly through his mouth when concentrating drove her crazy. And she wasn't even in his company often.

She drove through the imposing university gates and headed towards the river. She rarely came onto the campus, unlike her daughter Tiffany. When Tiffany passed her A-levels and got accepted to study engineering here, Whitney had been so proud. Her daughter was the first person in their family to go to university. It would lead to so many opportunities for her.

She pulled up beside the outer cordon and hopped out of her car.

'Guv,' Matt said, walking over as she opened the boot and took out a pair of disposable gloves.

She liked Matt. He worked hard and relentlessly until getting a result. If she asked him to do something, it would be done. He had a bright future ahead of him.

'Where's the body?'

'Under the tree.' He pointed towards a clump of oaks, close to the river.

'Who was the first officer attending?' she asked.

'PC Rogers. He's by the rendezvous point.'

'I see him,' she replied, after scanning the area. There were six officers strategically placed around the cordon to prevent anyone from entering the crime scene.

She headed over to Rogers and checked he'd taken the relevant steps to secure and protect the scene. They agreed he would continue in the role of keeping the scene log until someone else could take over.

Happy everything was in order and nothing was going to be compromised, she signed the scene log. 'Walk with me,' she said, turning to Matt. 'I've just left Jamieson. He wanted to talk about the Hodgson incident.'

'Did he give you a bollocking?' Matt asked as they navigated their way over the footplates which had been strategically placed so that those who needed could enter the cordon without worrying they were damaging evidence.

'Nothing I couldn't handle.'

'I wouldn't expect anything else.' He grinned.

'I do my best,' she replied, grinning back at him.

They headed towards the trees. As they approached, she drew in a sharp breath. It didn't matter how many times she confronted a dead body, it always got to her. It wasn't that she'd throw up. She'd got over that years ago. It was more the loss of life that sickened her, even more so when it was someone young.

'Who found the body?' She hoped it wasn't a group of students.

'Doctor Georgina Cavendish, a lecturer at the university. She knows the victim and identified her as Millie Carter, a student here,' Matt replied.

'I'll need to speak to her.'

'I've already asked her to wait near the rendezvous point. She's tall with short blonde hair. You can't miss her.'

'Good. Is the pathologist here yet?'

'Yes. Dr Dexter arrived about ten minutes ago.'

They were lucky the forensic pathologist was on duty. Without her there, who knew when they'd be able to move the body. And the longer it stayed out here, the likelier the press would get wind of it. 'Witnesses?'

'None at the moment, according to Rogers. The place was deserted when the doctor found her.'

They reached the tent which was being erected near the body. Their victim would have to be photographed where she was before they could move her into the tent and start their full investigation. Killers never thought about the implications of their body dumps, Claire Dexter had once whispered to Whitney at a particularly difficult dump site she'd had to circumnavigate.

'Hello, Claire,' she said to the pathologist, who was staring at the body, camera in hand. She'd known her for years, and although they weren't friends, they had a mutual respect for each other. 'What have you got for me?'

Claire was the best forensic pathologist in Lenchester. Her looks belied her toughness. She was short, a little overweight, with red hair and freckles. She always wore the loudest, clashing colours imaginable, apart from when she had on her protective clothing. Anyone who tried to cross her would do so only once.

'You know the drill,' Claire said. 'Can't tell you much, except it doesn't look like natural causes.'

Whitney got closer to the body, noticing the bruising around the girl's neck. 'Strangulation?'

'It looks like it. There are marks around the wrists, suggesting she'd been restrained. I'll know more when I get her on the table. I'd say she's been moved and placed in this position.'

Whitney scrutinised the body's position. She was leaning back against the tree trunk with her hands close to her chest. If the body had been moved and placed like that, it had to mean something. A relocated body was frustrating; it made their job harder as there would be less evidence to work with.

'She's fully clothed. Any indication of sexual assault?'

'I can't tell at the moment, though her clothes aren't on correctly. Her jeans are pulled up and zipped, but the button is undone. Also, the buttons on her cardigan are done up incorrectly,' Claire replied.

'Guv,' Matt said. 'There's a mobile phone on her lap.'

'Don't even think about touching it,' Claire said, and then proceeded to take pictures of the wasted life in front of them.

They waited until she finished photographing and allowed them to pick it up. Whitney was about to place it into the evidence bag when the wallpaper image came up.

It was a photo of the dead girl wearing nothing but her underwear. Duct tape covered her mouth, and her hands were tied to a slatted bedhead with what appeared to be cable ties. Her legs were wide open. Although the photo didn't show it, it looked like her ankles were tied, too.

Bile caught in her throat and she turned away. The girl was barely older than Tiffany.

She dragged in a breath, getting herself under control, determined her emotions wouldn't get in the way. This case had to be dealt with efficiently and by the letter. She couldn't afford it to go any other way.

'Crap.' She showed the image to Matt and Claire before dropping it into the evidence bag. 'We'll look closer when we're back at the office.'

As she paced the ground close to the body, she checked again for evidence. Nothing seemed to be disturbed; they'd know better once the scene of crime officers had scoured the area. She headed back to where Claire stood, dictating into her recorder.

'If she's been moved like you suggest, then where's the evidence? There are no tyre tracks or drag marks. If she was carried, then the offender must be strong. She's not exactly petite.'

Even from down on the ground, it was obvious the victim was tall and solidly built. Whitney would've struggled to move her at all.

'As I've already said, wait until we have her on the table. We'll know more once I've checked the trace evidence.'

'Okay. I'll come and see you later in the lab.'

'Fine. Now let me get back on with my work or I'll be here all day.' Claire dismissed her with a flick of her hand.

Not wanting to annoy her, Whitney moved away and headed towards the rendezvous point, anxious to speak to the woman who found the body.

Chapter Four

George shivered and wrapped her arms around herself. She was due in class soon, but the police officer had asked her to give her statement straight away.

The emptiness of Millie's eyes, devoid of any life, were etched in her mind. What had happened for her life to end so suddenly? She'd always liked Millie. She had an excellent attitude to work and a genuine interest in learning. And now she was dead.

George, trying to view it from a forensic psychologist's view point and not as someone personally invested, walked through the scene again in her mind. She'd been so stunned she hadn't looked too closely at the body after realising who it was. But what she did remember was how Millie's body had been positioned. Her hands held up to her chest resting on her breasts, elbows tucked in to her waist, and her fingers interlaced. It was the classic pleading pose. Almost religious. Like she was praying for her life.

Why was she positioned that way? Was it a message from the killer?

'Doctor Cavendish?'

George started at the sound of her name and glanced at the woman who had called it. 'Yes.'

'DCI Whitney Walker.' The officer, a short, attractive, dark-haired woman, who looked to be in her late thirties, held out her ID which George took a quick look at. 'I'd like to run through the events of this morning.'

Walker stood a few feet from her and looked George up and down. George's hackles rose, not liking the scrutiny. What had she done wrong?

'I've already told the other police officer,' George replied, harsher than she'd intended.

'I'd like you to tell me.'

'I was on my way to work at the university, and I came across Millie Carter, under the tree.'

'What time was this?' Walker took a notebook and pen from her pocket and began writing notes.

'Around eight. Maybe a few minutes earlier. I'm not sure.'

'Do you usually walk to work at this time of day?' Whitney asked, looking up.

'No. Most days I have a lift. Today I decided to walk.'

'Why?'

She wasn't about to discuss her run in with Stephen. It had nothing to do with finding the body.

'I wanted the fresh air,' George replied, immediately regretting it as Walker's face showed disbelief.

'It's not even ten degrees.' Walker shook her head.

'I wrapped up warm.' That sounded crazy and made her seem suspicious. 'Okay. I walked this way so I could have a cigarette before class.' Why did the admission make her feel guilty?

'So, walking here is unusual for you?'

'Yes. Even if I don't get a lift and do decide to walk to

work, there's a shortcut which takes me along the side of my building.'

'What was different about today?'

She now had no other choice than to explain. 'I had an argument with my partner and wanted some time to relax before work.'

'I can relate to that.' Walker's expression softened. 'Was there anyone else around when you found the body?'

'No. Yes. Well, a colleague was walking fairly close, so I ducked behind the tree. She turned off and headed towards the psychology building over there.' George pointed in the direction of the old Victorian building where she worked. 'That's when I noticed Millie's legs sticking out. I went to investigate and found her body. If I hadn't come off the path, I would never have seen her.'

'What did you do then?'

'I phoned 999 and reported it. It appeared to be a suspicious death. Is it?'

Despite being a forensic psychologist, she'd never been to a murder scene. She'd sat in on autopsies, and worked alongside other forensic psychologists doing profiling, but this was different.

'It's too early to say. The pathologist is over there.'

She glanced across at the crime scene and saw a familiar figure exiting the screen they'd put around Millie's body.

'Claire Dexter.'

'You know her?' Walker asked, frowning.

'Yes, she guest lectures for me.'

'For you?'

'I run the forensic psychology programme. We look into criminal behaviour and try to establish patterns, motives, and mindsets.' Was she trying to impress the woman? Why?

Judging by Walker's flat stare, it hadn't worked, anyway.

'Tell me about the victim.'

'Millie Carter was a third-year student in my department. She was also in my personal tutorial group.'

'What does that mean?'

'Students are all allocated a tutor to look after their academic needs. Millie's one of mine. We have a personal tutorial once a month to discuss her progress.'

'And how was she doing?' Walker asked, once again scribbling copious notes.

'Millie was an above-average student. Her assignments were usually submitted on time, and she did reasonably well in her examinations last year.' Her impersonal words made Millie seem like a number and not a person.

'Did she confide in you about anything?'

When had she last spoken to Millie? She hated to admit it, but tutorials seemed to blend into one another. When you had over thirty personal tutees, it was impossible to remember every encounter. But she would've remembered if there was anything which stood out as troublesome. She was sure of it.

'Occasionally, students talk about their personal lives. Millie was no different. She didn't tell me anything indicating she was in trouble.' George cringed. It sounded like a fob off.

'Did she have a boyfriend?'

George wracked her brain but couldn't remember. 'I'm not sure. I don't recall her mentioning anyone.'

'What about friends?' Walker's tone was impatient.

'I don't know her friends, but I can give you the names of others in her tutorial group. They might be able to help,' George offered, glad she could at least do something.

'I thought you saw them individually?'

'The tutorial group meets fortnightly, and there are also individual tutorials. It's standard practice,' she explained.

'Well, I didn't go to university, so wouldn't know.'

George stepped back. Had she touched a nerve? 'Sorry. The way the body was posed, have you considered that yet?' she asked, changing the subject.

'We haven't established whether it was posed. That's for the pathologist to decide.'

'Of course, I understand you have to wait for Claire's findings. But if Millie was murdered, which it certainly looks like, then the position of the body can tell us a lot about the person who did it. Let me help you with that.'

She didn't want to sit back and do nothing when she had the skills to assist.

'Dr Cavendish, I'm sure you mean well, but why don't you leave the investigation to the experts? I'm fully aware murderers leave signatures. But you're jumping the gun here. Dr Dexter will do her analysis, and we'll do the investigative work from there.' Walker closed her notebook and replaced it in the back pocket of the navy trousers she was wearing.

'I appreciate I'm not a police officer, but my skills could help.' George stared down at her. She wasn't used to having her knowledge brushed aside and didn't like it.

'I'll remember that, thank you. You can help by letting me have a list of the others in your tutorial group.'

'The list is in my office. I'll bring it down to the station later.'

'No need. Here's my card. Just email it to me.' Walker held out her card which George took.

'I'll do it as soon as I get into my office.' She glanced at her watch. She was already late for her first class and should've thought to text the departmental administrator.

Unless the Head of Department had cancelled all classes for the day, under the circumstances.

'Thank you. I'd also like details of your movements over the weekend, leading up to when you found the body.'

'Why?' Surely Walker wasn't implying she had anything to do with Millie's murder.

'Standard procedure. I'd also like you to think carefully about anyone else you saw on your walk to work.'

That was easy because there was only the one colleague.

'We don't know how long Millie was there for. I couldn't tell whether rigor had set in or not, so I doubt the murderer would be hanging around for me to pin point.'

'I wasn't asking for your professional opinion,' Walker said.

'I'm a forensic psychologist. It's what I do.'

'I appreciate that, but I'm a detective, and it's my job to investigate. The name of the colleague, please.'

'Geraldine Walters from the criminology department. As for my movements over the weekend, I was at home working on my latest research project.'

'Can anyone vouch for you?'

'My partner, Stephen Grant, was there for some of the time. Other than that, no. Unless you check my laptop. My saved documents will have the time and date on them.'

'Thank you. That won't be necessary. I'm just doing my job, as I'm sure you appreciate,' Walker replied.

'Of course. Now, if we've finished, I have to get to class.'

'Yes, that's all for now. Don't forget the list of names.'

'I won't. You'll have it within the hour.'

George walked away, her head a mass of conflicting thoughts. She got DCI Walker had a job to do, but didn't she realise George had found a dead body? A body of someone she knew. And—

She came to an abrupt halt and turned to look back at the crime scene. There had to be something she could do. There just had to be. She couldn't sit back and watch. Even if Walker did dismiss her view on the body and its posing. But to be of any help, she needed more information. She'd speak to the other students in Millie's tutorial group once she'd broken the news to them, which she was dreading. Then she'd visit Claire Dexter to see what other information she could glean.

Chapter Five

Whitney pinned up a photo of the victim on the board and wrote "Millie Carter" beneath it.

'Attention, everyone,' she called out over the chatter in the incident room. The team were huddled in small clusters, many of them standing, leaning against the desks. She waited a few seconds for the noise to die down. 'Our victim. Twenty-one-year-old Millie Carter. Third-year psychology student at Lenchester University. Suspicious death.'

'Do we know how she died, guv?' DC Ellie Naylor called out from the centre of the room, where she was sitting behind a computer screen. Ellie's research skills were extraordinary, and Whitney had pushed to get her permanently on the team. Ellie had also been trained to use the self-service kiosk for extracting data from mobile phones, which meant they could access data immediately, instead of waiting for the digital forensic unit to do it for them. It was brand new technology. Whitney kept well away from it; it was way too modern for her.

'Early indications are strangulation,' Whitney replied. 'We're waiting on the pathologist's findings.'

'Any sexual interference?' Ellie asked.

'Again, waiting for the pathologist. I wouldn't be surprised, as her clothes had been removed and replaced, as we can see from the photo on her phone. Matt, do we have a copy of the photo?'

'Here, guv.' He passed it to her.

Whitney placed it on the board. 'This is the victim. The murderer took it with her phone and saved it as wallpaper. At the moment, we have no idea where it was taken.'

'Dr Cavendish has emailed in the list of students you asked for. She's meeting with them all this morning. Shall we send someone along?' Matt asked.

They would, but it wouldn't be Whitney. She'd had enough of the stuck-up doctor to last a lifetime.

'Yes. You can go. You need the forensic psychology department. Interview the students individually and see what you can come up with. In particular, if she had a boyfriend.'

'Ellie, I want you to check out any CCTV at the university and any on roads leading there. Also, check the victim's phone and social media accounts. Find out what you can about her friends.'

'Yes, guv.'

'Do you think we should ask Dr Cavendish in to help?' Matt asked.

'Has she been talking to you?'

'No. It was just a thought,' he replied.

'She's already offered her opinion, and we don't need it. She's not a detective. As we all know, the majority of murders are committed by someone close to the victim. So, we can do without any complicated theories she'll have. Let's find out all we can about the boyfriend, if there is one.'

'Okay,' Matt said.

'I'm going to see the family. They live about half an hour away. We have to let them know before it gets back to them through other channels. Frank, you're with me. Sue and Doug, I want background checks on the uni staff, particularly those who taught the victim. Also, check if any sex offenders have been recently released into the area.'

She picked up her bag from under the table and was about to leave, when she glanced up and saw Jamieson open the door and walk in. Crap. What the fuck did he want?

'Good morning, team,' Jamieson said, striding up to her desk.

'Sir,' Whitney replied.

'Where are we so far?'

Whitney tensed. Was this how the investigation was going to go? He usually didn't interfere, so now because of her last fuck up he thought he would.

'Everything's under control, sir. I'm going to see the family. As yet, they don't know about their daughter's death.'

'I'll come with you.'

Out the corner of her eye Whitney noticed Matt and Frank exchange glances, smirks crossing their faces.

'Won't be necessary, sir. I'm taking Taylor.'

'I'm sure he could be better used elsewhere,' Jamieson insisted, his lips in a thin smile which didn't reach up to his eyes. 'We'll go in my car.'

'Yes, sir,' she replied through gritted teeth. 'Frank, you go with Matt and collect statements.'

Whitney left with Jamieson, following him to the car park and his brand-new Volvo. She didn't resent him the car. Actually, she did. She was fed up of driving around in an old Ford Focus. She'd have loved a new car, but she needed her money for Tiffany and to help out her mum, who had her hands full looking after Rob and wasn't able to work.

Whitney hated having to be the one to break the news about Millie's death to the family, but she couldn't leave it to Jamieson. If he spoke to the family the way he spoke to her, then it would be a total cock up.

Jamieson talked non-stop during the journey. Whitney learnt all about the work he'd done before joining the force. How good he was, and how he'd managed to save his previous company millions of pounds by implementing a reporting system, capturing everything. She had to stifle a yawn on several occasions. Not helped by the fact she'd missed out on her second cup of coffee. She timed her caffeine fixes. Every three hours was optimum.

'I think it's best if I explain to the family about their daughter,' Whitney said as they drew up outside the Carter home, a detached house on a small estate.

'No. Leave it to me.'

'Have you done it before?' Whitney asked, knowing full well he hadn't. At least, not in his role as a police officer.

'No. But there's always a first time.'

'Why don't you let me do it and you observe? It's often better coming from a female officer, in my experience.' Anything to stop him from going in and making the situation even worse, because after she'd delivered the news, she needed to talk to them about Millie.

She glanced at her watch before ringing the bell. It was nearly eleven. She hoped someone was in and they weren't all out at work. After a few seconds, the door was opened by a well-dressed woman with short grey hair, who looked to be around fifty.

'Mrs Carter?'

'Yes.'

'I'm Detective Chief Inspector Whitney Walker, from Lenchester CID, and this is Detective Superintendent Tom Jamieson.' She held out her warrant card, and Jamieson did the same. 'May we come in?'

'What is it?' Mrs Carter frowned.

'It's best if we talk inside,' Whitney replied gently.

Mrs Carter held open the door, which led into a long hallway. 'The lounge is on the left. We can talk there.'

'Is there someone else at home with you?' Whitney asked, following Mrs Carter into the room.

'My husband, Rex, is off work today with a bad back. He's in the kitchen.'

She hated all this small talk, but it was better to have both of them there, so they could support each other.

'Can you call him for us, please?'

'What is it?' Mrs Carter asked, her voice raising in tone and sounding anxious.

'Call your husband and we'll explain,' she replied.

While Mrs Carter went into the kitchen, Whitney took a moment to scan the room. Above the fire place were lots of photos. All of them Millie. Was she an only child? She shuddered, knowing in a few moments these people's lives would never be the same again. How would they cope? If anything happened to Tiffany—she couldn't even go there.

'What's all this about?' Mr Carter stood in front of them, his arm placed protectively around Mrs Carter's shoulders.

'Take a seat.' Whitney gestured to the sofa, and she sat

on one of the easy chairs next to it. Jamieson sat on the other.

Mr and Mrs Carter both sat down, and she took hold of his hand.

'Is it Millie?' Mrs Carter asked, her voice barely above a whisper.

Whitney drew in a breath. 'I'm sorry to have to tell you, but a body has been found on the university campus, and we have reason to believe it's Millie.'

The room fell silent. Then Mrs Carter let out an agonising scream. She sobbed uncontrollably, her whole body shaking. Mr Carter held her tightly in his arms, not uttering a sound. He just stared blankly at Whitney over the top of his wife's head, the colour drained from his face.

'Is there anyone we can call?' Whitney asked.

Mr Carter jolted back into alertness. 'No. Thank you. When can we see Millie?'

'We'd like one of you to come down and formally identify the body. It doesn't have to be straight away. Later today or tomorrow will be fine.'

'What happened to her?' Mr Carter asked.

'We're treating the death as suspicious. That's all we can say at the moment,' Whitney replied.

'Murder?' Mrs Carter said, lifting her head from her husband's chest. 'Who would murder my Millie?' Her voice cracked.

Whitney glanced at Jamieson, who was sitting back in the chair looking on.

'I know this isn't easy, but if we're to catch the person who did this, we need as much help from you as you can give.'

She hated this part of her job. She'd just given them the worst possible news ever, and now she needed them to give her some information. It just wasn't fair.

'Of course,' Mr Carter said, his back ramrod straight, as though he might totally collapse if he relaxed his body.

'When was the last time you saw Millie?' she asked.

'Two weeks ago,' Mr Carter said. 'She comes home for the weekend once a fortnight. And she phones two or three times a week, to speak to her mum. I'm not very good at chatting.'

'Did she have a boyfriend?' Whitney asked.

'N—' Mr Carter started to reply.

'Yes, she did,' Mrs Carter interrupted, giving her husband an apologetic look. 'She told me last week she'd just started seeing someone. I don't know his name. All I know is he's a student.'

'Why didn't you tell me?' Mr Carter asked his wife, frowning.

'Because it wasn't anything serious. And I know how protective you are of her. Oh my God. Was it him? Do you think he killed Millie?' Mrs Carter's hand slammed over her mouth.

'We can't jump to that conclusion. We'll find out who he is from her friends. May I take a look at Millie's bedroom?' Whitney asked.

'Yes. It's upstairs the first door on the right,' Mr Carter replied.

'Thank you. Sir, why don't you make everyone a cup of tea,' she suggested to Jamieson before she left the room.

Whitney walked back into the hall and headed up the stairs. When she reached the top, she noted there were four doors. She quickly peeped into all the rooms and then went into the one belonging to Millie. There were stuffed animals placed along the windowsill. It reminded her of Tiffany. She kept all the teddies she'd had from when she was a child. When Whitney had suggested getting rid of some of them, Tiffany had refused point blank.

They were still so young.

Whitney peered at some of the photos stuck onto the mirror of the dressing table. Most from picture booths. Millie appeared like a normal young woman having fun with her friends. There was a pile of magazines on the floor. She took a look. Some of them went back years. She opened the wardrobe. It was half full of clothes; nothing out of the ordinary in there either.

The double bed was covered with a blue and white striped duvet, and beside it stood a white cabinet. Whitney opened the drawer and found last year's diary. She flicked through it. Millie clearly wasn't one to pour out her feelings. The only entries were dates of birthdays, deadlines for assignments, and appointments with the dentist and doctor. Nothing useful.

Not wanting to be away from the Carters and Jamieson for too long, she went back downstairs. As she approached, she could hear Jamieson talking sympathetically.

'I'm happy to come back later and pick you up and take you to identify Millie's body. You let me know when.'

She walked down the stairs, just in time to see him giving Mr Carter his card. Maybe she'd misjudged him.

'Thank you for letting me go up to Millie's room,' she said to Mr and Mrs Carter. 'Are you sure there isn't someone we can call?'

'No,' Mr Carter said. 'We don't have any other children, and my sister is in New Zealand. Pat has a sister, but she's in Scotland.'

'Friends?' Whitney asked.

'We don't have many. We keep ourselves to ourselves. I'll come down to the station later to identify the body. No need for a lift.'

They left the house, and Whitney let out a long sigh. Delivering news of an accident or death never got any easier however many times she did it. If she was with anyone else, she'd have suggested they stopped at the pub for a drink to settle the nerves. She didn't think Jamieson would appreciate that. Plus, she didn't want to spend more time in his company than necessary.

'You did well,' Jamieson said once they were in the car.

'It's a horrible job. We go in and destroy their lives for ever. I don't know how they're going to cope.'

'The same as we all cope in these situations. They'll get on with the rest of their lives. The pain will always be there, but it will subside in time,' he replied.

Whitney glanced across at him, his eyes fixed firmly on the road ahead of them. She hadn't expected to hear compassion in his voice. Was he speaking from personal experience?

'You've had something like that happen to you?' she asked before she was able to stop herself.

'No. But I read a psychological paper on the delivery of bad news in my preparation for this job. I knew I'd come across situations like this, so I wanted to know what to expect.'

Just when she thought she'd seen a more human side of him, he showed his true colours. It was all academic theory to him. She didn't fault him wanting to be informed, but it didn't beat actually experiencing situations.

'Great,' she said, with little enthusiasm.

'What's your issue, Walker?'

'Nothing, sir.' She looked to the front, avoiding any eye contact with him.

'You really need to deal with that chip on your shoulder. Because if you don't, it will get in the way of your career. This is twenty-first century policing. You need to get your head out of the seventies and realise it's all about metrics and social media.'

Whitney tensed. How dare he imply she was stuck in the seventies? For a start, she hadn't even been born then, and she certainly didn't operate like the police did in those days. Convictions at all costs. She'd show him who the better police officer was, and it wouldn't be him.

Chapter Six

George stared out of her window onto the quad. She'd just come from the Head of Department's office. He'd decided to let classes continue, as there had been no official announcement of Millie's death. It would give him time to put in place some extra counsellors and to speak to the divisional head regarding how she wanted the whole affair to be managed.

She'd agreed with his response; however, she had her tutorial group in five minutes, and she'd decided to tell them. She wanted them to hear about it personally.

Picking up her briefcase, she went to the small lecture room where they were meeting. She'd deliberately arrived a few minutes late to make sure they were all there.

'You're late, Dr Cavendish,' one of them quipped as she entered the room.

'Sorry. Are you all here?' She quickly checked out the group.

'Except Millie,' Lisa, one of the more vocal students, said.

George pulled up a chair and joined the circle they

always sat in during a tutorial. It was more intimate than sitting behind desks and ensured everyone would contribute more to the subject under discussion.

Eager faces stared at her. They were totally unaware their day was about to be ruined.

Their lives changed forever.

Her fists clenched by her side. 'I've got some bad news for you about Millie. There's been an incident.' She paused. 'I'm sorry to tell you Millie's dead.'

After a couple of seconds of stunned silence, several of the students started to cry.

'What happened?' Seb asked.

How much was she allowed to say? DCI Walker hadn't said not to say anything. Which in George's view was remiss of her. But the murder would be in the media soon enough. Millie's fellow students deserved to know the truth.

'Her body was found near the river this morning. The circumstances of her death are suspicious.' She wasn't going to tell them she'd been the one to find the body, even though they'd probably find out.

She dug her nails into her leg and forced herself to breathe. It helped steady her, and she returned their gaze. 'The university counsellors are available if you'd like to speak to one of them. We won't have the tutorial today. I'm here if you want to stay and talk, or if you'd like to take the rest of the day off, I'll make sure your other lecturers know.'

There was a knock at the door, and the officer she'd seen earlier walked in. She got up and walked over to him.

'DS Price,' he said. 'We spoke this morning.'

'Yes. I recognise you. Do you need my help?' The DCI must have changed her mind.

'Not exactly. Have you told the students about Millie Carter?' he asked.

'Yes. Just now.'

'We'd like to speak to them. Is there somewhere we can do that?'

'There's an empty class next door. Go there and I'll send them in.'

She waited for them to leave and went back to the students.

'That was the police. They'd like to speak to you about Millie. They're in the class next door.'

They all shuffled out of the classroom, apart from Lisa who remained seated, her face pale. George moved and sat next to her. 'Were you very close to Millie?' she asked gently.

'We were in the same hall of residence in our first year. Our rooms were next door, so we saw a lot of each other back then. I moved in with my boyfriend in our second year, and she lived with several girls in a flat in town.' Tears filled Lisa's eyes, and George passed her a tissue, which she used to wipe her eyes and then scrunched up in her hand.

'Did you see Millie socially?'

'Not really. I tend to hang with my boyfriend and his friends. I'd sometimes see her at parties, or in the pub, but we haven't been out together in a long time. We mainly caught up during lectures and tutorials or for a coffee. I can't believe she's not here.' Tears streamed down her face, and she wiped them away.

George patted her gently on the hand, unsure whether putting her arm around Lisa's shoulders was appropriate. Physical displays of emotion always left her uncomfortable.

'Why don't you call your boyfriend and ask him to come and meet you? You don't want to be alone at a time like this.' It was all she could think of to suggest.

'I can't believe I'll never see Millie again.' Lisa's shoulders slumped.

'When did you last see her outside of classes?'

She couldn't sit back and wait for the police to come up with something.

She wanted to help.

She needed to help.

The fact she found the body. The fact Millie was her student. It had to mean something.

Millie's death, the way she was posed, was definitely a signature. If she could find out more information, she might be able to come up with a profile to help the police and catch the bastard who'd done it.

To make sure they didn't hurt anyone else.

Lisa was silent for a moment. 'I think it was the weekend before last. She was at a party I went to.'

'Where was it?'

'A house on Lloyd Road. It was a student party.'

'Which students?'

'Honestly, I don't know. There were hundreds of people coming and going. We only stayed an hour and then went onto another party. You know what it's like.'

'But you definitely saw Millie there?' George persisted.

'Yes.' Lisa nodded. 'She was standing with a couple of other girls. We didn't talk; I just noticed her across the room.'

She didn't pursue it, because Lisa was so upset. What she needed now was more information about how she died. Hopefully Claire would help.

After Lisa went next door to speak to the police, George called a taxi to take her to the mortuary. She had time as her next class wasn't until one. She'd been to the mortuary several times and had once sat in on an autopsy. Before studying forensic psychology, she'd gone into medicine, intending to become a surgeon like her father. But it didn't work out. With hindsight, she was pleased, because she'd found her true vocation.

The taxi dropped her off, and she walked into the new state-of-the-art mortuary which adjoined the local hospital. She headed down the wide, mildly antiseptic smelling corridor and pushed open the double door. Claire was seated at her desk in the office area. 'Hello, how's it going?'

'Hectic,' Claire replied, standing and walking over to greet her. 'Did we have a meeting?'

'No. I just popped in to ask you about Millie Carter. The girl found by the river this morning.'

'You know I can't discuss it with you.'

George had forgotten what a stickler for the rules she was. Much like herself. But that wasn't going to stop her from trying. She wanted justice for Millie.

'She was one of my students. I was the one who found her.'

'I'm sorry. But I still can't talk about the case with you. You know that,' Claire said, shaking her head.

'I understand. Can you confirm it was murder?'

'What made you ask? Did you spend time looking over the body?'

'Not really. But I noticed the way it was posed. It was unnatural, especially if the death was natural causes, suicide, or through a drug overdose.'

'Yes. She was murdered,' Claire confirmed. 'And that's all I can tell you.'

More than she officially knew before, which was a start.

She was just about to thank Claire when the door opened. They both turned to see who it was. Walker. Just the person she didn't want to see at the moment.

'Hello, Dr Dexter. Dr Cavendish, what are you doing here?' Walker arched an eyebrow.

'I called to see Dr Dexter.'

'What about?' Walker asked.

Should she tell her the truth? She expected it wouldn't go down very well. 'Dr Dexter guest lectures for me. I came in to discuss when we'll next be seeing her.'

Claire stifled a snort by turning it into a cough. George shot a warning glance in her direction.

'And you couldn't do that on the phone? Or via email? Are you sure you weren't here trying to find out about Millie Carter?'

George tensed. 'I realise Dr Dexter can't divulge any information.'

'Good. Now, if you wouldn't mind leaving, I have the case to discuss with Dr Dexter.'

'I'll call you later, Claire,' George said, turning to leave and refusing to acknowledge Walker's comments.

'Do you feel better after that?' Claire Dexter asked.

'I don't know what you mean,' Whitney replied, trying not to smirk.

She didn't appreciate Dr Cavendish attempting to muscle in on her case.

'Yes, you do.' Claire rolled her eyes upwards. 'Right. You want to know about our victim. She's over here.'

She followed Claire into the autopsy suite, the intense sterile hospital smell assaulting her nostrils. They headed over to one of the stainless-steel tables where the girl was lying. A big Y-shaped incision, which had been sewn up, covered her chest. Claire walked up close to the victim and turned on the directional light, illuminating her body.

'See here?' Claire pointed to purple marks on the victim's neck. Four on the right and one on the left. 'These bruises are from the strangulation. The killer was left-handed.'

'Yes, I see them,' she replied.

'And these red dots on her eyelids. It's what we call petechiae. Again, a symptom of strangulation.'

'And that's what killed her?'

'Yes.'

Whitney shook her head in disgust. It made her sick what people could do. 'Time of death?'

'According to the rigor, I'd say between ten and two Sunday night. Also, the body had been moved. She wasn't killed where she was found.'

Whitney wasn't surprised. There had been no signs of struggle at the crime scene. Also, no signs of the body being dragged.

'Any sexual assault?'

'Bruising around the vaginal area is consistent with the victim being raped. No semen. He would've worn a condom. There was soap residue on the body, indicating she was washed down after, hence no other sign of trace evidence, like pubic hair, in that region.'

Whitney honed in on the marks around the victim's wrists. 'Anything on the ties? We know they tied her up from the photo left on the phone.'

'If you look at the marks left on the wrists, they were from plastic cable ties, the sort you can buy in any DIY store.'

'Any chance of being more specific? Can we identify the make of tie?'

'Not possible, I'm afraid. I've examined under the nails for trace evidence. Skin. Fibre. Anything that might have accumulated under there, indicating signs of a struggle when she was taken. But there's nothing. The ankles were also tied, only more loosely and leaving only slight abrasions. I'd say laces were used. The sort found in trainers.'

'Make?'

'Again, impossible to identify.'

She fought down the frustration. The lack of evidence. The positioning of the body. It all pointed to a cold and calculated attack. They were the worst crimes to solve.

'If there are no signs of struggle, then it's likely she knew her attacker,' Whitney suggested.

'It seems so, yes,' Claire said. 'I've looked at her stomach contents. Her last meal was strawberry jelly and vanilla ice cream. With chocolate sprinkles.'

'The sort of food you give to children at parties.' What sort of deranged mind would feed that to their captive?

'I found traces of ice cream and several sprinkles an inch up her nasal passage, which leads me to conclude she'd been force fed and he cleaned her up, missing what wasn't visible.'

'How long before she died had she eaten?'

'Judging by the breakdown of the food, I'd say about three hours.'

'Is there anything else I need to know?'

'I'm waiting for the results of the blood test, from toxicology. I'll forward them once they've arrived.'

'Thanks. Let me know if Dr Cavendish comes sniffing around again. I don't want her interfering in my investigation.'

Whitney trusted Claire not to leak information, but she wanted her to know she wouldn't tolerate any interference.

'Up to you. If it was me, I'd be glad of her help. She's very well respected in her field. I'm sure she could be of great benefit to you.'

'Has she helped in police investigations before? I haven't heard, but you may know different.'

'I've no idea. I'm giving you my opinion based on her academic work,' Claire replied.

'You're entitled to your opinion. But good old-fashioned police work will catch the bastard who did this.' She didn't need a fancy education to do her job properly.

Chapter Seven

'Okay,' Whitney said to Ellie, once she'd returned to the incident room. 'Where are we on the CCTV?'

'I've accessed footage from the cameras covering roads into the university and also those on the campus, but so far there's nothing of note on there. Although there's still a lot more to go through,' Ellie replied.

'And the victim's friends?'

'We've had better luck there. I went through the list of contacts in her phone and checked out her social media accounts. Her boyfriend's name is Nathan Harris, and judging by the photos and comments, Millie had been seeing him for a couple of weeks. According to the university database, he's twenty-two and a third-year law student. He should be in class at the moment. He comes from Dorset and lives with four other males in a student house in Stanton Road. Number twenty-three. Here's a photo of him from the university records.' She handed it to Whitney, who placed it on the board next to the photo of Millie.

'Good work.' She turned to Matt, who was standing

close by. 'Go to the university and pick him up. We'll interview him here.'

'Yes, guv,' Matt replied.

'Frank. You and Sue go to Stanton Road in case he's at home. If he's not there, see if you can persuade any of the occupants to let you in for a look around. It will save having to wait for a search warrant.'

Time was crucial in murder investigations.

'What if there's no one there?' Frank asked.

For a seasoned officer, Frank could be infuriatingly dense. She didn't want to spell out everything, preferring her team to work on their own initiative.

'I'll leave that to your discretion. If you're at all concerned and think you've heard something worrying from inside, then you know the drill. Go and investigate.'

Whitney's concern was the longer they left the boyfriend at large, the more time he'd have to destroy any evidence. If they went by the rule book every time they came across something, investigations would be seriously hampered. She realised it had to be counter balanced with the need to have everything watertight for court, but there was always a way around things without crossing the line.

'Guv,' Frank replied.

'I'll see you later. I'm due in with the Super to discuss the press conference.'

She left the room and headed to Jamieson's office. The door was shut, so she knocked and waited for him to answer. She could hear him on the phone, his pompous voice coming through loud and clear.

'Enter,' he called out. 'Won't be a moment,' he mouthed to her once she'd walked in.

Watching him, she wondered how he'd ever cope if he had to chase someone on foot. He was considerably overweight, his shirt buttons straining against his protruding stomach. Much of the increase had occurred since joining the force. The result of spending most of his time behind a desk. She guessed it wasn't helped by all the lunches and dinners he had to attend. That was why she'd decided to stick at DCI. She had no desire to be tied to a desk. It would drive her bat-shit crazy.

The call Jamieson was on sounded personal, possibly his wife. She'd no idea whether he was married, divorced, single, or whatever. It sounded like he was making arrangements for dinner out that evening. Lucky for him, murder cases didn't interfere with his social life. She had choir rehearsal later but doubted she'd make it, which was annoying seeing as singing was her one release. The choir were rehearsing for a big concert to be held later in the month. She'd been asked to sing a solo, which was flattering, though she'd be a bag of nerves on the night.

'The press conference,' Jamieson said, dragging her back from her thoughts.

'Yes, sir. When is it?'

She'd already sussed how much he enjoyed doing them. The abduction of a ten-year-old boy a month ago was proof. Her team had successfully found the child within twenty-four hours of him going missing. At the press conference, Jamieson acted like he'd coordinated the whole operation and single-handedly carried out the rescue.

He clearly believed being in the public eye was good for his image. He'd also cleverly avoided being centre stage on the ones which were likely to have negative feedback. Then he'd step aside for someone else to take the flack.

'Sixteen hundred hours. I want you with me.'

Just what she didn't want. It was pointless having her there seeing as they had nothing of note to report, other than they were following all lines of enquiry and for anyone with information to contact the incident room.

'Might not be possible. I have an interview lined up.' She hoped that would get her off the hook.

'We have someone already? Good work, Walker.'

Praise … from him? What was going on?

'Nothing concrete, sir. We're bringing in the boyfriend for questioning,' she replied.

'Well, I'm sure you can leave him for a while when we meet the press,' Jamieson insisted.

'We really don't have anything to say to the press at the moment, other than there's been a suspicious death on the university campus and we're progressing with our enquiries. It really doesn't need both of us. My time is better spent elsewhere.'

Jamieson's right eye twitched. She'd already learnt it wasn't a good sign and braced herself for the onslaught.

'I'm not asking whether you think it's a good idea. I'm telling you I want both of us there. We have to instil the belief the public can trust us to do our job properly and we're working hard on the case. At the moment, thanks to you, our research shows they don't hold us in very high esteem.'

'From one incident? I find that very hard to believe.' She should let his words wash over her but was annoyed he wanted to involve her when she was so busy.

'Your fuck up wasn't the only one. Meet me here fifteen minutes before the conference. That's an order.'

The only other issue she was aware of wasn't anything to do with the running of a case. Another DCI had been caught taking a bribe from one of the newspapers to give up information on a case. He'd been set up.

'Sir.' She walked out of his office and went back to her

office, stopping at the vending machine for a packet of crisps and a can of cola, as she'd forgotten to have lunch.

After she'd been back at her desk for half an hour, Matt walked in.

'Nathan Harris is in the interview room.'

'Great. How is he?'

'So far, he's been very cooperative. He seems in shock over the victim's death. When I arrived at the university, he'd only just found out. He didn't object to coming with me.'

'Okay. Let's see what we can find out.'

They walked into the interview room, and Whitney quickly assessed Harris. Matt was right; he appeared shocked and there were red rings around his eyes as if he'd been crying.

Harris stood when they entered the room and Whitney was surprised at how short he was; at least six inches shorter than the victim. It was unlikely he could've carried Millie to where her body was left.

'Mr Harris. I'm DCI Whitney Walker. Thank you for coming in. We'd like to ask you some questions.'

'Do I need my solicitor?' he asked.

'That's up to you,' Whitney replied. 'You're legally entitled to one. Do you think you need one?'

'No. I've nothing to hide. But I know what can happen in situations like these,' Harris replied, no longer appearing so distressed.

'Situations like what?' Whitney asked.

'I'm not stupid. I study law. I know when there's been a murder the most likely culprit is someone close to the victim.'

'Mr Harris. We'll be speaking to everyone who knows Millie. Including you. Now, I can assure you at the moment all we want to do is talk. If you believe it's in your best interest to call a solicitor, by all means do so. I don't have time to waste, as I have a press conference to attend. So, what's it to be?' She locked eyes with him, and he shifted awkwardly in his seat.

'Let's get on with it,' he finally replied. 'I just want you to find the bastard who did this to Millie.'

'Thank you. I'd like to confirm you're here voluntarily. You're not under caution and can leave at any time. This interview will be recorded for our records.' She turned on the recording equipment. 'DCI Walker, DS Price, and Nathan Harris, Monday fourth November. Mr Harris, please confirm for the record you are here of your own volition to answer our questions.'

'I confirm,' Harris said.

'Thank you. Nathan, please could you tell me how long you've known Millie Carter?' She'd start with the easy questions, so he'd relax a bit.

'I'd noticed her for a couple of years, from around campus. I didn't actually get to speak to her until about a month ago when we got together one evening in the student bar.'

'Had you been wanting to get to know her before then?' Had he been fixated on her for years and then finally managed to get her to go out with him? Or perhaps she'd finished with him, and he couldn't take it.

'I suppose so,' Harris replied.

'Is that a yes?' Whitney asked.

'I'd always liked her but didn't think I stood a chance.' Harris looked down at the table.

'Why not?' Whitney pushed.

'The other guys I'd seen Millie with were all taller than me. I thought short guys wouldn't be her type. In case you hadn't realised, I'm at least six inches shorter than she is.'

'How did that make you feel?'

'Frustrated.'

'And how did you deal with this frustration?'

'I don't understand the question.'

'Did you get angry? Did you hang around Millie trying to get her to notice you?'

'No. I didn't need to.'

'Why not?'

'Mutual friends introduced us, and we got on really well. When I asked her out, she said yes. My height didn't come into it.'

'So, when you finally got together, how did you feel?' she probed.

'Good. It was good. Especially once we started seeing each other regularly.' He leaned forward in the chair, resting his arms on the table. His eyes glazed over with tears, and he blinked them away.

'How often did you see each other?' Matt asked.

'We'd meet for lunch on the days we were both at uni and saw each other most nights. Millie would come around to my house. She preferred it there,' Harris replied.

'Why?' she asked.

'It was quieter because my flatmates usually go out. We'd get the house to ourselves.'

'When was the last time you saw her?'

'That's the thing.' He shifted around in his seat. 'I haven't seen her since Friday. We met for lunch, as usual, and agreed to see each other on the Saturday afternoon, as she was going out with her friends that evening. But she didn't turn up.' His bottom lip quivered. 'I can't help thinking if I'd tried harder to find her or called the police, she might still be alive.'

'What did you do when she didn't turn up?' she asked.

'I called several times and left messages. After she

didn't respond, I thought she didn't want to see me anymore.'

'All it took was a couple of unanswered calls and messages for you to think it was over. I find that hard to believe. She could have had an accident. Been detained. Lost her phone. Didn't you consider any of these? And what about her friends? Why didn't you ask them?' His story didn't add up. What was he hiding?

'Well. We sort of … sort of. We—'

'What are you trying to tell me?' Her heart skipped a beat. She was onto something.

'At lunch on Friday, we had an argument. Millie stormed off.'

'What did you argue about?' She locked eyes with him, but he averted his gaze after a couple of seconds.

'I didn't want her going out with her friends,' he mumbled.

'Why not?'

'I thought she'd hook up with someone.'

'Had she done that before?'

'I don't think so.'

'But you didn't trust her.'

'You've seen her. You've seen me. Of course I didn't. She was way out of my league.' His voice wobbled.

Such insecurity. But did that make him a murderer?

'What did you do after she left you on Friday lunchtime?'

'I texted her to say sorry, but she didn't reply. Then I went to class, and after I went home.'

'And on the Saturday, you tried to contact her again.'

'Yes. I've already said so.'

'Do you have your mobile with you?' she asked.

'Yes. Why?'

'I want to see a record of the texts and calls you made.'

He pulled his phone from his pocket, unlocked it, and slid it across the table. Whitney's eyes travelled down the list of texts. He was telling the truth.

She gave him back the phone.

'Thanks,' he replied.

'What did you do on Saturday night, once you'd decided Millie had finished with you?' she asked.

'I went out with friends for a drink.'

'What time did you get home?' Whitney asked.

'I don't know. I got totally shit-faced. I don't remember anything until Sunday afternoon, when I woke up fully clothed on top of my bed.'

Whitney refrained from giving a lecture about consuming so much alcohol it caused a blackout.

'Where are the clothes you were wearing?' she asked.

'In my room,' he replied. 'Why?'

'Have you washed them?' she continued.

'No. I only do my washing once a week, if that.'

Whitney winced at the thought of how smelly his room must be, full of dirty washing. Still, his poor hygiene could be their good fortune.

'We'd like them for forensics, to eliminate you from our enquiries, if you don't object?' She could insist, but it was better to have his continued cooperation.

'Fine.'

'What exactly were you wearing? My officers can pick them up from your house,' Whitney asked.

'Blue check shirt, jeans, and a cream jumper,' he replied.

'Your underwear?' Whitney asked.

'I'm still wearing my boxers,' he replied, lowering his head sheepishly.

'We'll need them, too.' Thank goodness she had a girl and not a boy. Tiffany, if anything, was over the top clean.

She only had to wear something once and it was in the dirty washing basket. 'I'll ask my officers to bring you some underpants and socks. Do we have permission to go into your room?'

'Yes,' he replied.

Whitney pulled out her phone and texted Frank, asking him to bring in the clothes and saying they had permission to enter Harris's room.

'Thank you. You say you don't remember anything about Saturday night. Who were you with?'

'My flatmates.'

'And they can vouch for you, from Saturday through to Sunday night?' Matt asked.

'I think so. You'll have to ask them,' he replied.

'We will. I'd like you to tell me where you and Millie went over the last couple of weeks. I'm assuming you didn't stay in all the time?'

Harris sat thinking for a few moments. 'We stayed in most evenings, but two weeks ago, on the Saturday night, we went to a concert at a pub in town.'

'Who was the band?' Whitney asked.

'Dogbone.'

She'd never even heard of them. She must be old. 'Were you on your own?'

'No. A group of us went. The week after, we went out on the Wednesday night to the student union, as it was half-price beer night. Then, apart from lunches, we didn't go out until last Saturday, when we went to a birthday party in town.'

'Whose party?' she asked.

'Twins called Henry and Harriet. I don't know them well. One of Millie's friends invited us. There must have been over a hundred people there. We didn't stay long because Millie started a migraine.'

'Were you annoyed at having to leave?' Whitney asked.

'No. Why would I be?'

'I'm just asking. When did you see Millie this week?' Whitney asked.

'We had lunch on Monday, Wednesday, Thursday, and Friday. We went out Wednesday night, and that's it. Is there anything else you need to know? Can I go home?'

'For now. We'll let you have your clothes back once forensics have finished with them. We may wish to question you again, so don't leave the area.'

'I'm meant to be going home to see my parents in two weeks.'

'That's okay,' she replied, making a note of it on the file. 'Other than that, make sure you stay in Lenchester.'

'But…'

'This isn't up for negotiation. We're dealing with Millie's murder, and we will do everything we can do catch whoever did it. If our investigation happens to put you out, then deal with it.'

Chapter Eight

'Stop. I'm begging you. Stop. Please. Why are you doing this to me? Let me go. I won't tell anyone. I promise. I just want to go home. Let me go home. I want my mum.'

I rewind the tape.

I must have watched the "Millie Carter Experience" at least twenty times. It's so good.

I never tire of it. There's always something different to capture my attention.

Everything is recorded, starting from our contrived meeting in town, to how easy it was to persuade her to come back to the house. And the look on her face when she finally realised what she'd got herself into. When she understood there was only one way this was going to end.

It was utter perfection.

But it didn't stop the stupid girl begging me to stop.

Or promising to keep it a secret.

Did she really believe I'd fall for it? What an idiot.

If you ask me to choose my favourite bit, it would have to be the way her face distorted as my hand tightened around her neck and she drew her last breath.

That feeling of having control over a human life. To be the one who determines whether they should live or die. Wow.

Millie Carter was a great choice. She was so easy to play. Because playing is what it's all about. It's one big elaborate game. I made her think it would soon be over, that I'd let her go. There were times when she even started to believe me.

What a weekend it was.

She went from trying to appeal to my nicer side, to being angry.

She writhed in agony during the sex. Then cried after.

I saw every side of her.

Except she didn't laugh much. Actually, not at all.

She was told not to shout out, but when the post was pushed through the letter box, the dumb bitch did. Then the duct tape stayed on, apart from when I fed her.

Her favourite food was jelly and ice cream with sprinkles, so I gave it to her. It was the least I could do, knowing it would be her last ever meal.

She spat it out, the ungrateful slag. I forced it down her throat. She wasn't getting one over on me.

The only thing that didn't go to plan was how quickly she was found. Too quickly, really. My plan, which I believed was meticulous, had been for students to find her during morning break or at lunchtime, when the location was most populated, especially by couples who often go by the river for a session. I wanted to give them a session to remember. I even ensured she couldn't be seen from the path.

What was someone doing there, so early in the morning? Funnily enough, I'd gone down to check at nine, before class, and couldn't believe the police were already milling around. Millie had only been there a few hours.

Next time I'll make sure everything goes to plan.

And there will be a next time.

I can't even begin to describe the high I was on the entire weekend. Everything seemed lighter. Fun. Exciting. At times, it was almost too much to bear. Until the pinnacle. The moment her life was hanging by a thread, and I was the one to determine when the thread broke. I controlled, to the very second, when she expelled her last breath. Have I already mentioned that? Whatever. It's worth repeating.

Because when it happened, my head exploded like there were a thousand fireworks going up simultaneously. Lighting up my brain with a million watts. It was fucking awesome.

Then she was gone. And I came back down from paradise. Although I had a brief reprise when I laid out the body, in that special way. I wanted to show her begging for mercy. Mercy she wasn't granted.

Anyway, who to pick next? It took a while to decide Millie was the perfect specimen. She was my first, so it was important to get it right. Millie was chosen because she always came across as being fun and up for a good time. She reminded me of my mother, those times when my father wasn't there. Then everything changed. Nothing was right when he was home. But when he wasn't, Mum was great, and we always had a good time with her. She'd take us sightseeing. We moved around a lot, so there was always plenty to see.

Millie wasn't such fun while she was here. So maybe the likeness was a tenuous one. If she'd been more cooperative, she might still be alive.

No, she wouldn't. I'm just kidding. I make myself laugh, sometimes, I'm so funny.

Anyway, back to my next plaything. I'm thinking she

should be someone totally different from Millie. This time I'd like someone small and cute. Preferably with short dark hair and freckles. There are a few girls I can choose from.

I pick up my phone from the table and hit the photo button. Flicking through all the photos on there, I'm pleasantly surprised by the number of potential prospects. I take a lot of pictures, always have done. It's easy to do on campus because no one takes any notice. Just another kid taking a selfie.

After going through the gallery, a couple of girls stand out. One, especially, has all the attributes I'm looking for. We have friends in common, so luring her in will be easy enough. The luring bit doesn't excite me as much as everything else, so the easier that can be, the better.

Shivers shoot down my spine.

I'd better make my plans. Everything has to be just so. First of all, I need to find out what food she likes best. And I know exactly who can help me.

Chapter Nine

Whitney pushed her dinner around the plate, hardly eating anything. They'd come to a brick wall with the Carter murder. It had been almost two weeks since the body was found, and Jamieson was breathing down her neck about it. Everyone knew the more time progressed the harder it would be to find the perp. The only new thing they'd learnt was Millie had ketamine in her system. The trouble was, ketamine was so readily available, they had no idea where it had come from.

Despite their questioning and the scrutiny of all available CCTV cameras, there was no new evidence. It was like she'd disappeared off the face of the earth after Friday lunchtime. She hadn't gone out with her friends as planned, but that hadn't worried them because she was known for being unreliable. They'd assumed she'd decided to stay with Nathan for the weekend. There was nothing incriminating on Harris's clothing, or in his room, which didn't totally eliminate him, but made him much less likely to be guilty.

She glanced up at Tiffany, who was also sitting quietly

staring at her dinner. She'd been neglecting her, and it didn't sit right. Her daughter was her life and didn't deserve that.

'I'm sorry I've been so distant recently. It's this bloody case. It's going nowhere, fast. Let's do something together at the weekend. Your choice.'

She couldn't remember the last time they'd hung out together, work had got so demanding. Not just the murder but the screw-up case before, too. Not to mention all the paperwork she had to do. It was getting to the stage when she had to complete a form to request permission to complete a form.

'If you like.'

Not the answer she'd expected.

'Is everything okay?'

'Not really.'

'What is it?'

'I still keep thinking about Millie Carter. I've never known anyone to be murdered before.'

Tiffany's anguished face stared across at her. How come she didn't know Tiffany had connections with Millie? Tiffany shared everything with her. Didn't she?

'Most people don't, love. How well did you know her?'

'Not very. But that hasn't stopped me thinking about it.'

'It's a totally normal response. I wish you'd told me. I hate to see you upset like this.'

'I know how busy you are at work, and I didn't want to worry you.'

She'd spent very little time at home recently and hardly had time to say more than a couple of sentences to Tiffany when they bumped into each other.

'I'm sorry. But you know, you always come first, so

don't ever think you can't speak to me.' She picked up her glass of water and took a sip.

'What happened to Millie, it's so awful. It's still all anyone can talk about at uni. Do you think there'll be another murder?'

The sixty-four-thousand-dollar question. She hoped not, but her gut was telling her otherwise. The murderer was still out there. And if he could do it once …

'We've no reason to think there will be, so try not to worry. We'll find the person who did this. You have my word. But just to be safe, I want you to promise not to go anywhere alone, especially at night. Not until we have the killer locked up.'

'I never do. You've drilled that into me from an early age.' Tiffany smiled.

'Good. I'm glad you're still listening to me. You can't be too careful. Is there anything you want to know about the case? How did you know Millie, exactly?'

'You know what uni's like. Far from six degrees of sepa-ration, it's more like two. There's a girl on my course whose sister lives in the same house as Millie. She keeps moaning about the police not having found the person yet. That's why it's on everyone's mind all the time.'

'What do you say, when they talk about the police?'

'I don't tell anyone you're in charge of the case.'

She didn't blame her. If she was in Tiffany's place, she'd be the same.

'Wise move,' she replied.

'If they knew, they'd never leave me alone, wanting to know stuff all the time. They'd expect you to tell me how the investigation is going, and I know you can't.'

'Exactly.'

'Having said that, do you have any leads yet?'

'I'd love to say yes. But at the moment, I'm hitting a

dead end. I've got the Super on my back, too, which doesn't help. Something will turn up. Someone will remember something and phone the incident room, I'm sure of it. It's what usually happens in these situations.'

'I hope you're right. I hate constantly looking over my shoulder.'

'You'll be fine, it—' Her phone ringing interrupted her. 'I'm sorry, I've got to take this, it's work.'

'Okay.'

'Walker.'

'We've found another body, guv. Looks like the same MO,' Frank said.

Crap. Fucking crap.

'Okay. I'll be at the station in twenty.'

'What's wrong?' Tiffany asked.

'We've got another victim.' She immediately regretted saying it as Tiffany's eyes widened, and her face drained of colour.

'Oh my God,' Tiffany said.

'Right. Grab your things. I'm taking you to Granny's.'

With Tiffany at her mum's, she could concentrate on the case and not be worrying.

'I can stay here; you don't have time to take me,' Tiffany replied.

'I don't want to leave you on your own. I've no idea what time I'm going to be back tonight, if at all. It's not up for discussion.' She seldom laid down the law because Tiffany was such a sensible girl, so when she did have to be harsh, Tiffany didn't argue back.

'Okay, if you don't mind. To be honest, I'd rather not be alone.'

Five minutes later, they hopped in the car, and Whitney drove faster than she normally would with Tiffany in with her.

Fortunately, on a Sunday evening there wasn't much traffic on the road, and they arrived in record time. She hurried up the path to her mum's house and knocked on the door.

'Who is it?' a voice called through the letter box.

'It's me, Mum. I'm in a hurry.'

'Who's me?'

'Whitney. Stop messing around.' She was unable to hide her frustration.

The chain was pulled back, and the door opened.

'Hello. I wasn't expecting you.' Her mum blocked the doorway, so they couldn't walk in. 'What do you want?'

'Do you mind having Tiffany with you tonight? She's a bit upset, and I don't want to leave her on her own. I've got to go to work.' She glanced at her watch, anxious to get moving.

'Hello, Granny,' Tiffany said, coming out from behind Whitney so she could be seen.

'Come in, honey. Rob will be pleased to see you.' She stepped to the side and Tiffany walked in.

'Cool. I'll see you tomorrow, Mum,' Tiffany said, turning to Whitney.

'Aren't you coming in, too?' her mum asked. 'We can play cards. You haven't seen Rob for a while. He's always asking after you.'

She tried to call around most weeks to see her mum and Rob, but she'd been too busy with the case.

'I'm sorry, Mum. Not tonight. I've got to go to work. I'll call in as soon as I can. Promise. Tiffany, make sure you catch the bus to uni tomorrow. If you'd rather not go, then stay here with Granny. Is that okay, Mum?'

'Yes, of course. Would you like to stay tonight, Tiffany?'

'Thanks, Granny.' Tiffany shot a puzzled look at

Whitney over the top of her granny's head. Whitney gave a tiny shrug. Why was her mum acting so strange?

After her mum closed the door, Whitney headed down the path, frowning. This wasn't the first time she'd been confused. Perhaps she was just tired. Looking after Rob wasn't easy. Whitney would have to make more of an effort. Giving money helped up to a point, but she would have to do more.

She couldn't think about it now, though. She had a murderer to catch.

Chapter Ten

'In summary, what you need to remember when you're dealing with a suspect, is even if they're lying to you, they won't lie all the time,' George said to the students in her lecture on the use of forensic psychology in helping the police. She hated the early morning slot, as the turnout was never good, and those who were there seemed half asleep. 'Yes, if they're guilty, they will lie in respect of that, but there are other aspects of their life they'll tell you the truth about. It isn't easy to lie, and it takes a skilled person to maintain the lie without giving themselves away. Read the chapter on lie detection before your next tutorial, as we're going to engage in some role play on it.'

Role play. Was that all she was ever going to do? There'd been no noticeable progress with Millie's case, and yet she still hadn't been asked to help. Every day she'd been online scouring the newspapers for some news about the case, but there was nothing, apart from a bland statement from the police saying they were investigating lines of enquiry.

Her own investigation attempts had proved futile. She'd

spoken to everyone in her tutorial group, and they knew nothing. Though why she thought she'd be able to come up with something tangible just from speaking to them was a little ridiculous. It took more than a few, well-meaning conversations to solve a case.

Why had Millie been chosen? Was it premeditated? Or was she in the wrong place at the right time? And as for Claire not wanting to tell her anything, it wasn't like she was going to blab to the media. Claire was due to give a lecture to the new first years later in the week. She'd pump her for more information then.

She should leave everything to the police, but Millie's lifeless eyes had haunted her day and night since she'd discovered the body. Even in death, there was a look of panic on Millie's face. Her ending certainly hadn't been peaceful.

She dismissed the class, and as no one stayed to discuss anything with her, she left the lecture theatre.

'George. Wait,' her colleague Yvonne called, just as she'd walked into her office.

Yvonne hurried into the office.

'What?' she asked.

'Have you heard?'

'Heard what?' she asked her colleague. 'Who's hooked up with who? And how did you find out?' She grinned, waiting for the latest gossip.

Yvonne was the closest George had to a friend. She was a professor, married with two children. Her life seemed perfect. Except George had seen the occasional cracks. Usually over a few beers.

'They've found another body,' Yvonne replied, her face serious. 'Eric told me. But not down by the river, like before. This time in the ornamental garden, beside the water feature.'

George's jaw dropped. Another body. 'Are you sure? Is it a student? What else do you know?' *Please don't let it be another student I've taught.*

'All I know is the police are there now. I'm not sure who found the body, or who it is. But it's bound to be linked to the first murder. It would be too much of a coincidence if it wasn't,' Yvonne said, her voice matter-of-fact, like they were discussing some usual occurrence.

'If it is the same killer, they have to let me help their investigation. I can't just sit back and do nothing.'

Yvonne was one of the few people who knew she'd discovered Millie's body. She'd chosen to keep it quiet, as it served no purpose to let everyone know, and had only told Yvonne to shut her up because she'd kept asking what was wrong.

She grabbed her coat from the hook on the back of her door and slung her bag over her shoulder.

'Do you want me to come with you?' Yvonne asked.

'No, thanks. Could you pop along to room four and explain I've been held up? Ask them to read chapter six on victims of crime, and say I'll be back as soon as I can.'

It was a two-hour lecture, so she shouldn't miss too much of it. She could count the number of times she'd cancelled or been late for a lecture on one hand, with fingers to spare, over the last eight years. Even if she was dying, bad choice of words, or ill, she'd always drag herself into class. She owed it to her students to give them the best education she could. But this was different. She owed it to Millie to help stop this killer.

'No problem. Let me know what you find out.'

George hurried out of her office, which was situated on the east side of the university. She pushed open the side door and ran down the stone steps onto a path that circled the building. The ornamental garden, with geometrically shaped flower beds, and trees and shrubs on either side, was situated on the other side of the grounds. It was a lovely area, and she often walked around it at lunchtime to get some exercise and de-stress. The ornamental garden wasn't a popular place for students, which was part of the reason she went there. She'd take in the different smells and vibrant colours, especially in the summer.

Her heart went out to whoever had found the body because their dreams would be haunted from then on. How long had the body been there before it was discovered?

She hurried towards the water feature. It was a beautiful stone structure with cherubs spouting water, dating back from the eighteenth century.

She'd love a cigarette, but the campus was non-smoking, though there were areas where people went. On her way, she passed a group of students huddled together talking animatedly. Did they know?

Finally, she reached the garden. It was cordoned off, so she couldn't get any closer. She scanned the area to see if DCI Walker was there. As much as George didn't want to see her again, Walker was the one in charge, so she had no choice if she wanted to find out what had happened.

She approached the cordon and came across two uniformed police officers talking.

'I reckon it's definitely the same killer,' one of the officers said. 'The victim's body was in the same position, and her phone was in her lap.'

'With a killer on the loose, let's hope for lots of overtime. The wife's booked us a cruise next year, and I could do with the money,' the other officer said.

George's insides clenched. Was that all it meant to him? Overtime. What about the murdered girls? What about their families? Had he dealt with so many murders it just rolled off him like they were nothing? The guy only looked to be in his late twenties, so surely not.

The police should use her for their recruitment; she'd make sure they hired the right people.

She shook herself. What the hell was her problem? They were doing a job. Just like she did hers. She should cut them some slack. The murders had clearly affected her more than she'd realised.

'Excuse me,' she called out.

'No one's allowed beyond the cordon,' one of the officers answered.

'Yes, I know. My name's Dr Cavendish. I found the first body.'

'Makes no difference. You're still not allowed through,' the same officer replied.

'Is DCI Walker here? I'd like to speak to her, please.'

The officer clicked on his walkie talkie. 'Is Walker at the scene?'

'No, she hasn't been here this morning,' a voice replied.

'You heard?' the officer asked George.

She nodded. 'What about Dr Dexter, the pathologist?' Claire might let her view the body.

The officer sighed impatiently. 'I'm not a message service.' He clicked again. 'Is the pathologist here?'

'No, she hasn't been here this morning either,' the same voice replied.

'No one's here, Dr Cavendish, so if you wouldn't mind leaving the area.' He gestured for her to leave.

'When was the body found?' she asked, fully expecting them to tell her to take a hike.

The officers exchanged glances, looking like they wondered how much they could tell her. 'Last night.'

'Who found it?' And what were they doing in the ornamental garden on a Sunday night?

'We can't discuss the case. You'll have to speak to DCI Walker.' The officer turned his back on her and walked away, closely followed by the other one who'd remained silent.

George glanced at her watch. Her class should have started fifteen minutes ago. Should she go back, or go to the station to see Walker? She didn't want to be repri-manded for leaving her class alone for too long. But she couldn't let this go. She'd vowed many years ago, after an incident that was so clear in her mind it was as if it had happened yesterday, she wouldn't sit back and do nothing.

When she'd been at boarding school, her best friend committed suicide. Camilla was only sixteen. George had discovered her body. She'd panicked and totally froze, not knowing what to do. She'd just stared at her and screamed. If she'd acted immediately and given her mouth to mouth while calling for help, they might have been able to save her. George hadn't realised at the time, but Camilla had still been breathing when the paramedics arrived. She'd died in the ambulance, despite all the efforts to revive her.

Doctors, teachers, and everyone George knew, had said she'd done all she could, and she shouldn't blame herself. But they were wrong. They hadn't been there and couldn't possibly know. Five minutes was a long time when a person's life was in the balance. She'd never forgiven herself and never would.

Camilla was the first person to call her George, instead of Georgina, and for some reason, it had never occurred to her to mind, even though she hated that level of familiarity. It was why, from then on, she'd insisted on being called George, as a private tribute to her truest friend. Her parents were now the only people who got away with calling her Georgina.

Reflecting on Camilla made the decision for her. She'd see Walker and worry about her class once she got back.

Her car was at home. She rarely brought it in as a protest against the extortionate price of car parking on campus. It was only a twenty-minute walk, and the bus stopped on her street if she didn't fancy the exercise.

She broke a sweat walking as fast as she could and arrived home in fifteen minutes. She entered the kitchen and picked up her car keys from the glass bowl she kept them in. She tensed in annoyance. It had been tidy when she'd left that morning, but now it was like a bomb had hit. Stephen had clearly decided to cook his breakfast and not bothered to clear up afterwards. She was tempted to do the dishes and frying pan before everything stuck solid but stopped herself. He could do it when he got back. Though somehow, she knew she'd end up doing it. How could he live like this? She hated anything out of place and untidy.

Before she could change her mind about the cleaning, she left through the back door. The garage backed onto an alley way at the end of the garden. Opening the garage door, she smiled. A few months ago, she'd bought herself a top of the range, white Land Rover Discovery. She didn't get to drive it often, mainly at the weekends when she hit the open road and put it through its paces. People were surprised to learn she was a petrol head. She'd always loved cars. After much begging on his part, she'd reluctantly put Stephen on the insurance, though she seldom allowed him to drive it.

The police station was on her side of town, and it took around fifteen minutes to get there, thanks to the light traffic. She drove into the car park, but it was full. Fortunately, as she drove back out, a spot had come free on the street. It was only for thirty minutes, but she could always move it if Walker wanted to talk in detail.

She walked up the steps and into the station. As she stood waiting by the front desk, she shivered. Clearly, they'd dispensed with the central heating in reception. There was only one officer, who was on the phone.

'I'd like to see DCI Walker, please,' she said to the officer once she'd finished her call and come over to see her.

'What's it regarding?' The woman was in her late forties and had an *I don't take shit kindly* attitude.

She didn't want to tell her, but decided she'd have to, or they might not let her see Walker.

'The murders at the university.'

The woman leant forward over the desk. 'You have information regarding the crimes?' she asked.

'No. I'm Dr Cavendish. I found the first body. I'm a forensic psychologist, and I'd like to offer my help to DCI Walker.'

The officer's face showed no expression, making her hard to read.

'Okay. Dr Cavendish. Here to help,' the officer said while writing it down. 'Please take a seat over there, and I'll see if DCI Walker is available.'

Chapter Eleven

'Ah, Walker. I was coming to see you,' Jamieson said as Whitney walked out of the ladies' on her way back to the incident room.

Crap. Just the person she didn't want to see. He'd want a run down on the investigation and, so far, they had nothing. Well, that wasn't strictly true. They had another body and an identical crime scene and photo on the girl's phone. But no other evidence and certainly nothing enabling them to move forward. She hoped the killer had slipped up and Claire was able to find some trace evidence to guide them.

'Sir.' She tried to smile but suspected it came out more like a grimace.

'Any leads?' He stood in front of her, his arms folded tightly over his chest. He was a lot taller than her, and she had to strain her neck to make eye contact.

'Nothing yet, sir. I'm waiting to hear back from Dr Dexter. Everything points to it being the same killer. I just want to make sure, so we don't go heading off on a wild goose chase.'

'This can't escalate. I want you to use every measure possible to ensure we don't have a third body.'

'Will do, sir. I take it you'll authorise any overtime required?'

She'd already told the team they'd be working all hours until they solved the case, but it would be good to have Jamieson confirm it, so she wasn't reprimanded down the track for going over budget.

'I've already said, do what it takes. Public confidence is too low as it is. We need to ensure it increases. I want an update from you later today before we give a statement to the press. I want you with me again. To present a united front.'

Another press conference to take her away from her work.

'Yes, sir. If you'll excuse me, I need to get to the incident room.'

She walked away, relieved he hadn't decided to sit in on her briefing with the team. Although unusual for a Detective Superintendent to get involved, it did happen sometimes.

Pushing open the door to the incident room, the noise from everyone chatting hit her.

'Let's get started,' she called out. When no one stopped talking, she jumped onto the nearest desk. 'I said, let's get started,' she shouted.

That stopped everyone in their tracks. Now you could hear a pin drop. She might be small in stature, but she had a loud voice to compensate. She jumped down and stood by the board which now displayed both victims' photos.

'Thank you for your attention. Victim two. Olivia Griffin.' She pointed at the photograph. 'Twenty-one-year-old third-year history student at Lenchester University. Found on the grounds of the university last night. What else do we know about her?'

'I'm going through the contacts on her phone,' Ellie said.

'Family?'

'She comes from Devon,' Matt said. 'I've been in touch with the guys down there, and they're going to let the family know and arrange for someone to make the formal identification.'

At least she wasn't going to be the one to break the news to them.

'It appears the murder was done by the same person as Millie Carter. Same pose. Phone in the lap. Wallpaper on phone was a photo of the victim tied up. We're waiting for further information from pathology.'

'Unless it's a copycat,' Frank said.

The team groaned in unison. She'd worked with Frank for years, and he wasn't the brightest in the team. He hadn't got long until retirement. But she'd miss him when he did leave. He was part of the furniture, like the knackered old chair you didn't want to throw out for sentimental reasons.

'It's not likely, Frank. When we've given statements to the media, we've deliberately left out the detail of the phone in the lap with the victim's photo on it. And even though it's possible someone leaked the information, it's highly unlikely a copycat could have made the scene totally identical to the first. Even copycats tend to have their own signature.'

She stared at the two photos of the victims and the one of Nathan Harris which was directly under Millie. 'Has anyone been in contact with Millie Carter's boyfriend, Nathan Harris?'

'Yes, guv,' Matt said. 'He's got an airtight alibi for the

whole weekend, which I've checked. He was at his parents' house three hours away. They were having a silver wedding anniversary celebration.'

Whitney took his photo from the board. 'Yes. He did mention going home for the weekend. So, that rules him out.'

'What about the person who found the body?' Frank asked.

'People,' Matt replied. 'It was a middle-aged couple who live close to the university. They were walking their dog, and it ran off into the university grounds. We spoke to them last night, but they were in shock. I've asked them to come in for a longer interview later this morning. I'll—' He was interrupted by the phone on his desk ringing. 'Price,' he replied. 'I'll let her know. Hang on a second.' He put his hand over the mouthpiece. 'Guv, Dr Cavendish is at the front desk. She wants to speak to you about the murders.'

She rolled her eyes towards the ceiling. 'For goodness' sake, we don't need help from her. We're quite capable of working this case ourselves. Tell her if she has anything to say, to put it in an email, and I'll get to it when I can. In the meantime, we've got work to do.'

Whitney ignored the sarcastic oohs and ahhs from the rest of the team and listened as Matt relayed her message. She winced a little. She hadn't meant to be so aggressive, but she didn't like people trying to muscle in on her territory. It was bad enough having Jamieson, with his academic background, spouting theories which had little relevance in the real world, without adding Dr Cavendish into the mix.

'Let's look at similarities between the victims,' she said, dismissing further thoughts of the doctor and picking up a board pen. 'Both students at the university. Both early twenties. Anything else?'

'It doesn't seem like the killer has a type,' Ellie said. 'Millie Carter was nearly six feet tall, with long blonde hair and with a well-built physique. Olivia Griffin was small, with short dark hair. They were studying different subjects. We haven't found a connection yet, but we're still looking into both girls' lives to see if there's any crossover.'

Whitney's phone rang, and she saw it was Claire. 'I need to take this,' she said to the team. She headed to the back of the room and into her office away from the racket.

'Claire. What have you got for me?' Had she done Olivia's autopsy already?

'I haven't yet completed my investigation, but the various aspects of the killer lead me to suspect we're looking for the same murderer as for Millie Carter.'

Hardly a surprise.

'Thanks. Speaking of Millie Carter, when's the second autopsy report being done?'

'It was completed last Friday and the body released to the family. Didn't the coroner's office let you know?'

'If they did, it didn't reach me.'

Unless they'd informed Jamieson, and he hadn't bothered to pass it on. She'd ask him later before the press conference.

'The funeral is ten tomorrow morning, at the crematorium.'

'Thanks. I'll let you get on. When will you have more on Olivia Griffin?'

'When I've finished.' Claire's frustrated sigh echoed down the phone.

'I'll wait to hear from you.'

'I've just spoken to Dr Dexter,' Whitney said to the team as she walked back into the incident room. 'Millie Carter's funeral is tomorrow morning.'

'Are you going?' Matt asked.

'Yes. You can come with me. I'll pick you up at nine so we can get there early and watch who attends. The murderer could be there. The rest of you, continue with your investigations and report in after lunch tomorrow. We've got to make some progress on this. Soon.'

Chapter Twelve

George smoothed down her black coat, which she'd put on for Millie's funeral, as tears unexpectedly filled her eyes. She didn't do crying. Well, rarely. She blinked them away while the memory of her grandmother's funeral last year flashed before her eyes.

She'd spent most school holidays with her grandma because her parents were working. Her dad was always busy producing medical miracles as a heart surgeon or lecturing at conferences. And her mum spent most of her time preventing atrocities across the globe as a human rights lawyer.

Her younger brother, James, also now a surgeon, often spent his holidays with friends. So, it was mainly her and Grandma. They were hardly ever at home. There was always some charity event to go to. Some stately home to visit. Or just shopping, which her grandma loved with a passion. Everyone in Harrods knew her, and she greeted them all by their first names.

Stephen didn't understand why she wanted to attend Millie's funeral. He thought it would be for family and friends, and just because she was Millie's tutor didn't mean she was duty bound to attend. But every night since she'd found the body, she'd had bizarre dreams. Often involving Millie being alive, but she'd got to her too late and she died. She knew it came from what had happened with Camilla and wasn't anything to do with Millie, but that didn't make it any easier. She hadn't told Stephen about Camilla. She hadn't told anyone.

The drive took her just under an hour, and when she arrived at the crematorium, there were already people milling around outside. She had to park a couple of streets away, and by the time she'd walked back, they'd opened the doors.

Everyone poured in. Hardly anyone was talking. The silence was disturbing. She decided to sit towards the back and keep out of the way. The first two rows had older people in them, who she assumed were Millie's family. The rest of the chapel was mainly filled with students. She recognised several of them from her lectures. Millie was clearly popular. She could understand why. She'd always been lovely, and George had liked her.

On the other side of the chapel, at the back, were DCI Walker and DS Price. They were scanning the chapel. When Walker looked in her direction, she nodded. Walker said something to Price, and he stared at her. She didn't look away. She had every right to be there.

The music started, and the doors opened. The coffin, covered in a deep-red cloth, was carried in by four men. One of them had to be Millie's father; the family likeness was uncanny. Another, younger man, had the same family look. Was he also related to Millie?

She turned away. Such a waste of life. Millie had so much ahead of her. It surprised George the body had been released so soon. Not that she was up on procedures relating to murder victims, so she'd googled it and found in cases like this, an independent post mortem would have been carried out for use by the murderer's lawyer if they were ever caught. As much as she thought this was so the families could try to move on, she also knew it would be so the body didn't have to be held onto by the mortuary. Saving space and money.

Many of the people attending weren't wearing black, especially the students. The funeral was a celebration of Millie's life. A montage of photos played on a large screen that had been erected behind the podium, from when she was young, up until fairly recently. People stood up to talk about her and how much she'd meant to them. Although it was a celebration, it didn't stop the sobbing. When the coffin was finally put through the long red curtains, they played her favourite Adele song. A lump stuck in the back of George's throat, and she struggled to catch her breath.

The air was stifling, and once the family had left, Whitney and Matt quickly exited the building, along with other mourners. They stood back from everyone else, scanning to see if anyone, or anything, was out of the ordinary. In her peripheral vision, Whitney noticed Dr Cavendish heading in her direction. She started to move away, but Dr Cavendish picked up her pace and cut in front of her.

'DCI Walker.'

Whitney stopped. 'Dr Cavendish.'

'Do you have a moment?' she asked. 'I'd like to talk to you about the cases.'

'This really isn't an appropriate time,' Whitney replied, gesturing with her hand at all the mourners.

'Well, I've tried to speak to you before and sent you several emails, but you didn't respond.'

'What can I say? I'm in the middle of a murder investigation. You should understand that.'

'I don't understand what you have against using my help,' she continued. 'Plenty of police departments engage the help of a forensic psychologist in their investigations. Why not you?'

Whitney let out a frustrated sigh. 'I'm sure you'd be very useful in certain investigations, but not this one.'

'Why not?'

'We have our own methods of research and finding offenders that don't include using your type.'

Crap. Why had she said that? It gave credence to Jamieson's view of her being stuck in the past and not prepared to embrace modern policing. Which wasn't the case.

'My *type*? What's that meant to mean?'

'Nothing. What I meant to say was most murders are committed by someone who knows the deceased an—'

'Well, everything points to you dealing with the same killer for both murders,' Dr Cavendish said, interrupting her. 'Same pose. Phone in the lap. Left in the same vicinity.'

'Yes. Even using our antiquated methods, we've figured that out. More to the point, how do you know about the phone? That detail hasn't been released to the public,' she challenged.

'I overheard some officers speaking at the scene. That's why I went to the station yesterday. Thinking you'd actually welcome some assistance, though clearly I was mistaken.'

'It was kind of you to offer, but it's really not necessary,' Whitney said.

'Do you have any suspects yet?' Dr Cavendish pushed.

'I can't discuss an ongoing investigation,' she replied.

'So let me help. Show me the evidence, and I'll come up with a profile you can use. Where's the harm?'

'Anyone can come up with a profile. It's not hard. Let me see. The murderer's male, with a connection to the university.'

'Suit yourself. If you're so precious over your work you won't even consider taking any help offered, it's your issue. I'm sure the dead girls' families would be glad to hear you're limiting your enquiries to areas of which you're familiar. And not daring to think even slightly out of the box.'

'Are you threatening to go to them?'

'No. I'm not that petty. I was just pointing out a fact. Forget it. You know where I am if you change your mind.'

Whitney stared at the doctor's retreating back. Why had she been so awkward with her? The woman was offering to help. Claire Dexter recommended her. But she'd resisted. The trouble was, she couldn't warm to her. She didn't like her arrogant, condescending attitude. And her posh sounding voice especially grated.

'Why did you turn down her offer?' Matt asked.

'You must have read my mind. I suppose it's because I don't like the woman.' She cringed at how childish that sounded.

'You don't have to like her,' Matt replied. 'I think she'd be a useful addition to the team.'

She stared at Matt. She liked that he felt able to speak openly to her. She encouraged it in all of her team. Something she'd learnt from Don Mason, a DI who retired eight years ago, and who'd been instrumental in progressing her career. She still missed him. She also knew he'd tell her to pull her head in and stop letting her emotions get the better of her.

'You're right. I need to put my personal feelings to one side.'

She hurried after the doctor. 'Wait,' she called once she was within ear shot.

Doctor Cavendish turned. 'Yes?'

'I could do with some help, please.'

The doctor scrutinised her face for a few seconds. 'Okay. How would you like to proceed?'

'Come to the station and we'll go through the evidence. You can meet the team and answer any questions they might have.'

'Great. I'll meet you there.' She turned to leave when Whitney placed her hand on her arm.

Although Whitney wanted her there, this wasn't going to be some joint police/academic investigation, and that needed to be made clear.

'Just to let you know. This is my investigation, and you're invited at my request. What I say goes.'

Chapter Thirteen

Doctor Cavendish met Whitney at the front desk and followed her to the incident room.

'Listen up, everyone,' Whitney said as they entered the room. She headed over to one of the desks and dropped her bag onto it. 'This is Dr Cavendish. She's going to assist us in the investigation. She found the first victim's body. She is also a forensic psychologist and is here to offer her insight into the case and provide us with a profile of the murderer.'

She couldn't be a hundred per cent certain, but she thought she heard one of the team mutter, '*What the fuck?*' Understandable, based on her attitude before. But not polite. She glared in the direction of the comment.

She nodded in the doctor's direction, indicating she should speak.

'Good morning, everyone. And please call me George,' she said. 'As a forensic psychologist, I'm not just here to come up with a profile of the offender. Yes, I can do that, but I'm also trained to help you with the investigation.

Based on factors relating to the crime, I can recommend the direction you should take your search for the offender. I can also guide you in interviewing suspects or victims of the crimes.

'Thanks, George,' Whitney said. 'But for the moment we'd like your opinion on who we're looking for. Ellie, please let the doctor know what evidence we have on both cases.'

'So far, we have two bodies. Both students at the university. Millie Carter studied psychology, and Olivia Griffin studied history. Both were raped, strangled, and posed with their hands clasped together and brought up to their chests. They were left with their mobile phones in their laps, and the wallpaper had been changed to a photo of them in their underwear, with their wrists cable tied to the bed head and their legs splayed. The PM revealed the first victim had ketamine in her blood. We're waiting to hear about the second victim. There was no trace evidence found on either body, apart from soap, which we assume means the victims were washed. They were moved after death, and there is no evidence of them being dragged.' Ellie looked at Walker, who nodded at her.

'Thank you, Ellie,' George said. 'Based on what you've told me and the similarities in the killer's actions, we can assume it's the work of the same person.' She heard a titter and frowned. She obviously needed to get to the good stuff faster. 'The murderer is male. Possibly over six feet tall, young, and fit, to enable him to move the bodies. The nature of the rape and the use of ties suggests he has control issues. It's likely he had an upbringing during which, at times, he felt powerless. Perhaps he was moved from school to school and wasn't able to form stable relationships with others. Or he was subjected to bullying.'

Were they going to give her marks out of ten? It was like undergoing some sort of classroom test.

'Well, that's a start,' Walker said. 'Do you think he'll strike again?'

'Most definitely. And soon, judging by the cooling off period between the two murders, which was only two weeks. Serial killers, which these killings have all the markers of, tend to decrease time between murders, not increase. The pose and the photos are a message from him. He's telling us he had control over the victims. Control from tying them up. Control from the rape and ultimately, control over when they died. The pose represents them pleading for their lives. These things are inextricably linked and indicative of intelligence and psychopathy,' George said.

Whitney glanced at her watch and hoped like hell her frustration didn't show on her face. Doctor Cavendish might have hours to give her lectures and come up with her theories, but right now there was a killer out there. A real one. Not just an academic riddle to be discussed.

'So, what's the CliffsNotes version?' she asked.

George's jaw visibly tightened. 'All I'm saying is everything the murderer did was calculated and planned for maximum impact. Of course, it could've been worse. He could have mutilated his victims. That would have shocked, but probably wasn't the message he wanted to put across. Calculated and controlled was his message. This makes him far more dangerous. Because he's clever. Very clever. The whole set up was too well orchestrated for him not to be.'

'Which means catching him won't be easy,' Whitney said.

'What about leaving the photos on their phones?' Ellie asked.

'It's a message to us. To you. The police. It's a taunt. He's showing off. The same as leaving the bodies in a public place. If he wasn't trying to impress, he'd leave the bodies somewhere they wouldn't be found for a long time, if at all. That sort of killer gets different kicks from the death of their victims,' George said.

'Well, he's playing with the wrong people. Because we're going to find him. And it's not up for negotiation,' Whitney said.

'Geographical location can also tell us a lot. Offenders tend to work in a restricted area, close to where they live,' George said.

'In that case, for now I'm going to confine the house-to-house to a half-mile radius around the university,' Whitney replied. 'Matt, you come with me to Olivia Griffin's flat to question her flatmates. Hopefully they'll all be there.'

'Yes, guv,' Matt said.

'Ellie, go through the contact lists on both phones and look for any crossover. Then begin background checking Olivia's family.'

'Okay, guv,' Ellie replied.

'Doug. Start checking the CCTV for anyone hanging around the university over the weekend. Sue can help.'

'The rest of you divide up. Half of you can undertake a house-to-house and half can go to the university and assist uniform in questioning the students. Except you, Frank. Stay and answer the incident room phone. PR is issuing a statement to the press, so we're bound to get plenty of calls. Let's go, people.'

George joined Whitney. 'Would you like me to come with you? I can assess the people you question to establish whether they're telling the truth or not.'

'Thanks. But no thanks. We've got this. You go back to work, and I'll be in touch when we next want your help.'

Whitney picked up her bag and headed out of the door.

Chapter Fourteen

During her drive to Olivia Griffin's flat, Whitney pushed aside thoughts the doctor could be right, and she should be with them. Then again, Whitney could usually tell when people were lying to her, so having her there would've been overkill.

There was no doubt what she'd said about the murderer was useful. But the ridiculous long words she'd used seemed designed to make the rest of the team feel stupid, even if that wasn't her intention. They might not have had the doctor's education, but they were good at their jobs, and Whitney didn't want them developing inferiority complexes.

It was just more evidence the real world and the academic world didn't mix.

She wouldn't mind some of the doctor's height, though. Being only five feet four inches had its disadvantages. Especially when she was on the beat. Criminals used to think she was fair game when trying to avoid being arrested. Her nose had been broken several times, and the twist in the centre taunted her every time she looked at herself in the mirror.

'Just up here on the right, guv.' Matt's words cut across her thoughts, and she quickly shelved the guilt over her treatment of Dr Cavendish to the back of her mind.

She pulled up alongside a block of flats and parked. They got out of the car and made their way to the front entrance.

'Flat six.' She looked at the row of buttons in front of her on the wall, until spotting six and pressing it.

'Hello.' A voice came from the speaker.

'Detective Chief Inspector Walker and Detective Sergeant Price here to speak to you,' she replied.

'We were expecting you. We're on the second floor.'

The door was buzzed open, and Whitney and Matt walked in. The block of flats was typical of the nineteen sixties concrete monstrosities which were built after the war. Square and ugly, with aluminium windows. The building had clearly been renovated at some time or other, but nothing could change the cold feel of it. The lift had an *out of order* sign, so they walked up the two flights of stairs leading to the second floor.

The university owned many of these buildings, and they were mainly rented out to students. They were at odds with much of the historic city. Whitney loved Lenchester. She'd been born there and had never had the urge to leave. Of course, being pregnant with Tiffany at seventeen had put paid to her moving even if she'd wanted to, as she needed to be close to her parents. Her dad had died when Tiffany was ten. He'd thought the world of his grand-daughter. There were so many similarities in their person-alities. They both laughed at the same jokes and would sit for hours watching nature programmes on TV. He would have loved the young woman she'd grown into.

When they reached the second floor, the flat door was open, and they walked into a large square hall.

'Hello,' she called.

Two girls came out from a room on the left, both pale and their eyes red from crying. She instinctively had the urge to give them both a hug, knowing that's what she'd have done to Tiffany.

'Hello,' the taller of the two said. 'I'm Hannah and this is Lizzie. Peta's in the living room, if you'd like to come through.'

'Thanks,' she replied.

They followed the girls into the living room, which had two mismatched old sofas facing each other, and two single chairs. In the corner was a dining table covered in magazines and books. Dirty glasses and mugs were on the low coffee table between the sofas.

'Thanks for seeing us,' Whitney said, trying to put them at ease. 'I know it's a difficult time for you, but to catch the person who did this to Olivia, we need to get as much information as we can.'

The girls sat next to Peta on one sofa, and she and Matt sat on the other one.

'We want to help. We've talked about it non-stop but can't think of anything that might be of use,' Hannah said, a defensive edge to her voice.

What was she hiding? And how did they decide what was going to be useful?

'When did you last see Olivia?' Whitney continued.

The girls exchanged glances. The hairs on the back of her neck rose. She was on full alert.

'It's tricky.' Hannah avoided looking directly at them.

'What do you mean?'

It was obvious she was being lied to. Should she have brought the doctor with her, just to confirm? No. She was perfectly capable of dealing with the situation and should stop second guessing herself.

'We're not sure when she last was in the apartment. She goes out a lot and often doesn't come home,' Hannah said, her voice strained.

It didn't escape Whitney's notice Hannah was doing all the talking, while the other two sat in silence.

'Did she have a boyfriend?' Matt asked.

'No. Not exactly,' Hannah replied, after yet again looking at the others.

'Okay, you three. What's going on? And don't say, *nothing*. Because clearly something is.' Whitney didn't need a fancy psychology degree to see that.

Hannah looked out from under her eyelashes and flushed a deep shade of red. She looked directly at Whitney, even though Matt had asked the question about Olivia's boyfriend. 'If we tell you, please don't tell her parents. They wouldn't understand. They're old and uptight.'

'I can't make a decision like that until I know what it is. If it's possible to keep it quiet, I will. But no promises.'

'Olivia worked for Diamond Escorts. She needed the money to help fund her studies.'

She hadn't heard of Diamond Escorts before; they'd obviously kept themselves under the radar. Some agencies were more like brothels. She hoped this one wasn't. Olivia wasn't the first student, and wouldn't be the last, to go into that work. University fees were ridiculous. And she should know, as she'd been helping Tiffany with hers. She was grateful Tiffany had chosen to work at a garden centre to supplement her student loan.

'How often did she work for them?' She wrote the agency's name in her notebook. She'd call through to Ellie and get her to check them out.

'Maybe once or twice a week. That's all she needed, the money was so good,' Hannah replied.

'What about the rest of you? Do you work for them?' she asked.

'No,' they said in unison, vigorously shaking their heads.

'We tried to persuade Olivia to stop, but she wouldn't. Do you think it was one of her clients who did this?' Hannah asked.

A question Whitney had been asking herself.

'We can't make any assumptions at this stage, but we'll definitely check them out. Back to the last time you each saw Olivia. When was that?'

'I bumped into her at uni on Friday morning,' Peta said. 'She didn't say anything about working that evening, but I didn't actually ask her.'

Whitney jotted that down.

'I didn't see her but heard her in her room on Saturday morning at around ten,' Lizzie said. 'Our rooms are next to each other.'

'Are you sure it was her?' she asked.

'Not one hundred per cent, no. But if it wasn't, it had to be someone who had her key. I don't remember her ever giving her key to anyone.'

'Okay, we'll assume it was Olivia,' she said. 'Hannah, what about you?'

'I hadn't seen Olivia since Wednesday. But I stayed at my boyfriend's flat on Thursday and Friday night,' Hannah replied.

'I'll need his details, please, so we can confirm your story,' she replied.

'Why? Am I a suspect?' Hannah's eyes widened.

'It's just for our records. We have to account for the movements of those closest to her.'

Hannah went to the table and scribbled the details down while Matt continued the questioning.

'How often would you all go out together in the evenings?' he asked.

'If Olivia wasn't working, we'd sometimes go out together,' Hannah replied.

'Can you remember the last time?' Matt asked.

'Was it the party?' Lizzie asked the other two.

'I think so,' Peta said, nodding.

'Yes,' Hannah agreed. 'That was it. We all went to a birthday party a few weeks ago.'

A birthday party? Whitney was certain Millie had gone to a birthday party recently, too. Was it the same one?

'Whose party?' Whitney asked.

'Some vet students,' Lizzie said. 'I know them from uni.'

'You're studying to be a vet?' she asked.

'No. I'm doing medical science, but some of our classes are held in the veterinary science building,' Lizzie said.

'What are their names?' Matt asked.

'Henry and Harriet Spencer. They're twins.' Lizzie replied.

'Tell us more about the party. Did a lot of people go?'

'It was heaving,' Hannah said. 'If someone puts it on social media, you can guarantee a hundred or more attending. This party was no different. In fact, the house was so full, people were crowded in the garden. We had a good time.'

'Do you have the twins' details, Lizzie, please?' she asked.

Lizzie pulled her phone from her pocket and looked at the screen. 'I have Harriet's number.' She called it out, and Matt wrote it down.

'Thanks. While we're here, we'd like to take a look at

Olivia's bedroom, if you could point us in the right direction.'

'I'll take you,' Hannah said.

They followed her out of the lounge and into the hallway where she stopped.

'Before you go, I want to tell you something in private, without the others hearing.'

'Okay.' Whitney exchanged a quick glance with Matt.

'I lied about not seeing Olivia since Wednesday. I saw her on Friday night.'

'I thought you were with your boyfriend,' she said.

'On Thursday night I was. On Friday, I went with Olivia on a double date for the escort agency. It was the first time I'd done anything like that. No one else knew, especially not my boyfriend, or Lizzie and Peta. And I don't want them to. It was just a one off. Especially after what happened to Olivia,' Hannah said.

'We'll have to get in touch with the agency to confirm your story.'

'I understand. But you won't tell anyone here, will you?' Hannah pleaded.

'I'm sure it won't be necessary. I'm not so sure we can keep it from Olivia's parents, though. And it may come out at the inquest,' she replied.

'I understand,' Hannah replied. 'Olivia's room is the second on the left as you go along the hall.'

'Thanks. We'll pop back into the lounge once we've finished in there. Please don't go anywhere until we leave. And ask the others not to, either.'

Hannah left them and walked back into the lounge.

Matt looked at Whitney. 'What do you make of that?' he asked.

'The escort agency?'

He nodded.

'I think it's a sorry state of affairs that unless kids are rich, they can't afford to go to university. The fact these girls had to resort to being escorts is disgusting.'

'They can earn a lot of money,' Matt said.

'Yes. But at what cost? We all know what being an escort means. I'd be surprised if Olivia didn't have sex with any of her clients. I just thank God I'm able to help Tiffany out. The thought of her even contemplating doing that makes me want to vomit.'

'Tiffany isn't the sort, anyway. She's much too sensible,' Matt said.

'It must be the good example I've set her. Or something. Come on, let's see if we can find anything useful in the bedroom.'

Chapter Fifteen

Whitney and Matt were back in the incident room after lunch. Olivia's bedroom had given them little in the way of evidence, apart from her bank statements which were crazy. Olivia had been making thousands a month from her escort work. More than Whitney earned. Would she ever consider that sort of work? She could take care of herself if there was a problem. And the money would be amazing. But no. She wouldn't swap her job as a police officer.

She headed over to where Ellie was sat peering at her computer screen.

'Guv,' Ellie said, once she'd noticed her standing there.

'What have you got from the contact lists?' she asked.

'I split them up into male and female. There were a few similarities. They both had over a hundred contacts in there. There were ten matching females on both and eight males.'

'Right. Let's look at the men. We'll speak to them first.'

Ellie handed Whitney the list, and she scanned through it. Ellie had obviously been working hard, as she'd added their addresses and other relevant information, including whether they were students or staff, and their subjects.

'Good work. Take Frank and make a start on interviewing all the men on this list and obtaining alibis for both dates. If you can't see them face to face, phone them. Report back to me anyone who can't provide one.'

'Will do. Come on, Frank.'

He got up from the desk. 'I can't work too late. I've arranged to go out with the missus,' he said.

Whitney rolled her eyes towards the ceiling. 'This takes precedence over you pissing it up the wall at the pub.'

Frank scowled in her direction and then walked towards Ellie, who was waiting at the door.

'Matt, we're heading to Diamond Escorts.'

'Lucky bastard,' Frank said, turning his head and speaking over his shoulder.

'You win some, you lose some,' Matt quipped, grinning.

'Give me a break,' Whitney groaned. 'Keep it in your pants, or I'll go on my own.'

'Just joking, guv.'

The office for Diamond Escorts was listed at a residential address in one of the posh areas of Lenchester. It was on the outskirts of the city and took twenty minutes to get there.

'I'm in the wrong job,' she said as they drew up to the gate belonging to a large modern house, built in mock Tudor style. She opened her window and leaned out, pressing the entrance buzzer.

'Hello,' a woman answered.

'DCI Walker and DS Price, to see Diamond Escorts,' she replied.

'What's it about?' the woman asked.

'We need to talk in person. Please open the gate.'

The black iron gate slid open, and she drove around the circular gravel drive until they reached the front of the house. They walked to the front door and before she had time to ring the bell it was opened by a tall, fifty-something, glamorous, well made-up woman. Whitney couldn't help notice the six-inch heel gold shoes she was wearing and wondered how on earth she could stand in them, let alone walk.

'Please come through. I'm Annabelle De Souza. I run Diamond Escorts.'

Whitney and Matt showed their warrant cards and followed her into a large rectangular hall, with a highly polished light wooden floor. A huge stone coloured vase full of grasses was situated in the corner, and large pieces of modern art adorned the walls. A white marble staircase was the main focus of the room, rising up the centre, and splitting off to the left and right, with open banisters over-looking the room below. Her eyes were drawn to the large chandelier, with hundreds of tiny glass droplets, which hung from the high ornate ceiling.

'We'd like to talk to you about one of the women you have working for you,' she said.

'We'll go to my office,' Annabelle said. 'My young grandchildren are here with their nanny, and I don't want them hearing anything.'

To reach the office, they went through the kitchen. It was white and chrome, complete with every appliance imaginable. A square island, with a double sink, dominated the middle, and there was an Aga, a huge hob, and oven. Whitney had never been much of a cook, but she loved fancy kitchens and had a cupboard full of recipe books. She just enjoyed looking at the photos. The odd occasion she managed to watch the TV, cookery programmes were her viewing of choice.

The Diamond Escorts' office was locked, presumably to keep the grandchildren out. She'd seen some home offices before, but this took it to a whole new level. It was huge. A large antique desk was situated in the centre of the room, and there were photos on the wall of a number of women. She quickly scanned them and saw Olivia.

'We're here about Olivia Griffin.' She pointed to the photograph on the wall.

'You mean, Kirsty?' Annabelle said.

'Her real name's Olivia Griffin. How long has she worked for you?'

'All my girls are self-employed sub-contractors.' Annabelle leaned against the desk.

'You know what I mean. How long have you been using her services?' She was losing patience by the second.

'What's this about? The reason many of my girls use an alias is to be discreet about what they do,' Annabelle said.

'Olivia was murdered. We're trying to work out her recent movements.'

Colour drained from Annabelle's face, and she grabbed hold of the desk with both hands. 'Murdered? When? What happened?'

'Sometime over the weekend. We know she worked for you on Friday evening, and Hannah was with her. We'd like contact details for the men they were with.'

'Not possible, I'm afraid,' Annabelle replied adamantly.

'Why not?'

'Look, DCI Walker. My business runs on discretion. If my customers found out I'd given their details to the police, they wouldn't be my customers for long.'

Whitney glared at her. Did the woman care nothing about the girls she employed? Did she seriously believe her customers' privacy was more important than finding Olivia's killer?

'I understand you want to be discreet, but this is a murder enquiry.'

'My clients are men of a certain standing. I can't betray their confidence.'

'Your decision, but if I have to get a search warrant, you might find those *men of a certain standing* will go elsewhere. Because once we go down that track, it will be out in the open. If you let me see your records now, it stays between us.' She hoped her words would do the trick. It would also save the rigmarole of getting a search warrant, assuming she could get one.

'Okay,' Annabelle replied as she walked around her desk and opened one of the drawers in the filing cabinet behind it. She took out a folder.

'You don't have it electronically?' Matt asked.

'I'm not good with computers, and I don't want to risk being hacked,' Annabelle replied as she handed the manila folder to Whitney. 'This is the file on Olivia's Friday evening client, Richard Reid.'

'Had Olivia seen him before?' she asked.

'Yes. Olivia stood in for his previous favourite once, and now he requests her whenever he comes to town.'

Whitney wrote down his contact details and handed the file back to Annabelle. 'What's the name of the man he was with?' she asked.

'I don't know his name. You'll have to ask Richard.'

'You were happy to let Hannah go out with someone you hadn't even vetted? That doesn't seem like sound business practice to me,' she said.

Annabelle shifted awkwardly on the spot. 'It's not something I'd usually do. It's different with Richard; he's been with me since the beginning of my business.'

'What about Hannah? Did you interview her first before allowing her to go out with Olivia?' she asked.

'Yes. I'd already met Hannah. She was thinking of joining us. Students make good escorts. My clients like beauty and brains. My students have both.'

'And what about sex?'

'As I mentioned, my girls are self-employed. I provide escorts for my clients. Anything happening during the evening is between the two of them. I'm not saying it doesn't happen. I don't know whether Olivia and Richard had sex. I don't ask, and I'm not told. That's the way it has to be.'

'Olivia's the second student to be murdered. Please check your records and let me know if Richard Reid was in town on the weekend of the third of November.'

'I read about the other student. She didn't work for me. Are the murders connected?'

'We believe so, yes,' she replied. 'Your records,' she added.

'Richard usually only books once a month when he travels to Lenchester on business. But I'll check.' She looked in her diary. 'Oh. Yes, he was. But that doesn't mean he had anything to do with the murders. He has a strict routine. He arrives in Lenchester on a Friday and leaves first thing Saturday morning on an early flight to Scotland, where he lives.'

'You seem to know a lot about his movements.'

'As I mentioned, he's a longstanding client. When you speak to him, please make sure he knows you forced me to hand over his details. I don't want to lose him.'

'We'll try our best not to lose you business, but right now our main concern is finding Olivia's murderer before he strikes again.'

'You think he will?' Annabelle asked.

'He's done it twice, already.'

'If that's all, I have an appointment with my accountant shortly. I'll see you out.' Annabelle brought the meeting to an abrupt end.

'We can see ourselves out. Thank you for your time.' Whitney opened the door to the office and went out into the kitchen.

In the distance she could hear small voices. The grandchildren. What sort of mother would allow their children to be in the same house as an escort business? Because surely the escorts would be visiting on a regular basis. There was no way she'd have let Tiffany be anywhere near one.

Once out of the house, she turned to Matt. 'What do you think?'

'She seemed legitimate enough. It's ridiculous how much men pay for the services of an escort,' he replied. 'It would be hard to afford on a copper's salary.'

'You seriously want to go there?'

'I just wondered.' Matt shrugged.

'I'm more interested in Olivia's client, Richard Reid.'

'We need to speak to him.'

'Agreed. We'll also check with the airport to see if Annabelle De Souza's account of his routine is accurate. In the meantime, let's get back to the station to see if Ellie's managed to find anything on the men who knew both girls.'

Chapter Sixteen

George left the lecture theatre, relieved it was over. Her concentration had been shot and several times she'd had to refer to her notes. She doubted the students would notice. Many lecturers kept their noses in their notes the whole time while speaking. She knew her stuff so well, it wasn't necessary. Usually at the end of a class she hung around in case anyone wanted to discuss an aspect of what she'd taught. Not today.

Once in her room, she went into the drawer of her desk and pulled out a cigarette and lighter. She'd given a good profile to the police. Something they could work with. But she wanted to do more. Her time with DCI Walker's team hadn't gone well. She'd almost heard Stephen's mocking laughter in her head when Walker had asked for the CliffsNotes version. He often accused her of being unable to communicate in a non-academic way. And judging by the unimpressed look the detective had given her, her attempt at doing so had backfired spectacularly.

She slipped the cigarette and lighter into her coat pocket. She'd never smoked as much as she was doing now.

At least she'd finished teaching for the day, so no one would smell it on her. She was just about to leave the office when her door opened, and Stephen strolled in.

'Hello.' She smiled, inwardly breathing a sigh of relief he hadn't come in a few seconds sooner. He knew she smoked but hated it with a passion. She made sure to keep it away from him, always carrying around breath mints and hand sanitiser.

'What's wrong?' He placed his arm around her shoulders.

'What do you mean?'

'It's written all over your face. Tough lecture? The first years still need to be licked into George shape.' He laughed.

'It's not funny. And no, it's not the students. It's the murder investigation. I've screwed up.' She pulled away from him and folded her arms across her chest.

'You admitting to screwing up. That's got to be a first.'

'Because it's not something I usually do.'

'Well, it's good to screw up occasionally. It makes you more human. Everything doesn't have to be perfect all the time.' He dropped down onto one of the easy chairs she'd placed under the large bay window, leaning back with his hands behind his head and stretching out his long legs in front of him.

She slipped off her coat and hung it up on the back of the door and sat on the chair opposite him. The cigarette would have to wait until he'd gone.

'I like order. Without it, everything turns to custard. Why is that so bad? If I wasn't so organised, my work would suffer. Or are you now saying there's something wrong with that, too?'

Stephen leaned forward and took both of her hands in his, relaxing her almost immediately. 'Of course I'm not saying that. But you're allowed to be a little vulnerable now and then.'

She didn't even know what that meant. Vulnerable? How? Was she meant to burst into tears at the drop of a hat? She did cry, sometimes. At her grandma's funeral. And at Millie's tears stung her eyes, until she'd managed to blink them away.

'Well, this has nothing to do with me wanting order. Or not being *vulnerable*—whatever that's meant to mean. If you must know, I'm frustrated by my mistake and how DCI Walker is excluding me.' She pulled her hands from his and balled them into tight fists.

'What did you do?'

'She didn't like the way I explained my theory. Even asked for the CliffsNotes version.'

'I can relate to that. I've often thought you must have been born with a thesaurus in your hand.'

She stared at him. What the hell was going on? He should be supporting her, not siding with someone he hadn't even met. 'Whose side are you on?'

'Yours. You know that. But sometimes you give off this arrogant air and can be intimidating.'

And he thought his words were going to pacify her, did he? Make things okay?

'I disagree. I'm totally able to work with normal people, it—'

'Normal people,' Stephen interrupted. 'Are you sure you meant to say that? Do you consider yourself to be different from the norm? On a higher plane?'

She stared at him. Was he right? She might come across as standoffish, sometimes, but not arrogant. Surely not. It was hard being in other people's company. It made her uncomfortable. She wasn't like Stephen, who was the life and soul of the party. She always held back a little. If she wanted to dig deeper, she might imagine it was something to do with her family life, but she wasn't going there. Some things were best left untouched.

'I didn't mean it,' she conceded. 'It's frustrating to be excluded when I know my input could make a difference. Two students have been murdered. It's only a matter of time until there's another. I'm sure of it. I can't sit back and do nothing. My conscience won't let me.'

'Why don't you contact the DCI and sort things out between you?' Stephen suggested.

'It's not easy. The last time we spoke, she told me to go back to work, and if they needed my input, she'd be in touch.'

Stephen laughed. 'The mighty Dr George Cavendish put in her place by a lowly police officer. You have to admit, it's funny.'

When he put it like that, she could see his point. Sort of. But he still didn't seem to get it. He couldn't understand why it was so important for her to help.

Maybe if she told him the real reason for wanting to be involved, because of what happened with Camilla, he'd be more understanding and supportive. But that wasn't going to happen. It was staying in the past where it belonged.

'Debatable. She's a DCI, hardly lowly. Anyway, I don't want to discuss it any more. Let's go to the pub later and grab something to eat.' She couldn't face the stack of marking she had waiting for her. One evening off wouldn't hurt.

'That's what I came to tell you. I'm going to be late home tonight,' Stephen replied.

'Why? Don't tell me you're staying late to work because I won't believe you.' She grinned. It was good getting everything off her chest, even though it hadn't been resolved. She'd never known Stephen to work late. In fact, it beat her how he ever got anything done, because he seldom brought work home or spent time in his office. He could invariably be found in the staff room or one of the university cafes.

'One of my PhD students is having a crisis. I'm taking him out for a drink to sort out what's going on.'

That was a first. Maybe her commitment was rubbing off on him, which had to be a good thing.

'Which pub are you going to? I could come along later, once you've finished,' she suggested.

'I'm not sure. I'm waiting for him to get back to me with a time and place. I don't know how long it's going to take, as he's pretty down about it all. His computer crashed, and he lost a whole raft of interview data. Why don't you wait for me at home? We'll open a bottle of wine when I get back.' He leaned forward and kissed her lightly on the lips.

She pulled back. 'Stop. My door's open. People will see.'

'So what? Everyone knows we're living together.' A belligerent expression crossed his face.

She hated this *laissez-faire* attitude. That sort of behaviour at work simply wasn't acceptable.

'Students don't. Anyway, it's not appropriate.'

Stephen stood up. 'This is exactly what I've been talking about. Lighten up, won't you? I'll see you later.' He stormed out of her office without a backwards glance.

What the hell just happened? One minute he was all over her and the next he'd thrown a wobbly.

She definitely needed a cigarette now. She might even have two, seeing as she'd gone from being relaxed to tense in a matter of seconds.

As she was pulling on her coat, her phone rang. She looked at the screen. Walker. What did she want?

'Dr Cavendish.'

'It's Whitney. DCI Walker.'

'What can I do for you, Detective?'

'I'd like you with me at the morgue to speak to Dr Dexter. If you've got time?'

She hadn't been expecting that. But she wasn't going to let the opportunity pass her by.

'I'll be happy to. When?'

'Meet me at the station, and we'll go together. There are a few things I'd like to run by you. I need some advice.'

'Give me twenty minutes.' She might never find out what had caused this sudden change in Walker. And she didn't need to know. The main thing was she was back assisting in the case.

Fortunately, she had her car on campus from when she drove back from the station earlier.

'I'll see you soon.'

Chapter Seventeen

Whitney kept her head facing the road as she was driving to the morgue, but in her peripheral vision she kept an eye on George, who was sitting upright in the passenger seat, her hands clasped firmly in her lap.

She couldn't work the doctor out. Whitney had been pleasant and courteous to her, even though the response she'd received had been cool, to say the least. Should she consider apologising, or was that going too far? It wasn't like they'd had some massive falling out. Whitney had just been a little disrespectful. Not even disrespectful, more thoughtless. She didn't mean anything by it.

Fuck it. She'd say sorry.

'George. I want to apologise for the way I dismissed you earlier when you wanted to stay and help.' She turned her head to see the response. Nothing.

'I accept your apology,' George finally replied.

'Cool. Thanks. I'll fill you in on what happened at Diamond Escorts.'

She gave her a quick run-down of what they'd found out, including the amount of money Olivia earned from working there. Even George raised an eyebrow. Like Whitney, she clearly had no idea it could be so lucrative. Although, unlike her, she doubted George would consider for one moment a situation when she might be tempted to become an escort.

When they arrived at the morgue, she parked in the car park, and they walked into the building.

'Are you and Claire good friends?' she asked as they walked down the sterile corridor.

'Work colleagues, mainly. We've been out for a drink several times, but I wouldn't say we're friends. Why do you ask?'

'Just curious. I suppose you academic types like to stick together. So you can talk about intelligent things people like me don't understand.'

George came to an abrupt halt and turned to face her. 'I don't spend my entire life discussing ground breaking theories in order to side line anyone who doesn't understand them.' She shook her head.

Wow. What had got into her? She'd only been joking. Well, not joking exactly, because she did assume they all hung out together. She certainly hadn't meant it as an insult.

She held up her hands in mock surrender. 'Sorry. Didn't mean to offend.'

'It's fine.' George paused for a moment. 'Has Claire given you any indication of what she has for us?'

'Not really. You know Claire. She likes to keep everything to herself until she's sure of the results. She doesn't like to make rash predictions.'

'That's why she's so good at her job,' George replied.

'True. She's the best pathologist we have. Her evidence always stands up in court.'

'Good to know,' George said as she pushed open the

door to the lab, and they walked in. 'The lectures she does for me always prove very popular. Not least because of the gruesome photos she puts up on the screen. Though not all students can take it. On most occasions, one or more of them will race out of the room to throw up.' George laughed, and Whitney joined in, amused at the thought.

'What the fuck's going on with you two?' Claire stood there with her hands on her hips, staring at them through her enormous black-rimmed glasses which practically covered her entire face. Although she had on her scrubs, her vivid green and black striped trousers could still be seen.

Whitney and George exchanged a glance, both frowning.

'What do you mean?' Whitney asked.

'Best buddies all of a sudden? Have I missed something? The last time you were together it was heading for pistols at dawn,' Claire replied.

'A slight exaggeration, Claire,' George said. 'Let's just say we've sorted out our differences and are intent on solving the case together. Which is why we're here.'

Whitney shot George a conspiratorial look. Maybe working together would be okay after all. 'Agreed. What do you have for us?'

They followed Claire to the back of the lab, where Olivia Griffin's body was laid out on a stainless-steel table. Claire put on her gloves.

'First, I can confirm this killing is identical to that of Millie Carter. Check out the bruising on the neck.' She pointed to the purple marks. 'Identical sized bruises, from the pressure of the fingers. No prints unfortunately, so he must have worn gloves. Again, although there is no semen, there is evidence from bruising around the vaginal area penetration has taken place.' She lifted up one of the victim's hands. 'Marks to show restraint. The difference in this case is they're more jagged, indicating signs of a struggle.'

'Was she drugged?' George asked.

'I'm getting to that,' Claire barked in her usual no-nonsense way.

Whitney was glad it wasn't just her who could be subjected to Claire's sharp tongue.

'We've had the toxicology report back,' Claire continued. 'We found both alcohol and ketamine in her blood.'

'There wasn't any alcohol in the first victim's blood, was there?' she asked.

'No. Just the ketamine, which I suspect was mixed in with some food. Though we don't know for certain. As it didn't show in her last meal, I can only make an assumption it was administered in a previous one.'

'Interesting,' George said. 'Was the ketamine given with the alcohol in this victim?'

'We can't tell. But the fact she struggled leads me to conclude she had a greater tolerance to the drug than victim one. Especially as she'd also consumed alcohol, which ought to have added to the effect.'

Her mind was racing. One reason for someone to have a tolerance for the drug was previous consumption. Did she take it before going out as an escort? Was she a regular drug user? She'd need to revisit the girls in the flat.

'Were there any other drugs in her system?' she asked.

'I'd have told you if there were,' Claire said.

'What about her stomach contents? Her last meal. Not jelly and ice cream by any chance?'

'I'm afraid not. The last thing she ate was pizza. A meat-lovers, judging by what was in there. She was strangled before it had time to digest. I'd say around two hours before death.'

'The murderer fed her pizza. Interesting,' George said. 'Did he force feed her?'

'I don't believe so. There's no trace of sauce anywhere, other than under her fingernails, which you'd expect. There was nothing up her nose, or round by her ears.'

'So, he untied her to eat, and she willingly did so. That makes no sense,' she said. 'What do you think, George?'

'They could've eaten first, and then he tied her up, indicating either she knew him well enough to spend the weekend with him, or he'd promised to release her if she ate with him. Probably the latter.'

'Agreed. Anything else to tell us, Claire?' she asked.

'Time of death, somewhere between one and three Monday morning. Body definitely moved. No other trace evidence apart from a miniscule piece of sponge used to wash the body. The same detergent as the first victim was used. A very basic washing up liquid. The sort you can buy in every supermarket.'

'Thanks, Claire,' she said.

'You're welcome. I'll email my report later.' Claire turned away from them, indicating their time with her had come to an end.

When they got outside of the lab, she turned to George. 'Fancy a drink, so we can discuss evidence?'

George looked at her watch. 'Yes. I have time for a quick one.'

George wasn't impressed by the pub Whitney had chosen for them. It was around the corner from the station. It was everything she hated in a pub. Huge, with lots of chrome, red plastic seating, and several TV screens strategically placed to ensure everyone had a view. It had about as much character as a dead body.

Probably not the best analogy under the circumstances.

'What would you like to drink?' Whitney asked as they got to one of several bars in there.

'It's okay, I'll get my own.'

'No. It's on me. Expenses.' Whitney waved her hand dismissively.

'I'll have a sparkling water, with ice and a slice of lemon, please.' She'd get the next round.

'Nothing stronger?' Whitney asked. 'I'm having a bottle of lager.'

'I've got work to do when I get back.' A tiny lie, as she'd already decided not to do anything that evening. But she still didn't want anything to drink. She'd rather keep a clear head while discussing the case.

'Suit yourself. There's a free table over there.' Whitney pointed towards the rear of the pub. 'You grab it and I'll order the drinks.'

She sat at the table, taking in her surroundings. Considering it was so early in the evening, it was remarkably busy. She wondered how many of them were police officers. Quite a few, if the number of people Whitney had said hello to on their way in was anything to go by.

She focused her attention on Whitney, waiting to be served. She was standing on tiptoes, leaning over the bar, waving her money. It surprised her how short Whitney was. She'd always assumed police officers had to be tall. In fact, didn't they have a minimum height range? Or had that been stopped? She supposed it would have to be, on the grounds of equal opportunities. She doubted Whitney let being short get in the way of doing the job. She was fierce. Maybe as a result of her height.

You could have knocked her down with a feather when

she'd apologised earlier. No one liked doing that, and from what little she knew of Whitney, she'd have thought it would have been especially hard for her. At least it meant George could now be a part of the case.

When Whitney reached the table, she placed George's drink in front of her. 'Here you are. Don't drink it all at once. We can't have you falling down all over the place.'

'Thanks.' She took a long sip while watching Whitney knock back half the bottle.

'That's better,' Whitney said, placing the bottle on the table. 'It's got rid of the antiseptic stench from my nostrils. The mortuary is even worse than being in a hospital.'

'It's worse when there's a decomposed body. The smell is enough to make you want to throw up.'

'I know. I actually did vomit the first time. And Claire being Claire, she omitted to tell me to put vapour rub under my nose to stop most of the putrid smell from getting through.'

'She didn't tell me either. It's her little joke.'

Whitney took another swig from the bottle. 'Yes. That seems like Claire. You've heard all the evidence. What are your thoughts?'

George was silent for a few moments, wanting to choose her words carefully, so she wouldn't be accused of not speaking in everyday language.

'Research indicates there's a link between criminals' actions in committing crimes and how they act in normal life. If you consider he fed both girls while they were being held captive, it could, in a perverse way, be an indicator of him being a considerate person.'

'Or an act of control.'

'Exactly. Which is why profiling isn't an exact science, rather an aid to the investigation as a whole.'

'I get that. What are your thoughts on our next steps?'

'Now we have two victims, it's important to look at what we know about each victim and look for similarities.' She leaned back against the hard chair, trying to get a little more comfortable. Was she now making this too simplistic?

'Agreed. I've been wondering about both bodies being left on university soil. What's your take?'

'There could be several reasons. Both victims were students, so the killer took them back there. Why? Is it because he's a student? Is it because he applied to study at the uni but was turned down and is taking his revenge? Is there a sexual reason? Maybe both girls turned him down. These are all pointers for considering alongside the other evidence.'

'Do you think the revenge scenario is likely?'

'It's possible, but in my opinion not likely. Controlling behaviour, like he's exhibiting, isn't about revenge. We also need to consider the exact location the victims were left. Beside water. The implication is water has some significance. We just don't know what, yet.'

'Can you guess?'

'No. I don't base my profiling on guess work. You might as well call in a psychic if that's what you want.' Her words came out harsher than she'd intended. 'Sorry. No offence meant.'

'None taken. What do you make of the food? Jelly and ice cream. Pizza. Children's party food. Anything significant, do you think?'

'Too early to say. Both foods are eaten by adults, too. I hate to say this, but we need more victims before we can assess properly the food and its relevance.'

'Okay, let's park that. One definite link we have is the twins' birthday party both victims went to. The murderer could have been there, too. In the morning, I'll go and speak to the twins. Would you like to come?'

Her heart sank. She'd been desperate to get back onto the case, and the one time when she could be extremely useful, she couldn't make it.

'Sorry, I can't. I've got a meeting with one of my PhD students. I can't let him down. His viva's next week, and I've promised to go through it with him.'

'Viva?'

'He has to defend his thesis. It's like an oral examination. Not a pleasant situation to be in.' Her mind flashed back to her viva. It was firmly imprinted on her brain as the worst moment in her academic career.

'No problem. I'll take Matt and let you know the outcome.'

'Ask them for photos. They're bound to have taken some. Or check out their social media. And their guests' accounts, too. We might get something there.'

'You read my mind. We'll make a police officer out of you yet.' Whitney arched an eyebrow.

'I think I'll stick where I am for now.' George grinned.

She picked up her drink and finished it. She didn't mind helping, but the thought of actually being in the police. No, thank you. Although it could be worth it, just to see what her father thought of the idea. She smiled, just imaging the scene when she told him.

'Another drink?' Whitney asked, nodding at her empty glass.

'No, thanks. I really need to get going.' She picked up her coat from the back of the chair and her bag from under the table.

'I'm going to stay for another. I'll join the rest of the team over there.' Whitney nodded towards the bar. 'I'll let you know how we get on tomorrow.'

Chapter Eighteen

Whitney rang the bell of the end of terrace house where Harriet and Henry Spencer lived. Matt was standing behind her. She'd phoned ahead and spoken to Harriet to ensure they would both be there. According to Harriet, they didn't have a lecture. Whitney already knew from Tiffany's timetable, a full-time course wasn't full-time in the way she understood it. She realised they had assignments to do as well, but even so, fifteen hours a week of lectures? They'd be in for a shock when they got out into the real world.

'Hello, are you Detective Walker?' A tall, blonde-haired girl with large almond-shaped grey eyes, was smiling at her. 'I'm Harriet Spencer.'

Whitney warmed to her immediately. 'Yes. I'm DCI Walker and this is DS Price.'

'Come in. Would you like a cup of coffee? I've just put the machine on.'

'That would be lovely, thanks.' As much caffeine as possible was Whitney's motto, and she'd only had one cup so far today.

They followed Harriet down a narrow hall until they got to the rear of the house, where there was a kitchen with an archway into a dining room. The house was nothing like Olivia's flat. It was clean and tidy. Clearly not all students were slobs.

Sitting at the table was a male version of Harriet. No mistaking they were brother and sister. They were stunning.

'You must be Henry.' She offered her hand for him to shake.

He stood up, towering over her. 'Pleased to meet you. Harriet said you wanted to talk to us about our party. Is there a problem? It's rather late for neighbours to be complaining, as it was over three weeks ago.'

When she'd called, she hadn't mentioned any link to the murders, not wanting to worry them.

'Did the neighbours complain?' Matt asked.

Henry shook his head. 'This is predominantly a student street. Every weekend someone holds a party. There's an elderly couple living four doors down on the opposite side of the road, but they're hard of hearing, and on the weekend of our party they'd gone to visit their daughter in Bournemouth for a week.'

'How do you take your coffee?' Harriet asked.

'Milk with one sugar for both of us, please,' she replied.

Harriet handed out the coffees, and they all sat around the dining table.

'Is it just the two of you living here?'

'No, Lydia lives with us. She's upstairs. Would you like me to call her?' Harriet replied.

'Not at the moment. How do you know Lydia?'

'We're all in the veterinary science department. Lydia's studying for her Masters, and we're in our final year of vet training,' Henry said.

'Sounds interesting.' She loved animals but didn't have a pet because of the hours she worked. They'd always had dogs at home when she was growing up.

'We enjoy it. It's hard work, though. It's unusual for us not to be in college studying at this time of day. If we don't have lectures, we're often in the library,' Henry said.

Whitney fought the urge not to respond to the *hard work* comment. 'Tell me about your party. Who was there? How long it went on for. Anything else you remember.'

'Are you allowed to tell us why you want to know?' Harriet asked.

She exchanged a glance with Matt. If she did, maybe they'd try harder to help. 'You're aware about the two student murders recently.'

'Yes,' the twins replied in unison.

'According to our investigation, both students attended your birthday party.'

Harriet's eyes widened. 'But we don't know them, do we, Hal?'

'Hal?' Whitney asked.

'It's what I've always called him, since we were children. I didn't even recognise their names when it was reported, did you Hal?' Harriet said.

Henry shook his head. 'No. That doesn't mean they weren't here. The house was totally packed. You know what parties are like. Someone knows someone, who knows someone. And they come along.'

Whitney took out her phone and showed the twins photos of Millie and Olivia. 'These are the two victims. Do you recognise them?'

They both stared for a few seconds, and then looked at each other. 'They sort of look familiar,' Henry said. 'But that could be because their photos have been in the media.

I don't remember them being at the party. Then again, we did have a lot to drink. And as I said, the house was full.'

'Same for me,' Harriet said. 'I was drinking the punch we'd made for most of the night and had the hangover from hell the next day.'

'Did you take any photos at your party?' she asked.

'Loads. I put them all up on social media,' Harriet replied.

'Please forward them to me.'

'Friend me, and then you can see them all,' Harriet replied.

'That's not something we're allowed to do. It goes against protocol. Please could you email them to me.'

'Sure. No problem,' Harriet said.

She took a sip of her coffee. The good stuff. The twins obviously lived well.

'If you do remember anything else, let me know. Just for our records, what were your movements between two and four in the afternoon of Sunday the third, and the early hours of the morning on Monday eighteenth?' she asked.

'I think we were at home, both times. Weren't we, Hal?' Harriet looked at Henry.

'No. Sunday, we went into town at around three, remember. You wanted to buy Mother's birthday present. Monday we were at home.'

'Oh, yes. That's right.'

'Can anyone corroborate this?' she asked.

'Are we allowed to corroborate each other?' Harriet said. 'If not, Lydia might. I can't remember if she was here or not. She often stays at her boyfriend's flat.'

'Yes, you can. But we'll have a chat with Lydia too, if you could ask her to pop down.'

Harriet jogged out of the room, and Whitney could hear her footsteps as she ran up the stairs.

'Would you like another coffee?' Henry asked.

She was impressed by his manners. She'd love it if Tiffany could find someone like him to settle with. Not necessarily as posh as him, but with his personality and manners.

'No thanks.'

They sat in silence until Harriet arrived back, with Lydia following behind.

Whitney and Matt stood. 'Hello, Lydia. We're investigating the murders of two students, and we'd like to ask you a few questions. It appears both attended the party you had here recently,' she said.

'Yes. Harriet told me,' Lydia replied.

'Were you at the party?' Matt asked.

'Yes. But I didn't stay overnight. I stayed with my boyfriend. We left around midnight.'

'Were you here on Sunday afternoon on the third and Sunday night, going into Monday morning, on the eighteenth?' Whitney asked.

She paused for a moment. 'Not on the first Sunday afternoon, but yes. I did stay overnight on the second Sunday.'

'Thank you,' she said.

'Do you think the Campus Killer will strike again?' Lydia asked.

She rolled her eyes at the crass nickname the media had already given the killer. Then again, it was the most obvious.

'We hope he won't, but until we've caught him, make sure you don't go out alone. Pass that message on to all of your friends.'

'I won't let Harriet go anywhere on her own. I make sure I'm always with her,' Henry said.

'He even tries to go into the ladies' loo with me.' Harriet rolled her eyes.

'I don't care what you say. Until the murderer's caught, you'll have to get used to it,' Henry retorted.

'But you're always together, anyway,' Lydia said as she laughed.

'The main thing is you're careful. Here's my card. If any of you remember anything more about the party. Anyone acting strange. Anything out of the ordinary, please call me.' She pulled out a couple of cards from her pocket and handed one to Henry and one to Lydia.

'Will do,' Henry said. 'I'm sorry we couldn't have been more help.'

'You've been fine. And don't forget the photos,' she said.

As they left and headed to the car, her phone rang. 'Hello.'

'Jamieson here. We've called a press conference, and I want you with me. Where are you?'

'On my way back to the station.'

'Head straight for my office when you arrive.'

'Yes, sir. I'll be back in fifteen.' She ended the call.

'Crap.'

'Problem, guv?'

'More an inconvenience. The Super wants me with him at the press conference he's decided to call. He's perfectly capable of managing on his own, so why the fuck he can't do this alone, I do not know.'

Chapter Nineteen

Panic is rife, everywhere I go. And I love it. There are so many stupid girls acting like someone's going to pounce on them at any minute. Constantly looking over their shoulders in case the "Campus Killer" is walking behind them. I can't say I'm enamoured by the nickname. It's totally predictable. They could've been more creative. Like—like — "The Student Strangler". That has a good ring to it.

Anyway, back to these frightened girls. They should be so lucky to find themselves on my radar. I don't choose randomly. They've got to be very special to have the privilege of being my next target. I want to march up to them and explain they have nothing to worry about. But where's the fun in that?

What everyone fails to realise is Millie and Olivia were chosen for specific reasons.

Reasons only I know, and I'm not prepared to share. So, don't ask.

You have to keep an air of mystery over these things. To be honest, my reasons aren't deep, but they are reasons, nonetheless. And they're all mine.

Now it's time to make plans for number three. Every time I think about what I'm going to do to her, excitement courses through my whole body. I imagine savouring every squeeze on her neck. Enjoying every ragged breath she takes, each one closer to her very last one.

The preparation's been fun and is mostly done. I've yet to make a decision on the actual date, but it will be sometime soon. Her favourite food is sushi, which needs to be bought, as do the drugs. Once the bed's been stripped and clean sheets put on, there's nothing left to do.

It's surprising how different it feels now I'm up to number three. The first time, I was hesitant, lacking in confidence. I wasn't sure how hard to press down on her neck before she'd stop breathing. In fact, it happened so suddenly it was over before I'd realised. The second time was easier and more enjoyable, apart from how much she wriggled and squirmed, despite having the same drug dose as number one. That taught me a valuable lesson.

I'll be giving number three a larger dose. I don't want a repeat performance of number two trying to escape. I say trying to escape, but she wasn't going anywhere. The ties on her wrists and ankles made sure of that. But it was messy. And I don't do mess.

Number three is going to lay there unable to do anything other than stare up at me. So all she has are the horrendous thoughts in her head. The agony of not being able to express them, suffering so badly inside all she wants to do is scream. But she can't. She'll have to endure the pain. And endure the knowledge she's going to die in silence.

Having no release is something I've experienced. It eats you up inside. When you long to scream and scream without let up. But in reality, all you can do is bottle it up inside, until it explodes. I don't remember much about the day I totally lost it, but my hands were covered in blood from where I'd ripped apart the furniture and punched through the glass of the patio doors. I had to be restrained to stop me from destroying everything in my path.

But I got through it. I'm here to tell the tale. It's amazing what money, drugs, a good psychiatrist, and six months in a secure wing can do to fix everything. Now if you asked anyone, they'd never believe once I'd had such a severe breakdown I couldn't speak for months.

Now I'm perfectly normal.

Just ask my friends.

Chapter Twenty

Whitney popped into the ladies' to inspect her appearance. Looking at herself in the mirror, she was glad she'd taken the time, as her eye shadow had mostly come off and mascara flakes were on her cheeks. After reapplying her make-up and smearing on a fresh coat of lip gloss, she brushed her hair and retied it. At least now the person staring back at her was passable. She had no desire to be dubbed the UK's female version of Columbo.

Fronting up to the press was not her idea of fun, but she'd been given no choice. It came with the territory. As much as she loved being a DCI, there were certain duties she'd give up in a heartbeat. Especially all the strategy meetings she was supposed to attend.

She was just about to leave when the door opened and Sue, one of the DCs on her team, came rushing in, tears streaming down her face.

'What is it? she asked, reaching into her bag and passing Sue a tissue.

'Sorry. I know I should be focusing on the case, but I'm

finding it so hard.' Sue sniffed and wiped her nose with the tissue.

'Why? Tell me what's happened.'

'My dad's in hospital having heart surgery today. A triple bypass. I stupidly googled the procedure this morning and read all the risks with the surgery. I haven't told Mum because I don't want to worry her.'

She pulled Sue into her arms and gave her a hug. 'I'm sure it will be fine. It's a routine operation. I remember my granddad having one, and he was perfectly okay after. It gave him a new lease of life.'

'I know. But I can't stop worrying about it.' Sue pulled away from Whitney's hug and wiped her eyes again.

'Take the rest of the day off and go to the hospital. Be with your mum. You'll feel better if you're close by.'

'Are you sure? What about the case?'

'We can manage without you for the afternoon. Family comes first.'

'Thank you. I really appreciate it.'

'You're more than welcome. Now I better be going, before the Super sends out a search party,' she said, checking her watch.

She left the ladies' loo and headed for his office, knocking on the door once she arrived. He called her in.

'Sit down, Walker.'

He'd got his full uniform on, but the jacket didn't hide his prominent stomach, which was straining the silver buttons to within an inch of their life. Any moment now she expected them to pop off in revolt against their torture.

'Sir.' She sat on the seat in front of his desk.

'I know we don't have anything new to report, but the DCSI has been on my back. She's been getting it in the neck from the public. They're concerned by the lack of progress we're making.'

Easy for them to say, as bystanders. She hadn't had a decent night's sleep since the first murder. They'd all been working their socks off: background checking, interviewing, trawling through mountains of CCTV footage, following up on potential leads from the public. But she got it. Hard work meant nothing if they didn't have results to back it up.

'I wouldn't say lack of progress, sir. We're pursuing lines of enquiry. Although we have no solid leads, we have been able to eliminate possible suspects from our enquiries. I'm using a forensic psychologist to help with the profiling. Dr George Cavendish, who works at the university.'

'Interesting.' Jamieson arched an eyebrow. 'I wasn't aware you liked bringing in outsiders to the team.'

'Dr Cavendish offered, and I accepted. It's not costing the department anything. In the past, budgetary constraints meant we were unable to use this type of service. So, contrary to what you believe, it's nothing to do with my personal preferences.' She immediately regretted her flippant response, as a dark expression crossed Jamieson's face. She flinched. He held her career in his hand and annoying him for no real reason wouldn't do her any favours.

'And how's that working out? Is he coming up with anything you can use?'

Good question. How was it working out? Well, underneath all that poshness, George wasn't as bad as she'd first thought. Okay, they'd never be best friends, not least because George was way too single-minded and serious. Whitney would never mock anyone for hard work, but that was all George seemed to do. And certainly, all she ever talked about. Then again, they weren't friends, so why would she share any personal details? She hadn't either. Anyway, it didn't matter. All she cared about was finding the killer before he took another life.

'He's a she, sir. Dr Cavendish has provided us with a detailed profile and has also contributed to our investigation.'

'Good.' He nodded.

'Do you want me to speak at the press conference?' She assumed he'd be the one doing all the talking. It was good for his image, his major preoccupation.

'I'll lead and pass to you any questions you're better placed to answer.'

Of course he would. Questions which are tricky and might not put her department in such a good light. Because all that was going to come out of the conference was that they were no closer to cracking the case than they were a week ago.

'Okay. Are you ready to go now?' She glanced at her watch, noting the conference was due to start in five minutes.

He got up from behind his desk, picked up his cap, and put it on.

'Let's go.'

When they reached the conference room, Jamieson opened the door for her to go in. The room was full. There were reporters sitting on chairs, and TV cameras at the back. Whitney sucked in a breath. This wasn't going to be easy. They wanted answers, and at the moment she didn't have any.

Michelle, the PR officer, was waiting for them beside the table which was situated along the front. She ushered them along and sat at the end.

'Good afternoon. Thank you for attending the press conference,' Michelle said. 'Detective Superintendent

Jamieson will read out a short statement, and then we'll take questions.'

Jamieson held the statement that had been prepared by the PR department, took a sip of water from the glass in front of him, and cleared his throat.

'We've asked you in today to give you an update on what's happening with our investigation into the murders of two female students from Lenchester University. We are making steady progress and following some potentially good leads. We are treating the crimes as linked. We believe the killer is male, probably between twenty-five and forty, and has a connection to the university. We ask the public to be vigilant, and in particular request young women do not go out alone. Also, if you are suspicious of anyone you know or have come in contact with, please contact our incident room, so we can investigate. All calls will be treated confidentially. Any questions?'

'The leads you mentioned. Are you holding anyone in custody?' a reporter in the front row called out.

'I'll leave DCI Walker to answer questions about the leads.' Jamieson smiled and nodded at her.

She should go into fortune telling, she'd called it right. Leave the difficult stuff for her to deal with.

'Thank you, sir. At the moment we don't have anyone in custody.'

'Does that mean you have no leads whatsoever regarding who's committing these crimes?' another reporter called out.

In a word. Correct. But if she said that, then she'd be off the case quicker than she could say serial killer.

'Not at all. It means we have a number of leads we're pursuing which I can't talk about without jeopardising the investigation. But I will reiterate what Detective Superintendent Jamieson has said: we're anxious to hear from anyone who thinks they might have some information. Don't worry how trivial it might seem. We want to hear it.'

Asking for the public's help was a double-edged sword. On the one hand, they might get that one piece of information which could lead them to the killer. On the other, every Tom, Dick, and Harry would call in. Often with totally useless information. Or, and this is what got her so angry, people would phone in with a fabricated story. Or fabricated confession.

'Is it true the killer took photos of the victims with their phones and left them for you to see?' a female reporter towards the back called out.

What the fuck?

They'd deliberately held those details back. She glanced at Jamieson, whose face was set hard. She mentally ran through those people who knew about the phones and photos. All of her team. The officers at the scene, plus a few others. Also, some of the top brass. And the pathologist. Even George had known about it from overhearing officers speaking. Too many people.

But who leaked it? What if it was George? She could've discussed it with her colleagues and they mentioned it to the media. She'd have a word with her once she left the press conference.

'I'm not sure where you got that information, but it's not entirely accurate.'

'Are you saying the killer didn't do anything with the victims' phones?' the reporter persisted.

'What I'm saying is it's not entirely accurate,' she repeated, trying to keep her cool.

'Can you be more specific?' the reporter continued.

'You heard DCI Walker,' interrupted Jamieson. 'Thank you all for your time.' He stood up. 'Walker, with me,' he said quietly, through gritted teeth.

She followed him out of the room, and they walked in silence until they reached his office. After entering, he closed the door behind them. She braced herself for the onslaught.

'What the hell happened in there?' His cheeks were red, and he looked about ready to explode. 'Who told them about the phone?'

'I don't know, sir. It was as much of a shock to me as to you,' she replied.

'You need to bring your team in line, because from where I'm standing, you're looking less than competent.'

He had no proof it was anything to do with her team, and she wasn't going to stand there and let him get away with accusing her like that. She didn't care how much it went against her.

'I'll be speaking to them. But it's not just my team who know about this evidence. Some of uniform are aware of it, as are you and others.'

'I hope you're not implying I leaked the information to the press.'

She was certain it wasn't him, but that didn't mean she shouldn't point out he knew about it.

'No, sir. But maybe someone was discussing the case and inadvertently mentioned the phone. Unfortunately, too many people had knowledge of it. I'm not pointing the finger at anyone, just letting you know it's not just my team who could've done it.'

'What about the forensic psychologist you brought in?'

'I'll be speaking to her, and if I find out she was the one, we will no longer be using her.'

She left the office and went back to the incident room, glad to get away from him, but not happy with something else to divert her attention from what was important. Finding the killer before he killed again.

Chapter Twenty-One

George grabbed a table while Stephen queued for their coffee. It was a pleasant surprise when he'd popped into her office and asked her to join him in the university café, as she'd been unable to concentrate on her work. She'd been preparing a report for a meeting of the department research committee, which she chaired. Usually she had no trouble writing her monthly report, but her mind kept wandering to the murders. It was only a matter of time before the killer struck again, and they were no nearer finding him. Was it her fault? Had she missed something?

'Here you are.' Stephen placed their coffees on the table.

'Thanks, I could do with this.' She wrapped her hands around the mug and inhaled the rich coffee aroma.

'I've got something to ask you,' Stephen said hesitatingly. 'Hear me out before you say no.'

'Why do you automatically assume I'll say no?'

Did she always say no to his ideas? She didn't think so. Okay, so she'd been refusing to go out recently during the week because of all the work she had on. But they did go for a meal at the weekend and had a good time.

'I'm just saying, that's all.' The narrowing of his eyes was a clear indication he was troubled about something.

'Tell me what it is,' she said, determined to say yes, whatever it was. Well, within reason.

'My folks were going to their cottage in the Lake District this weekend, but now they can't. They asked if we'd like to go instead, and I said yes.'

Her body tensed. If there was one thing she hated, it was people making plans for her. It was just plain rude.

'Without asking me first?' She tried to keep her voice light but didn't succeed.

'I had to make a decision straight away, or they'd have offered it to someone else. We can leave after work on Friday and come back first thing Monday morning. If we leave early enough, we'll be back in time for your nine o'clock start. It's a beautiful cottage. I've been wanting to take you there for ages. Open fire. Views over the lake. It'll be just what you need. You've been looking peaky recently because of all the work you've been doing,' he cajoled.

Under any other circumstances, she'd have loved a few days in the Lake District. It was one of her favourite places. But how could she justify the time away? Not counting her research and marking, there was the investigation to think about. What if the killer decided to strike again while she was away relaxing? She'd be no good to Whitney if she wasn't available when needed.

As for her looking peaky, she didn't agree. Yes, she was a little tired, but no more than usual for the first term in an academic year. According to him, it sounded like she had one foot in the grave and had let herself go.

'I feel fine, so I'm not sure why you think I need a

break. That said, I think it's lovely of your parents to offer us the cottage,' she said, working herself up to turning him down.

'So, we can go?' he asked as a broad smile marched across his face.

Crap. She hadn't meant to lead him on.

'I'd love to, but not this weekend. Sorry.' She leaned over to put her hand over his, but he pulled it away.

'Why not? Surely you're on top of your work. You must be, you're at it so often.'

She resented the tone in his voice, but now wasn't the time to discuss it.

'It's the case. We need to catch the murderer before he strikes again.'

'The case,' Stephen scoffed. 'You're kidding yourself if you think your presence is going to make that much difference. I'm sure they're only letting you be part of the investigation because you pestered them so much. It's not like you've actually contributed anything. The killer's still out there.'

She bristled. Where did he get off insulting her like that?

'That's really uncalled for. And for your information, I've provided the police with a good working profile. We will find him.'

'It's not *we*. You're an academic, not a police officer.' He rolled his eyes upward and gave a callous laugh.

'Fuck you, Stephen Grant. And your weekend in the Lakes. You can go by yourself, because I'm not going.'

'Your choice,' he replied, glowering at her.

'Yes, it is.'

Their eyes locked in anger, then suddenly Stephen's softened.

He rested his hand on top of hers. 'I'm sorry. I didn't mean what I said. It was out of order. It's just these past weeks I've been feeling neglected. It seems like you have time for everyone else except me.'

His words took the wind out of her sails, and guilt inched its way into her head. She knew she had a tendency to be single-minded, and in the past it hadn't mattered. Looking at it from his perspective, maybe she wasn't being fair. They were in a relationship, and that meant give and take on both sides.

'I'm sorry, too. I just don't want to let Whitney down. I couldn't bear it if another student lost her life because I hadn't been there to help.'

'It's not all down to you. I'm sure your DCI will understand if you go away for a couple of days.'

She was determined she wouldn't be going, but she'd wait until later to tell him. Let him think she was going to see what she could work out. If that made her a bad partner, then so be it. Once the case was solved, she'd make more of an effort. It annoyed her Stephen had become so needy. Nothing like her parents, who were both single-minded in the pursuit of their careers. They understood each other. They recognised the passion which accompanied being a success in their chosen fields. Why couldn't Stephen be more like that? Actually, she knew the answer. Because he wasn't passionate about what he did. In fact, what was he passionate about? Nothing, as far as she could see. Apart from having a good time and hanging out with colleagues in the pub or the staff room.

It was times like these when she questioned why she'd got together with him in the first place.

'I don't want to agree just yet. Let me see what I can do. I promise I'll let you know by the end of the day, if that's okay with you?' There, she couldn't be more accommodating.

'I'll take that as a yes then.' He beamed at her.

'I'll confirm later. But—'

She was interrupted by her phone ringing. She picked it up from the table, and Whitney's name was on the screen. 'Sorry, I've got to take this. Hello, George speaking.'

'It's Whitney. We've got another body. When can you get to the station?'

Hell. She knew it had been likely, but hearing it had actually happened sent shivers down her spine. She checked her watch, her heart thumping against her chest. 'I've got a class now which I can't get out of. I can make it in a couple of hours.'

Whitney's frustrated sigh was audible. 'Okay. Just get here as soon as possible.'

She ended the call and looked over at Stephen, who was staring at her, an indefinable expression on his face. 'Let me guess. Your friendly neighbourhood police officer has requested your presence. I wish I had some of what she does; then maybe you'll be at my beck and call.'

'There's been another murder. I don't have the details, but it's likely to be a student from this university. Doesn't that mean anything to you?'

'That's below the belt. Of course I'm concerned about the spate of murders. It's just I don't share your view of your indispensability to the case. But clearly, I'm fighting a losing battle. Do what you want.'

'I will. Thank you for being so understanding.' She could've kicked herself. She didn't do sarcasm, as a rule.

'My pleasure,' he retorted.

'I'm going. I'll let you know later about the weekend.'

'Don't pretend you're going to consider it. We both know that's not the case. I'm going whether you come or not. It will probably do us good to have some time apart.'

She picked up her bag from the back of her chair and marched off.

Chapter Twenty-Two

As George pushed open the door to the incident room, the cacophony of sound hit her. The place was buzzing and straight away she got caught up in the intensity. Whitney was over to one side, talking to Ellie.

Whitney glanced up and waved for her to come over.

'Hi,' Whitney said. 'Glad you could finally make it.'

She prickled, then reminded herself sarcasm seemed to be Whitney's go to response, especially when the pressure was on.

'I came as soon as I could. Tell me about the latest victim.'

'Before we discuss that, I want to speak to you in private. We'll go to my office.' Whitney pointed to the back of the room, where there was an open door.

'Sure.' She wondered what couldn't be said in front of other members of the team. Unless it was something personal. But how likely was that?

'I want an honest answer from you,' Whitney said once they were alone.

Whitney could almost be intimidating if she wasn't so much shorter than George.

'Of course.'

'Have you mentioned to anyone about the mobile phones being left in the victims' laps?'

She hadn't discussed the case with anyone outside of the team. She'd automatically assumed she was confined by a confidentiality agreement. 'No. Other than when we've discussed it here with the team.'

'Are you sure?' Whitney persisted.

The hackles rose on the back of her neck. She didn't lie.

'Yes. Why?' She was unable to hide her annoyance.

'At the media conference one of the reporters asked about it. We hadn't released the information.'

'And you think it's me?'

'You're just one of the people we're asking. Unfortunately, too many people know.'

So, she was accusing her because she wasn't actually part of the team. Now she got it.

'You think because I'm the outsider, it's more likely to be me than anyone else?'

'Whoa. What's got into you? I'm just asking a question.' Whitney shook her head.

'Sorry. It's been a difficult day. I didn't mean to take it out on you. I haven't discussed the case with anyone. Especially not the phone, as you'd already mentioned keeping quiet about it.'

'Who the fuck was it then?' Whitney mused. 'I doubt it's a member of the team. I'm more inclined to believe uniform had something to do with it. Some of them have no idea about keeping their mouths shut.'

'Did they know we were withholding the information?'

'Yes,' Whitney replied. 'Anyway, I'll have to deal with it another time. We need to talk about the latest murder.'

'I hate to say this, but having a third body does give us more to work with.'

They walked back into the incident room, stopping next to the board.

'Latest victim. Poppy Brooks. Second year English student. Aged twenty. Found at nine-thirty this morning by Rushton Lake.'

She tensed as Whitney pointed to the photo of a young pretty girl with long dark hair. Nausea washed over her. They had to get the bastard who did this.

'By water again. I think we can safely confirm water is important to the killer.'

'Exactly what I thought. Doug, print me off a map of the university grounds and surrounding area,' Whitney called over to the DC who was sitting at his desk.

A few moments later, he brought the map over. Whitney put it up on the board and took hold of the pen, marking the locations where the three bodies had been found.

George glanced again at the photo of Poppy Brooks. She didn't recognise her. Then again, that wasn't surprising, seeing as there were over twenty thousand students studying at the uni.

'I take it she was left in the same pose?' she asked.

'Yes. Phone in the lap and photo of her as the wallpaper.'

'May I see the photo?'

'Ellie's been looking at the contact list. Ellie, here a minute,' Whitney shouted over the chatter.

'Guv,' Ellie said once she'd walked over.

'Do we have a copy of the wallpaper photo on Poppy's phone? I want to show George.'

'Yes, it's on my computer. Over here, Dr Cavendish.'

She followed Ellie to her desk and examined the photo on the screen. It was identical to the others. All that could be seen was the victim, the headboard, and her splayed legs. Nothing to give them any indication of where they were. It was impossible to see exactly what the ankles were tied to.

'Thanks. What about the contact list? Have you come up with any matches on all three yet?' she asked.

'I'm going through it now. The latest victim has over two hundred names in there.'

'Okay.'

George walked back to the board and stood next to Whitney.

She ran her fingers through her hair. 'With three victims we can now establish a pattern of behaviour and make inferences.'

'The patterns being the rape and strangulation, where the bodies are left, and they're all students?' Whitney said.

'It's more than that. These crimes are meticulously planned. Implying our murderer is intelligent and has been educated. Also, his violence is controlled. The forensic evidence indicates the rapes aren't frenzied. He likely sees the victims as representing women in his past who he has something against. I suspect he has violent tendencies in his normal life.'

'That's all good, but how can we use it in our investigation?'

'By continually building on what we have. We need to look at the victims themselves. Physically, there are no similarities. None of them lived in the same location, and they weren't all in university accommodation.' She paused to think. 'What about college?' It was a longshot, and not something she'd considered before because the students weren't first years and didn't live in halls.

She hurried over to Matt, who was by one of the computers. 'Do you have access to the university records on each of the victims?'

'Yes. The administration department emailed me their files,' Matt replied.

'Check out what college all the girls were in.'

'College?' He frowned.

'The university is divided into eight separate colleges, which aren't subject related. They have their own halls of residence and their own pastoral care.'

'Godwin,' he said after a minute. 'They're all in Godwin.'

Finally. They had something.

She headed back to Whitney. 'We have a link. It's a tad on the tenuous side, but it's the first one we've found, other than the party, which we can't count, as we don't know yet whether the latest victim had gone to it. They are all in Godwin College.'

'Fantastic. Does it have its own separate building at the university?' Whitney asked, some of the tension around her eyes easing.

'No. The colleges have their own halls of residence for first years. But in later years, students tend to mix. The administration staff for all the colleges are in one building. An—'

'Guv,' Ellie called. 'I've found him.'

Whitney, George, and Matt rushed over to Ellie's desk. 'Who is it?' Whitney asked.

'Kevin Vaughan. He's in the contacts of all three girls. It's a landline number.'

'Haven't you already spoken to him regarding alibis for the first two murders?' Whitney asked.

Ellie opened a file on her computer and scrolled down.

'According to my notes, he was shopping at the time of the first murder and alone in bed at the time of the other. There was nothing to follow up on.'

'Why didn't you tell me?' Whitney asked. 'We should have brought him in for further questioning.'

'I used my judgement. I'm sorry.' Ellie blushed as she bit down on her bottom lip.

'Don't worry. We all make mistakes,' Whitney said, resting her hand on the young detective's shoulder. 'The main thing is we've identified him now.'

Ellie visibly relaxed. Impressive leadership skills from Whitney. She could've so easily hauled Ellie over the coals.

'A university extension,' George said. 'Go into the university website and see where he works.'

Ellie keyed in his name. She turned to them, her eyes bright. 'He's a Junior Dean in Godwin College.'

Whitney and George exchanged glances.

'We've got the bastard,' Whitney said. 'George, you come with me. We're going to bring him in.'

'Me?' she asked, puzzled why she wasn't going to take Matt.

'We don't want to alert him. You can show me the way without us having to involve anyone else at the university. The fewer people who know the better.'

That made sense. 'We'll go in my car, then we can park close to the administration building.'

'Attention, everyone,' Whitney shouted across the noise. 'We've got a lead. I'm going with Dr Cavendish to pick him up for questioning.'

A cheer went up, and a chorus of 'well done' echoed around the room.

'His name's Kevin Vaughan, and he works at the university. I want a background check on him. Where he lives. His family. His friends. His social media presence. Whether he holds a firearm licence. You know the drill. Also, any links to our victims. Check out CCTV from the university, the centre of town, and anywhere close to where he lives.' Whitney turned to George. 'Come on, let's go.'

The drive to the university didn't take long, and after feeding the parking meter, she was soon parked in her usual spot. 'The building's through there,' she said, pointing at the Victorian archway to the left of them.

'I don't want to alarm him,' Whitney said. 'We want him to come with us voluntarily. We'll use the fact the girls are all from his college and we need his help.'

'Good tactic. It's a psychopathic trait of many killers—they want to get close to the investigation and offer to help. They get off on it.'

They got out of the car and walked together under the archway and into the door leading to the administration building. She approached the board beside the entrance door, which listed rooms and occupants.

'Second floor, room six,' she called over her shoulder to Whitney. 'This way. It's quicker than waiting for the lift.'

They hurried up the stairs to Vaughan's office.

Whitney gave two sharp knocks on the door. 'Come in,' a male voice answered.

They walked in and were faced with Vaughan sitting behind a desk. A very ordinary looking man in his mid-thirties, with mousey-brown hair cut in a traditional short back and sides style. He certainly didn't give the impression of being a manipulative serial killer, but appearances were often deceptive.

'Yes?' He smiled at them.

'DCI Walker and Dr Cavendish,' Whitney said. 'We were hoping you could help us.'

'Certainly. Please sit down.' He gestured to the two chairs in front of his desk.

'We've come about the recent student murders,' Whitney said.

George kept her eyes firmly fixed on Vaughan's face, looking for any tell twitches, nervous movements. Anything to signify his unease.

'It's dreadful. I did know the two students, as I've already told your officer.'

'Three,' Whitney said.

'There's been another?' he asked, blinking several times. 'That's dreadful.'

'Agreed. Also, like the other two students, she was a member of Godwin College.'

'Who's the third one?' he asked, shaking his head slowly.

'I'm sorry, we can't disclose that at the moment. Not until her family has been informed.'

'Of course. I totally understand. How can I help?' he asked, seeming to recover slightly.

'We wondered if you'd come to the station with us? We'd like to ask you some questions.'

'Any chance we can do it here, as I have a meeting to go to in half an hour?'

'It would be easier if you could come with us.' Whitney smiled at him. 'We'd like to run some things by you, photographs, CCTV, etc. We can wait until after your meeting, if that helps?'

She glanced at Whitney. Her relaxed demeanour meant alarm bells wouldn't be ringing for the suspect. A good call on her part.

'I could send my apologies. I doubt anyone will miss me,' Vaughan said.

'We really appreciate it. Thank you. We'll wait for you outside in the corridor.'

They left Vaughan making a call about the meeting.

'I'm impressed,' she said to Whitney.

'About what?'

'The way you handled Vaughan. Offering to wait until after the meeting gave the impression you valued his input and suspecting him was far from your thoughts.' She nodded her head appreciatively.

'Thanks.'

Had Whitney just blushed slightly? Maybe she wasn't used to having compliments thrown her way. Interesting.

'What did you make of him?' she asked.

'I was about to ask you the same,' Whitney replied.

'He's definitely hiding something. His body language was a dead giveaway. Did you notice his rapid blinking? That can indicate stress, in particular from lying, because he was trying to be careful about what he said.'

'Really. I was thinking how relaxed he came across. He didn't look at all guilty to me.'

'You'd be amazed what you can tell from the tiniest of twitches. The slightest body movements. Or lack of movement, which can be just as important. When someone is totally rigid, it's often because they're forcing themselves to appear calm and in control.'

'Well, now it's up to me to get a confession out of him. I'd like you to watch from outside. I'll wear an earpiece, so you can advise me on areas of questioning based on his responses.'

At last Whitney seemed to be valuing her input.

'I'd love to. Thanks.'

'I'm not doing this to be nice. There's a lot hanging on it, and we can't afford to fuck up.'

Chapter Twenty-Three

George stood by the window of the interview room. Whitney and Matt were sitting opposite Kevin Vaughan. She was wearing headphones so she could hear what was being said and a mic to speak to Whitney in her earpiece.

'Can we get you a cup of tea or coffee?' Whitney asked Vaughan.

'No, thanks. I'm fine,' he replied. 'Is this going to take long?'

Whitney flashed him a smile. 'I hope not.'

Yet again, Whitney's manner was impressive. She was putting him at ease. Great job. She'd like to have said something in the earpiece to that effect, but she doubted it would go down well. She'd already complimented her earlier, and if she did it again Whitney would probably interpret it as George being condescending towards her.

It was fascinating to be involved in real police work. So far, most of the work she'd done was theoretical. Apart from the few times she'd worked with inmates at a local prison, when doing her research.

Several times throughout her career, she'd considered

going into private practice, but changed her mind as she enjoyed researching and teaching so much and really didn't have the business acumen to call on. She'd heard of several psychologists who'd lost their livelihood because of neglecting the business side of their practice. She didn't want that to happen to her.

'Good, I really can't spare much time.' Vaughan's response cut across George's thoughts. He moved awkwardly in his seat.

'He's getting anxious,' she said into the mic. 'Maybe regrets agreeing to come in to talk.'

'Mr Vaughan. Kevin. Do you mind if we record our conversation? It's so much easier than taking notes,' Whitney asked.

'No. That's fine,' he replied.

'Thank you.' Whitney opened the wrappers of two discs and loaded them into the recording equipment. She pressed the record button, speaking after the alarm had finished. 'DCI Whitney Walker, DS Matthew Price, and Kevin Vaughan. Interview. November twenty-fifth. Mr Vaughan. You're Junior Dean in Godwin College. Please could you explain what that involves?'

'I look after the pastoral care of all students in the college, especially the first years,' Vaughan stated.

'So, you're responsible for over two thousand students? That's a lot.' Whitney sat back in her chair, looking relaxed.

George approved of her non-threatening approach.

'Not all of them. There are three of us, and we all live on-site in the college. As I've mentioned, we mainly deal with welfare concerns. We're also there to ensure they behave properly when they're in the college and ensure noise is kept to a minimum, especially after the college bar closes. We work with security, too, if there are any issues.' Vaughan nodded.

'The girls who were murdered—Millie Carter and Olivia Griffin—how well did you know them?' Whitney asked.

Vaughan sat ramrod straight, a sure sign to George he was trying his hardest to concentrate and come across as being truthful. It was an interesting change in his demeanour and likely indicated he was hiding something.

'They're in Godwin College. I remember them during their first years. They were both friendly and good students. Neither of them caused any problems.'

'Interesting he remembers them in such detail,' George said into the mic.

'Do you remember all of your students? Or just the girls?' Whitney asked, leaning in slightly and resting her arms on the table.

'I don't remember every student who comes into the college. I just happen to remember Millie and Olivia,' Vaughan replied.

'Why's that, do you think? What about them was memorable?' Whitney asked.

Vaughan's face gave very little away, apart from a slight pink tinge to his cheeks, and even then, she wasn't sure whether it was just the light.

'Nothing I can put my finger on. I remember lots of students, just not all of them,' he replied.

'What did you think when you found out they'd been murdered?' Whitney asked.

'I was shocked and devastated, of course. The same as everyone else in the college. How else would I react? Why are you asking me these questions?'

'Ask him about Poppy.' George needed them to press

him more, so she could study his reactions when under pressure.

'How well did you know Poppy Brooks?' Whitney asked.

Vaughan frowned. 'The name rings a bell. Is she in Godwin?'

He was being too slick. Frowning at the right time. Trying to appear concerned.

'I thought you knew all the students. Especially the girls,' Whitney said, her tone a lot less relaxed.

'I've already said I don't know all of them,' Vaughan replied. 'Do I need a solicitor?'

'Why do you think that?' Whitney answered.

'This questioning. It's like you're accusing me of something.'

'Mr Vaughan, as I said earlier, we just need your help. If you'd rather have legal representation, that's your right. But I don't understand why you'd think it necessary, unless you have something to hide.'

'I don't have anything to hide,' Vaughan said.

His fists were clenched in his lap. 'I disagree,' she said to Whitney, who gave an almost imperceptible nod of the head.

'Good. So, shall we continue?' Whitney asked.

'Yes,' he agreed.

'Returning to Poppy Brooks. You don't remember her?'

'I'm not sure. Is she the third victim? You said you couldn't tell me who she was until her family had been notified.'

'I can't say. Are you sure you don't remember her?'

'I'm not certain. There are a lot of students in Godwin, as you've already pointed out.'

'Yet you clearly remember Millie and Olivia, who

haven't even been living in the college for two years,' Whitney persisted.

Beads of sweat formed on his forehead. He really was a contradiction. On the one hand, his body language was showing he was lying. The way he was concentrating so hard on looking like he was in control. And then he was displaying the characteristics of someone who wasn't lying but anxious in case he wasn't believed.

'It isn't adding up. He's definitely hiding something. I can't be sure it's to do with the murders. But I can't be sure it isn't, either.' She could tell from the way Whitney tensed, she wasn't happy with her comments, but she had to tell it as she saw it. 'Show him Poppy's photo,' she added.

'Here's a photo of Poppy Brooks.' Whitney slid the photo across the table. 'Please look and see if you recognise her.'

Vaughan stared at the image for a few seconds and then slowly nodded his head. 'I may have seen her. Yes.'

'You may? What does that mean exactly?'

'She definitely looks familiar. But I wouldn't have known her name if you hadn't told me.'

'Thank you,' Whitney said.

'Can I go now?' he asked.

'Kevin. Please could you tell me what you were doing between two and four in the afternoon of Sunday the third and between one and three in the morning of Monday the eighteenth?'

'Why?' he asked.

'We're asking this of everyone who comes in to help. Just to eliminate them from our enquiries. It's standard procedure.'

Vaughan looked upwards to the right, indicating he was thinking. Was it fake or genuine? It depended on how clever he was. If he knew a little about body language, it was a basic tell-tale sign which he could use.

'On the Sunday, I'd been to the garden centre to pick up a plant for Moira's birthday. She works in the admin office. I got back home around two-thirty, I think.'

'Can anyone vouch for you?' Whitney asked.

'I might be able to find my receipt from the garden centre. Other than that, no. I live alone.'

'What about Monday the eighteenth?' Whitney asked.

'I was home in bed. It was the middle of the night. No one would be able to vouch for me,' Vaughan answered.

'Thank you. Tell me, Kevin, do you have a girlfriend?' Whitney asked.

A flush crept up Vaughan's cheeks, and he looked down at the table. 'Not at the moment,' he replied.

'When was the last time you had one?' Whitney asked.

Vaughan coughed. 'I don't remember.'

'How can you not remember?' Whitney pushed.

She edged closer to the window. 'You're onto something. Keep on with this line of questioning.'

'It was a while ago,' Vaughan finally said.

'Please could you give me the name of your last girlfriend?' Whitney smiled sweetly at him.

'Why?' Vaughan asked, his flush getting deeper.

'Just for the record,' Whitney replied.

Vaughan stood up and placed both hands on the table. 'Look. I agreed to come in to help you, and now you're treating me like a suspect. I don't have to take this. I want to leave.'

'Please sit down, Kevin. You have every right to leave. But I'd advise against it. At the moment, you're here voluntarily, but if you insist on leaving, I might have to arrest you.'

'On what charge?' He remained standing, glaring at Whitney.

'Let's put it this way. You have links to the victims and won't discuss them with us, which means you're obstructing a police investigation. So, it's up to you. Stay here voluntarily or I'll be forced to arrest you for obstruction, and then we can hold you for questioning for at least forty-eight hours.' Whitney sat back in her chair.

'I want a solicitor. I'm not saying another word until I get one.' He sat back down.

'That's your right. Do you have one in mind?' Whitney asked.

'I don't know anyone,' Vaughan said.

'Would you like us to call one for you?' she asked.

'Yes,' Vaughan replied.

'Okay. Wait here. Interview terminated at fourteen hundred hours.' Whitney switched off the recording. 'DS Price, please contact a solicitor for Mr Vaughan.'

She left the interview room and joined George by the window.

'What do you think?' Whitney asked.

She slipped off her headphones. 'You certainly put him on the back foot. He's hiding something, for sure. Whether it's the murders, I don't know. He fits the profile and appears strong enough to lift the girls and take them to their resting places. He clearly has problems with relationships. It all fits.'

'Agreed. Our application for a warrant to search his flat has been approved on the grounds it might contain evidence relating to the case. We're going now.'

'Can I come?' she asked, keen to see where he lived and what his flat was like. She'd hazard a guess it would be immaculate. Everything put away and kept perfectly tidy.

She wouldn't be at all surprised if he even kept his books and CDs in alphabetical order.

'We don't need you, thanks. You get back to work. I'll let you know how we get on.' Whitney turned and left the room, leaving George staring at her retreating back.

Chapter Twenty-Four

'Yes.' Whitney punched the air. 'We've got him.'

The digital forensic unit had forwarded hundreds of images of women taken from bondage websites, which were on the laptop they'd seized from Kevin Vaughan's flat. He also had photos of students on there, including both Millie and Olivia. Not Poppy, but that didn't worry her. He was their guy; she was convinced of it.

She'd debated phoning George to let her know the outcome, then decided to do it later, once they had the confession. She didn't want to keep interrupting her, in case it got her in trouble at work. She was perfectly capable of interviewing Vaughan on her own, without George's help. She'd managed to secure hundreds of convictions over her career, and this would be no different.

'Matt, come with me. We're off to nail the bastard,' she said as she passed his desk.

'Coming, guv,' Matt replied.

Before they left the incident room, she asked Ellie to print off some of the photos found on Vaughan's laptop, including the two of the victims.

They walked to the interview room in silence while she ran through in her mind her plan for the interview. Before entering, she drew in a long calming breath. As much as she wanted to swing for him, she couldn't. This had to be played by the book, and she wouldn't deviate. Having said that, she would go in soft and then hit him hard.

She pushed open the door and saw Vaughan's solicitor sitting beside him.

'About time, too,' the solicitor said. 'My client has been here for over four hours.'

'Sorry to keep you waiting. We were searching Mr Vaughan's flat.'

'What?' Vaughan exploded. 'You can't do that.' He turned to his solicitor. 'She can't do that, can she?'

'I assume you had a search warrant?' the solicitor asked.

'You assume right.'

'Bu—'

'No buts, Mr Vaughan. The search was legal.' She sat opposite them and Matt next to her.

She placed the file on the table in front of her and prepared the recorder. She picked up the remote and pressed it. 'This is an interview with, please state your full name.' She nodded at Vaughan.

'Kevin Lawrence Vaughan. And I want to say I've bee—'

'We'll get onto your comments shortly,' she interrupted. 'I am DCI Whitney Walker. Also present is—' She nodded at Matt.

'DS Matthew Price.'

'And ...' She looked at the solicitor.

'Timothy Anders, solicitor for Mr Vaughan.'

'Thank you. Kevin, you stated earlier you remembered Millie Carter and Olivia Griffin from when they were first years and lived in Godwin College. Is that correct?' she asked.

'Yes. I've already told you that,' Vaughan replied in a belligerent tone.

'You also stated you don't remember every student who comes into Godwin.'

'Yes.' Vaughan leaned forward, resting his arms on the table.

'Would you say you remember the young women more than the young men?'

'Not necessarily. No. Where is this heading?'

Whitney eyeballed him for a few seconds until he averted his gaze.

'Do you take photos of the students in Godwin College and keep them?' she continued.

'I don't know what you mean. We have photographs of all the students on record, so I wouldn't need to keep any.'

She opened the file in front of her and pulled out the photos of Millie and Olivia. 'In that case, please can you tell me why we found these on your laptop? For the recording, I'm showing Mr Vaughan photographs of Millie Carter and Olivia Griffin.' She slid the photos across the table and allowed a tiny smile to escape her lips.

Colour drained from Vaughan's face. He looked at his solicitor.

'You don't have to answer,' Anders said.

'You don't,' she agreed. 'But I strongly advise you do. It won't look good if you don't.'

'No comment,' Vaughan said.

She opened the file again and pulled out photos of women tied up in a variety of positions. 'Okay. What about these?' She pushed the photos towards him.

Vaughan stared at the them and then looked up at her. 'No comment,' he said weakly.

She let out a long sigh. 'Kevin. You're really not helping your case. Let me make it clear, none of these images are illegal. All we want from you is an explanation as to why you have them on your laptop. Do you get off on seeing women tied up?'

'No comment,' Vaughan repeated.

'Does it make you feel manly? Do you like having control over women?' she persisted, the tone of her voice getting colder with each word she spoke.

'No comment.'

'And why the images of Millie and Olivia? Did you fancy them? Did you want to take them out? Maybe tie them up and take photos of them to add to your collection?'

'No comment. No comment. No comment!' Vaughan shouted, banging his hand on the table.

Anders rested his hand on Vaughan's arm. 'That's enough, detective,' the solicitor said.

'All I want is an answer to my questions,' she said, her voice steady and calm. 'Kevin. I'll ask you again. Why do you have photos of Millie Carter and Olivia Griffin on your laptop?'

'I just wanted—'

A knock on the door interrupted them, and Frank popped his head around the door.

'What?' she snapped.

'A word, guv.'

She groaned. She had the bastard, and now he'd have time to regroup. Whatever Frank wanted it had better be good or there'd be hell to pay.

'Interview suspended.' She got up from her chair and went outside with Frank.

'What the fuck do you want?' she blasted. 'I'd got him on the ropes, and you gave him an out.'

'Sorry, guv. But I thought you'd want to hear this.' Frank shifted awkwardly on the spot.

'Well?'

'We've just found out Kevin Vaughan uses Diamond Escort Agency and has used the services of Olivia Griffin.'

Excitement coursed through her veins. Now let the fucker wriggle out of that. It was the information she needed to nail him. 'That's fantastic. Thanks, Frank. Great work.'

She hurried back into the interview room and whispered into Matt's ear, telling him the news.

'Interview recommences. Mr Vaughan. It's come to my attention you use Diamond Escort Agency. Is that correct?'

Vaughan looked at the floor. He remained silent.

'Mr Vaughan. Is. That. Correct?' she repeated.

'Yes,' he muttered under his breath.

'And is it also correct one of the escorts you've used is Olivia Griffin? Also known as Kirsty?'

Vaughan shrugged and gave a small nod.

'For the tape, please.'

'Yes. It's true,' he said.

'Kevin Vaughan. I'm arresting you on suspicion of the murders of Millie Carter, Olivia Griffin, and Poppy Brooks. You do not have to say anything, but it may harm your defence if you do not mention something which you later rely on in court. Anything you do say may be given in evidence. Do you understand?' she stated.

'Yes.'

'Right. You will be remanded in custody for further questioning.' She stood up. 'DS Price, please take the prisoner down for processing.'

After Vaughan and his solicitor were escorted out, she retrieved the recording and left the interview room. Jamieson was waiting for her.

'Sir,' she said.

'I hear you have some good news for me.' He smiled, and it actually reached his eyes.

'Yes, sir. We've got our man. It all fits. He has no concrete alibis. He lives alone on the university campus. He's a perv. His laptop's full of disgusting images of women. And he's used Olivia Griffin as an escort. It's all there. All I need to do is break him and get a confession. At least then we won't have to go to trial. The evidence is circumstantial, but there's too much of it for it not to count. I've got forensics going through his flat for any trace of the young women being there. He won't get away with it.'

'Good work, Walker. Press conference tomorrow morning. The sooner this is put to bed the better.'

Chapter Twenty-Five

'Hi, Mum,' Tiffany called as she walked into the kitchen. She dropped her bag on the floor next to the table and sat down. 'Mmm. Smells good.'

Whitney looked up from stirring the sauce she was making for dinner. Spaghetti bolognaise and chilli were the most adventurous dishes she ever cooked, as even she couldn't ruin them. Well, apart from when she forgot she was cooking and got so engrossed in other tasks they burnt. That had happened on more than one occasion. Usually they made do with ready meals or whatever could be zapped in the microwave, like jacket potatoes.

'I wasn't sure whether you were in for dinner. We can have this tomorrow if you're not,' she said.

'I just assumed you'd be busy at work, seeing as I've been feeding myself for the last few weeks.'

A smidgeon of guilt flashed through her, but she pushed it aside. Years ago, Whitney had worked through the *you shouldn't be working full time with a child to care for* attitude prevalent among certain people. Her job gave them the life they had now. It also meant Tiffany was able to fulfil her dreams. And she'd never been short of love and attention, despite what some antiquated people thought would happen.

'We've had a breakthrough in the case,' she said as she turned and smiled at Tiffany.

'Have you caught him?'

'It certainly looks like it.'

She'd spent the last couple hours singing at the top of her voice while doing some much-needed cleaning and generally being happy. She'd be lying if she said it was more than catching the killer. That was important, obviously, but after the balling out she'd received from Jamieson over the fucked-up drug raid, and his warning, she was relieved to no longer be on unofficial probation. She could get back to what she enjoyed doing and what she did well. Catching criminals.

'Thank goodness. It's been so bad at uni recently. Everyone looking over their shoulders, second guessing what others were doing, and worrying about going anywhere on their own. Can I tell anyone, or is it secret?'

'I'd rather you didn't mention anything until tomorrow, after the press conference. Now what about dinner? Do you want any?' She gave another stir and her stomach rumbled.

'Actually, I've planned to go out for dinner with my new boyfriend.'

She stopped stirring and turned to face her daughter, who had flushed a delicate shade of pink.

'New boyfriend. Since when? And how come you didn't tell me?' She couldn't hide the disappointment in her voice. Why had she kept it from her? Usually she told her everything. They had that kind of relationship.

'You were so busy, and I've hardly seen you. We've only just started seeing each other.'

'Is he on your course?' she asked, determined to keep her voice light. She didn't want her to clam up.

'No. He's studying to be a vet. You've actually met him already.' She grinned.

'I have?'

'Henry Spencer. He's got a twin sister called Harriet.'

'Isn't he a little old for you?' she asked, then immediately regretted it as Tiffany's expression darkened.

'No. He's only four years older than me. He's twenty-four.'

'I suppose four years isn't much. He seems very responsible. In the short time I spoke to him, he impressed me. A bit posh though,' she said, hoping she'd said enough to defuse the situation.

'Mum, you're such a snob.' Tiffany shook her head.

'A snob. That's ridiculous. He's the one who's posh. I'm just common old me.'

'Okay, you're an inverted snob. Anyway, his family background doesn't matter to me. It's him I'm seeing, not his family,' she said, her tone making Whitney realise these feelings for Henry ran deeper than Tiffany was letting on.

'How did you meet him?' she asked, changing the subject before she said anything else to upset her.

'He had a birthday party a few weeks ago. I went with Chloe. One of her friends invited us.'

'That party.' Whitney shook her head. 'It seems like the whole student population of Lenchester University went.'

'It was crowded, for sure. Their parties are legendary, so I've been told. It was the first one I'd been to. It was fun; we had a great time. And I got to meet Henry and Harriet.'

'I'm happy for you. Really. But don't let it affect your work.'

Tiffany rolled her eyes towards the ceiling and laughed.

'Yes, Mum. Whatever you say, Mum. I am allowed some time off, you know. I'm up to date on all my assignments, and my grades are good. What about you? Haven't you got choir tonight?'

She checked her watch. Crap. She'd never make the rehearsal now. The investigation had messed so much with her social life she'd got out of the routine. She'd have to leave it until the following week.

'I'll go next time. They understand I can't always make rehearsals.'

'You don't mind me going out, do you? Are you okay on your own?'

She went over and gave Tiffany a big hug. 'Of course I am. I'll probably go out for a celebratory drink.' She hadn't planned on doing so, but now the thought had popped into her head it seemed a good one.

'Who with?'

'I'll find someone. Or go to the pub near the station. There's bound to be people in there I know.'

'Okay. I'm going upstairs to get changed. I'll take the bus into town and walk to Henry's. I don't mind going on my own now it's all safe.' She left the room and ran up the stairs.

Whitney turned off the sauce, leaving it on the side to cool. She didn't fancy the local cop pub. It would be rowdy, and she'd end up getting hammered, knowing her. A quiet drink to relax and ruminate over her success was just what she fancied. Except she didn't know anyone who would be up for that.

Actually, she did. George. It seemed her sort of outing. Except what would George think if she phoned out of the blue and asked her out for a drink? She could use the excuse of wanting to update her on the investigation, as she'd promised.

She reached for her phone and called.

'Hello,' George answered after a couple of rings.

'It's Whitney. I wanted to let you know we've arrested Kevin Vaughan. At his flat we found images of women tied up. There were photos of students, including Millie and Olivia. Also, he's a client of Diamond Escorts. Certainly enough for an arrest.'

'Well done. Excellent news. Congratulations.'

Should she ask? The most she could say was no.

'I wondered if you'd like to go out for a drink to celebrate?'

'Sorry, I've got a lot of work on.' George didn't even appear to consider it.

'That's okay. I asked on the off chance.'

'Where are you all going? I might be able to pop out for a short while,' George said, seeming to have a change of heart.

'It's not the others. Just the two of us.' She felt stupid saying it like that. Did it seem like she was asking her out on a date?

'Oh. Right. Okay. Yes. I'd love to. Where do you want to go?'

'Somewhere where there aren't any raucous police officers,' she replied, laughing.

'There's a pub in Hollowton, a village about five miles out of the city. I've been meaning to try it. We could go there. I'll pick you up, if you like,' George offered.

'Sounds great. Pick me up at six-thirty. I'm at sixty-eight Lutterbridge Road. Shall we get something to eat while we're there?' she suggested, eating alone suddenly not appealing to her.

'Great idea. I'll see you soon.'

Chapter Twenty-Six

George pulled up outside Whitney's house, a small semi-detached in a quiet cul-de-sac on the west side of the city. The last thing she'd expected was for Whitney to ask her out for a drink. On their own. Not even with the rest of the team. Normally she would have said no, as she steered away from going out socially, especially with people she didn't know, but Stephen wasn't there, and for some reason sitting down in front of the TV wasn't doing it for her.

She was just about to get out of the car when Whitney opened the door, closed it behind her, and walked down the small path leading to the gate. She'd changed out of her usual dark trousers, lace-up shoes, and jacket and instead wore some light-coloured jeans with a maroon knitted poncho over the top.

George's eyes were drawn to the garden, which was bare and unkempt. The small blocks of lawn needed mowing, and there wasn't a flower bed or bush in sight. A marked difference to the neighbours either side, whose gardens looked pristine, even though it was winter. She loved gardening when she had the time, and her fingers itched to do something to Whitney's.

Whitney opened the car door and slid in. 'Nice car.' She nodded appreciatively as she stroked the black leather seat. 'A Land Rover?'

'Yes. I love it. Especially on the open road.' She started the engine and headed off in the direction of the pub she'd chosen for them.

'Thanks for coming. I didn't fancy being stuck at home all evening. And it will be good to run through the case if you don't mind.'

'I'm happy to. Why didn't you go out with other members of the team?'

'I'm their boss. It makes socialising a little difficult at times. I've got to watch how I behave. Especially at the moment, with Jamieson on my back for what happened before.'

'I get it. What did happen before? If you don't mind talking about it.'

'I fucked up big time. Orchestrated a drug raid on the wrong house. I got duped by an informant.'

It didn't seem such a big deal to her.

'But surely they understood it wasn't your fault? This sort of thing must happen all the time.'

'True. Except the house we raided wasn't in a known drugs area. And to top it all, the family who live there are good friends of the Chief Constable.'

'Ouch. Not good.'

'You can say that again.' Whitney gave a hollow laugh.

'Well, at least now you've earned back your credibility.'

'Exactly. Which is why I wanted to celebrate. And seeing as I was too late for choir, I gave you a call.'

They drove for a few miles, chatting about nothing in particular, before pulling into the car park of the Black

Swan. The setting was idyllic, beside a village pond and overlooking fields, not that they could see much, as it was dark, and there was very little street lighting. 'It looks charming doesn't it?' she said.

They got out of the car and walked through the wooden door, so low she had to duck her head. The warmth from the open fire hit them as soon as they entered the small bar. Large wooden beams lined the ceiling, and the furniture was traditional, with dark wood tables and chairs with floral cushions. The floor was flagstones.

'It's lovely,' Whitney said.

'My treat,' she said as they stood by the bar. She scanned the bar to look at all the beers they had on tap. 'What would you like?'

'Half a cider, please.'

'Yes, ladies,' the barman said as he approached where they were standing.

'A pint of Bodsworth Mud and half a cider, please.'

'You drink pints?' Whitney said, her eyes wide.

'Only real ale.'

'I'd never have had you down as a beer drinker. You seem way too … too…' Whitney paused.

'Posh?' George suggested. She'd heard it all before. Girls like her didn't drink beer. People thought she was a gin and tonic person. She liked that, too. But real ale was her passion.

'No, not that.' Whitney paused, before letting out a rueful groan. 'Actually, yes that is it. Sorry.'

'It doesn't matter. I'm used to all the comments. Let's sit over there.' She pointed to an empty table next to the wall leading into the restaurant.

After sitting, there was an awkward silence. She often struggled with starting a conversation. She'd never been good at small talk. Especially when she was with people she didn't know very well. Then she remembered Whitney had mentioned her choir.

'What choir do you belong to?' she asked.

'The local Rock Choir. We meet weekly, but I can't always get there.'

'I can't hold a note, so you'll only hear me singing in the shower. Actually, you won't hear me. I only do it when there's no one around.' She laughed. 'Are you any good?'

'With a name like Whitney? What do you think?'

'What do you mean?' She was totally lost.

'My mum's a huge Whitney Houston fan, which is how I got my name. And lucky for me, it turned out I can sing. I love it.'

'You didn't think about taking it up professionally?' she asked.

'In my dreams. But in reality, there was no way. I had my daughter, Tiffany, to consider. I wouldn't have been able to go on tour, stay out late. All that stuff.'

She hadn't realised Whitney had a child. 'How old is she?'

'Twenty. She's studying engineering at university.'

'Twenty? You must have had her when you were very young. Sorry, didn't mean to pry.' Not only was she crap at small talk. She also had the habit of putting her foot in it.

'It's fine. I'm happy to talk about it. I got pregnant at seventeen. The father isn't on the scene.' Whitney waved her hand dismissively.

'It must have been hard, joining the force with such a young child.'

'My mum and dad helped me. Dad died ten years ago.' Whitney's voice faded.

'Sorry, it can't have been easy.'

'It wasn't. Especially for Mum because she was left with very little money and my older brother to look after. He's got learning difficulties after being attacked as a kid. The police were next to useless when it came to solving the case. That's why I became a police officer. I wanted to make a difference. Make sure what happened to us didn't happen to any other family.'

She'd never been able to spill everything like Whitney had just done. She kept most stuff to herself. She envied her the ability to do that. It had to be better than locking everything up inside.

'I get your reasoning behind going into the police. The motivation must have been extremely strong.'

'It was. I sometimes wonder whether it was the right thing to do. When you get the likes of Jamieson coming in on the fast track path. Having no real knowledge of policing and then wanting to tell you what to do.'

The more she got to know Whitney, understand her motivations, the more she found herself warming to her. It hadn't been easy for her. She also understood why Whitney had been resistant to her coming in. Whitney probably saw her as another academic trying to muscle in on her territory.

'I'm sure it was the right thing for you. To get to your level is a fantastic achievement.' Did she sound condescending? She hoped not.

'What about you?' Whitney asked. 'Have you always wanted to be a forensic psychologist?'

'I fell into it accidentally. I originally wanted to go into medicine.'

'Why medicine?'

'My father's a surgeon. I wanted to follow in his footsteps.'

'What stopped you?'

'Blood.' She took a large swallow of beer. 'Or, more

precisely, it turned out vast quantities induce a strong reaction in me.'

'What sort of reaction?'

Am I really going to share this?

'Non-discriminatory projectile vomiting.'

George leaned forward and placed her hands over her cheeks as the memories came flooding back. It was funny and embarrassing all at the same time. And not something she'd ever thought to share.

'Non-discriminatory? What do you mean?' Whitney asked.

'I wasn't fussy who I vomited over. Fellow med student or consultant, it didn't matter,' she replied, laughing.

She could laugh about it now. But it took a while for her to get to that place.

'You vomited over your boss? That's hilarious. Did you get kicked out of med school?'

'I left.'

'But I don't get it. How can you now go into the morgue and see dissected bodies and organs covered in blood?'

'I went to a good hypnotherapist. I'm not great with blood, but I can handle it.'

'Was your father disappointed when you dropped out?' Whitney asked.

More like embarrassed. He'd rolled his eyes and said he was annoyed she'd made him look so bad in front of his colleagues. He then patronizingly told her he'd never believed she'd cut it. He suggested she should forget about forging a career for herself, should find a man, and get married. Her mother was away at the time, so didn't stick up for her. Not that she would have. She was all for fighting your own battles.

'He wasn't surprised. He never thought I was smart enough.'

She didn't want Whitney to feel sorry for her. She'd got over it a long time ago.

'But not being smart wasn't the problem,' Whitney said.

'That didn't matter to him. Anyway, let's not talk about it anymore. I'd rather have another drink.' She finished off her pint.

'You're driving, remember,' Whitney reminded her.

'True. I'll have a half and order some food,' she said.

'Good idea.' Whitney picked up the menu from the centre of the table. 'I'll have a burger and chips.' She handed her the menu.

She scanned it. 'Same for me.'

Whitney went to the bar to order the drinks and food, and George leaned back in her chair. The pub was full and she could just see into the dining room. There was a couple close to the open fire who stood up from their table and walked to the back door. They got close to her, and she did a double take.

What the hell?

Going out of the door was Stephen, with his arm resting protectively around a petite woman, who was gazing up at him with an adoring smile on her face.

Chapter Twenty-Seven

Whitney strolled into the station, her steps lighter than they'd been in a long time. For the first time in months, she'd had eight hours undisturbed sleep. And she felt great. Last night had helped. She had to admit she hadn't enjoyed herself so much in ages. George was actually good company once she let down her frosty barriers. And as for her drinking beer. That was a surprise. Though George had been quieter over their meal than she had beforehand. But Whitney had enough to say for both of them, so it didn't put a damper on things.

She headed for her office and then the incident room. When she walked in, everyone stood and applauded.

'Stop it,' she said, trying unsuccessfully to suppress a smile. 'We're not there yet. There's still a lot to do. Matt, contact the digital forensic unit and see if there's anything on his work computer.'

'Yes, guv,' Matt said.

'Ellie. Visit Annabelle at Diamond Escorts. We want dates and times when Vaughan used their services, and names and contact details of all escorts he's been with.'

'Yes, guv.'

'I'm doing the press conference with the Super and later will begin questioning Vaughan again. For the moment, I'm happy to leave him sweating in the cell.'

She went back to her office and gathered her bag and the Vaughan file and headed for Jamieson's office. When she got there, she could hear him on the phone, so she waited outside. 'Yes, ma'am. We're speaking to the media shortly.' He paused. 'I'll make sure of it.' He replaced the phone on his desk.

'Come in, Walker,' Jamieson said after she knocked.

'Sir.'

'Where are we?'

'We're working the evidence and pulling everything together. Dr Dexter's report has come in for Poppy Brooks confirming same MO. The victim's last meal was sushi. I'll be grilling Vaughan hard later. He'll break. No question. There's so much stacking up against him.'

It was funny, even Jamieson didn't seem so bad to her at the moment. She hadn't changed her mind about his ability. But she could live with it. She'd have to. Maybe she'd make more of an effort to be involved in departmental strategy. As DCI her remit was to take a more strategic role, but she tended to spend most of her time hands on with the cases. It didn't help Jamieson hardly ever valued her input on anything outside of operational matters.

'I like to give praise where it's due. Well done, Walker. Have you spoken to the Crown Prosecution Service, yet?'

'I've run it by them, but they'd prefer either a confession or more evidence. Understandably. I'm confident we'll have what they need soon.'

'Excellent. Right, the media. They'll be here in ten

minutes. Are you ready? I'll leave it for you to tell them. I'll be sitting by your side.'

'You want me to lead?' she asked, unable to hide her surprise.

This would be his time to shine. She'd have put money on him wanting to take the lead.

'Yes. You've made the arrest. You can take the credit.'

The day was getting better and better.

'Happy to, sir.'

They walked together to the conference room, and Jamieson chatted all the way. She learnt about the golf competition he was entering at the weekend. About how his wife complained constantly because he was either at work or on the golf course. He also mentioned the Christmas party he was planning to give at his house, which he hoped she'd be able to attend.

It was like she'd entered a parallel universe. But she loved it. Whether she'd go to his party remained to be seen. He asked her about her family life, and she did tell him about Tiffany studying engineering at university. Why wouldn't she? She was so proud.

Jamieson made the appropriate noises and commented how clever Tiffany must be, as engineering was one of the hardest degrees to take.

By the time they reached the press conference, it was like they were best buddies.

They walked into a packed room. As usual, reporters sat in the front rows and cameras were at the back. She wished she'd had time to do something better with her hair, rather than the usual scraped off her face into a hair tie.

Michelle was already there. 'Thank you all for coming,' she said to the reporters once Whitney and Jamieson were seated. 'I'll pass you over to Detective Superintendent Jamieson.'

Jamieson nodded. 'And I'll pass you on DCI Walker.' He nodded for her to begin.

'We're pleased to report we have a male in custody for the murders of Millie Carter, Olivia Griffin, and Poppy Brooks.'

'Who is he?' one of the reporters called out.

Whitney stared at him. 'You know I can't tell you.'

'Does he work at the university?' another reporter called out.

The question took Whitney by surprise. How the fuck did they know? Surely not the leak again. As soon as this case was sorted, that would be her next priority. She glanced across at Jamieson, who gave a tiny shake of his head.

'I'm not in the position to say where the accused works,' Whitney replied.

'But you're not denying it,' the reporter persisted.

'I'm neither confirming nor denying. All I will say is at this point in time we're not looking for anyone else in connection with the case.'

'Are you withdrawing your warning to female students in Lenchester to not go out alone?' the reporter continued.

'As I've already said. We have someone in custody and we're not looking for anyone else at this time. I believe Lenchester is now a lot safer, but I still recommend women go out in pairs at night.'

She didn't want to come across as sexist, but she wouldn't want Tiffany out on her own at night. Daytime was fine.

'You believe Lenchester is an unsafe place for women at night, chief inspector?' a female reporter asked.

She'd had a feeling her words were going to open up this debate.

'No area is one hundred per cent safe all the time. Before the student murders, I would always recommend women didn't go out alone in unlit, remote areas of town. The same for men, too. I'm not here to discuss that. The aim of today's press conference is to report on the student murders. Are there any more questions?'

There were none, so Whitney and Jamieson left the room.

'I thought you were over the top in there, Walker,' Jamieson said as soon as they were away from the room.

'Why, sir?'

'We want to instil confidence into the general public. Now, you've made it appear we live in a violent city, and no one is safe if they're out on their own. Not quite the image we want to put across.'

Why was he twisting her words? He knew exactly what she'd meant. And she stood by it.

'I was stating my opinion. Would you be happy if your daughter walked the streets alone in the middle of the night?'

'No. Of course not.'

'That's all I meant. We want our children to be safe. I also mentioned men. My comments weren't just restricted to women.'

'Yes. And that's worse. Are we now saying our streets are unsafe for everybody at night?'

Maybe she had gone too far, but she didn't regret it. It could be because her job made her jaundiced, but she'd seen far too many attacks to change her mind on this.

'I'm sorry if you view it like that, sir. I believe everyone should be careful, that's all. What's more important is we've now got someone for the murders, and the public will be reassured we've done a good job.'

Jamieson stared at her for a few seconds. 'It depends on how it's reported. When are you interviewing the suspect again?'

'I'm going back to the incident room now to see what the team have got. I'll speak to the suspect again in an hour or so.'

'Good. Keep me informed of progress.' He turned and headed down the corridor, leaving Whitney staring at him, wondering whether she'd imagined his civility from before the conference. Who cared? She had a job to do and didn't care whether he invited her to his stupid party or not.

Chapter Twenty-Eight

I nearly pissed myself laughing when I heard on the radio the police have caught the "Campus Killer", and they've stopped looking for anyone else. Luckily, I was on my own, because even with my awesome acting skills, which I've successfully put to use over the years, I doubt I'd have been able to contain myself.

I mean, really, people pay their taxes to fund this ineffective police force of ours. Or maybe it's because I'm so clever at what I do.

Whatever. I have news for DCI Walker and her pathetic little team, who think they have the killer in custody.

No.

You.

Don't.

Watching that self-satisfied bitch Walker speak at the press conference gave me the urge to punch her in the face. She sat there acting all smug, like she'd won the lottery or something, when really all she'd won was the booby prize. And as for when she went on about women still having to be careful—actually, that was probably the only accurate statement she made.

Not that I'm planning another kill.

Or am I?

That's for me to know and the rest of you to wait for.

This is such fun. It's like the icing on the cake. The cake being the life and death control I have over people of my choosing.

I'm curious about the guy they've arrested for my crimes. What evidence do they have? Because there isn't any. I'm one hundred per cent certain. I made sure of it. It was the whole point in the thoroughness of my planning. To make sure absolutely nothing could be tied back to me. I'd stake my life on it.

I wonder if he actually confessed to the murders. It can happen. Some deranged people feel the need to confess to crimes they haven't committed, just for the notoriety. But even Walker isn't stupid enough to take a confession at face value. She would have investigated it and come up with something to prove her case against this guy.

Idiot.

Of course, if the murders now stopped, I'd get away with them. It's certainly worth considering. At the moment, no way will they ever be able to pin anything on me. The police will think they've got their murderer, and he'll go away for years. Case closed. Leaving me free to do what I want with the rest of my life. Whatever that is. I haven't thought that far ahead.

Stopping now is the logical thing to do. The safest option. But since when have I ever done safe? And, more to the point, I don't want to stop. I haven't had so much fun since the day I set fire to the Wendy house in the garden, killing next door's cat.

No one ever suspected me. It was blamed on a boy who

lived close by. I ran rings around my family in the same way I'm now running rings around the police. The way I do to everyone. I don't let my 170 IQ go to waste.

One thing I've been contemplating is, if I do stop, then what am I going to do for an outlet? There's something extremely therapeutic about murdering someone. Therapeutic. Invigorating. Liberating.

And what will happen to me? I'd have to go back to being boring and normal.

Joke.

I've never been boring and normal. I'm way too exciting to be around for anyone to think that of me. I've spent my whole life fooling people into believing I'm the nicest and most fun person they'll ever meet. I always offer to help anyone in trouble. I lend money if they need it. I go out drinking and have a good time with them. I'm the perfect companion.

What they don't know is behind the normality lurks a monster. A monster who thrives on destruction.

That's right. Decision made.

For now, I'll continue. The next girl is lined up. Preparations already done, to ensure if I decide to proceed, I can. I don't need to remind you being methodical and well prepared is my modus operandi.

And because of that, it's going to happen soon.

Very soon.

Chapter Twenty-Nine

Whitney came in early to work, to prepare for another interview with Kevin Vaughan. She'd been disappointed he hadn't yet cracked, and she'd had a good go at him yesterday. She was waiting to hear back from forensics to see if anything connected Vaughan to the victims. His flat had come up clean, but that didn't mean he was innocent. He probably had somewhere else he used to restrain and rape them.

She knew it was only a matter of time until they'd got something incriminating.

'Morning, guv,' Matt said as he walked into the incident room. 'Are we interviewing Vaughan again today?'

'Yes, but this time I'll take Ellie. I want you to look deeper into Vaughan's background. His flat's clean, so he must have taken the victims somewhere else. Check out other places he might have access to. Find out more about his family. Where they live. What properties they own. Investigate everything.'

She'd find something to nail him, if it was the last thing

she did. She knew in her gut he was the one who'd done it. And her gut was seldom wrong. Well, apart from that lousy snitch of hers, who she still hadn't found. Though, to be fair, looking for him was now so far down on her list of priorities, it wasn't surprising he was still at large. Fortunately, the Chief Constable had let the matter rest while they'd been following through on the murders. Once it was over, he'd no doubt be back wanting answers.

'We've already done that. But we can look again. We might've missed something,' Matt said. 'We know it's him. It all fits. We'll nail him. At the moment I'm running down a lead from the hotline. Someone who claims to have seen Poppy walking through Riverdale Shopping Centre the afternoon before her murder. I'll check the CCTV.'

'Good. Maybe they saw Vaughan in there, too. He could've been stalking her.'

'That's what I'm hoping,' Matt said.

The phone on the front desk of the incident room rang, and Whitney reached over to answer it. 'Walker.'

'We've got another body. Under Tile Bridge. Looks like same MO.' Her hand gripped the edge of the desk, and she sank down onto the chair.

No. It can't be. They'd got their man.

'Thanks. I'll be right there.'

She replaced the phone on the handset. How the fuck had this happened?

'Guv?' Matt's puzzled expression stared back at her.

'There's another body.' The words stuck in the back of her throat.

'Shit. That mea—'

'Vaughan couldn't have done it. He was in custody. Unless it's a copycat. We'll know more once I've been to the scene.' She grabbed her bag from under the table.

'Where's the body?' Matt asked.

'Tile Bridge. It's by the stream, on university grounds.'

'Water again,' Matt said.

'Yeah. Speak to your lead about Poppy. I'll meet you back here later.'

She hurried out of the incident room. Another young woman murdered. She cursed herself for saying at the press conference they weren't looking for anyone else. How many women took that as they were now safe? She'd even told Tiffany she'd be fine to go out on her own. Okay, she'd said women should still be careful, but would they have listened? Or would they have assumed, like most young people, they were immortal and it didn't apply to them? Was this young woman's death on her?

Stop.

She forced the thoughts to the back of her mind. It was pointless jumping to conclusions before assessing the situation.

She turned on her siren and drove as fast as she could to the crime scene. By the time she arrived, Claire Dexter was already there. She recognised her old red MG soft top.

Running down to the cordon, she pulled on gloves as she went. She signed in and ducked under the tape, heading in the direction of the body.

'Hello, Whitney,' Claire said, looking up from taking photos of the body.

She moved closer to take a look at the woman, immediately recognising the victim. 'Shit. That's Lydia Parker.'

'You know her?'

'I met her when we interviewed the twins who had a party the victims all attended. Lydia's their flatmate. She was a really sweet girl. Had everything going for her and now—' She swallowed hard. 'I take it this murder's the same as the others?'

'From my findings so far, yes.'

'Could it be a copycat?'

'I'll know more when I get the body back to the lab.'

'Tiffany will be devastated.'

'Are they friends?'

'Tiffany started dating Henry Spencer, one of the twins, so she's bound to know her.' She dragged in a long breath. She had to get on with the case. She couldn't dwell on having to tell her daughter.

'Here's the phone, which was in her lap.'

'Thanks.' She took the phone and pressed the button. Her insides clenched as she viewed the photo of Lydia restrained on the bed. She placed the phone in an evidence bag and skirted around the body to look more closely at the scene. No drag marks. Nothing. She'd get forensics onto it, but she doubted they'd find anything.

'I've done all I can. I'll get back to the lab and will be in touch once I've got something to tell you,' Claire said.

'Thanks. I better get back to the station. I don't want to release Vaughan until we have confirmation it's not a copycat.'

She drove back to the office. How had they managed to get it so wrong? The evidence against Vaughan was compelling, though circumstantial, but had she been too quick to pin the murders on him? What was she going to tell Jamieson? She'd be the one blamed in the media because she'd done all the speaking. Had he done it on purpose, in case it all backfired? Usually he loved to be the centre of attention and having his name out there in the media. Yet this time he'd handed it to her.

She didn't have time to think that one through.

When she got back into the incident room the team was there.

'There's no easy way to say this. It looks like we've

fucked up big time. I've been to the crime scene. I recognise the body. She's Lydia Parker, and she lives with the Spencer twins. Ellie, find her family's address. They need to be informed. Matt—'

The phone on the incident desk rang, interrupting her. 'Walker,' she answered.

'It's Jamieson.'

'Yes, sir.'

'My office now.' He hung up before she could even reply.

Her heart sank. What she wouldn't give for a stiff whisky right now. He was going to give her both barrels. 'Jamieson wants me in his office. I want a run down on where everyone is when I get back.'

'Yes, guv,' Matt replied, the pitying look on his face reflecting her thoughts.

She got to Jamieson's office and found the door open, so she tapped on it and walked straight in.

'Sir.' He was sitting at his desk, staring into space.

'Close the door.'

After doing as he'd asked, she sat in front of him. The look on his face unsettled her. It wasn't angry, more determined, and his eyes were cold as they fixed her with a stare. She involuntarily squirmed in her seat.

'What do you have to say?'

'About the latest murder?' she asked, just to check he already knew. Which was stupid, because of course he did.

'No. About what you watched on the TV last night. Of course the murder,' he growled.

'It appears we might have arrested the wrong man. Unless this is a copycat, which I doubt, Kevin Vaughan didn't do it.'

'You don't say. How could you fuck this up so badly? I thought it was an open and shut case.'

'We thought it was. The evidence was circumstantial, but there was so much of it we believed it to be only a matter of time until Vaughan confessed.' She flicked non-existent fluff from her trousers, not making eye contact with him.

'Yet even though we had no confession, or concrete evidence, you took it upon yourself to focus everything on Vaughan and look no further. Do you think that was a wise move?'

'In hindsight, probably not. But you knew all this,' she added before being able to stop herself.

'I was being led by you. You're the officer in charge of the case, and you insisted you had your man. If I'd have imagined the evidence was so tenuous, I'd have made sure you continued investigating other leads.'

Did he really believe what he was saying? Or was he just trying to distance himself?

'We're back investigating the case and following up on anything that's come through the hotline. We do have a lead on someone who saw Poppy Brooks at one of the shopping centres. We'll catch the bastard, sir.'

'We'll have to call another press conference. That will make us look incompetent in the eyes of the public. The Chief Constable won't be happy.'

'I understand. Do you want me with you at the press conference?' she asked, hoping he'd say no so she could get on with the investigation. But she'd understand if she had to be there. She was the one who'd told the good news, so it was only right she was the one to admit their failure.

'Are you joking?'

She frowned. 'No. I just thought you'd want me there. I'm happy to leave it to you and get on with solving the case.'

'You don't get it, Walker. Not only are you not going to

be present at the press conference, you're not going to be involved in the case.'

She swallowed hard. Surely he didn't mean he was taking her off the case? Why would he do that? 'Not involved in the case?' she repeated.

'Well done. At least you managed to get that right. I warned you if you fucked up again then you'd be put on other duties. And that's exactly what's going to happen. We can't afford this case to drag on any more. We need someone in charge who's a lot more competent than you.'

She could hardly breathe. She'd worked hard to succeed in her career, and now it was over. How could she continue on the force if all she was doing was traffic rotas, or worse?

'Who, sir?'

'I'm calling in DCI Masters.'

Talk about rubbing salt into the wound. Masters was the biggest arse around. An arrogant son of a bitch who pissed everyone off. He didn't care whose toes he stood on as long as he got the results he wanted.

'Do you want me to work with him, to bring him up to speed?'

'I do not. He's on annual leave at the moment and comes back from overseas in forty-eight hours. You have that time to tie up any loose ends and write a report which can be handed over to him on his return.'

'But if we don't continue investigating, that's forty-eight hours we've lost.'

'I didn't say stop investigating. Your team can work the case, and you can advise where necessary. In the meantime, concentrate on getting everything in order for DCI Masters. You can go now.' He dismissed her with his hand and averted his eyes to some papers on his desk.

Her eyes filled with tears, but she blinked them away, grateful he didn't get to see them.

There was a killer on the loose, and they had no idea when he'd strike again, yet all she could do was sit back and watch.

Chapter Thirty

George hadn't slept for two nights after seeing Stephen in the pub with that woman. She'd decided to work from home, as she couldn't face going in, which was fine, as she didn't have any lectures or tutorials. How could Stephen cheat on her? They had a good thing going. Okay, she was more dedicated to her work than he was, and she didn't want to be around other people as much as he did. But he'd never complained in the past. Well, not much. And relationships were give and take, weren't they? She'd given up a lot when he moved in. Her privacy. Her need for quiet when working. She even put up with his untidiness. Yet it clearly wasn't enough, because he was seeing someone else. And who the hell was she? Certainly no one she recognised.

What should she do? Could she forgive him? Should she even mention it? Deep down, was she surprised? He was a good-looking guy, and women were always throwing themselves at him. So many questions, for which, at the moment, she had no answers.

She'd sat at her jigsaw all morning, hoping it would

help her think clearly about what to do. It usually had that effect when she was stuck over something. But for some reason, it wasn't working. Her mind was still as conflicted now as it had been earlier. She'd asked him to pop home for lunch, using the excuse she'd enjoy the company, as she was stuck there working.

The front door banged, and her heart flipped. This was it. She either faced him or pretended nothing had happened. Burying her head in the sand wasn't the way she usually operated, so she had her answer. But it wasn't easy. And was now the right time? Should she wait until the evening when they'd have more time? But could she stand another five or six hours of uncertainty? Too many questions.

'Hello.' Stephen walked into the dining room where she was staring at her puzzle and dropped a kiss on the top of her head. 'I thought you were meant to be working. Or are you just taking a break?'

'I couldn't settle to work.' She tried to make her voice sound normal, but it didn't.

He frowned as he looked at her. 'Are you okay?'

'Fine.' She bit down on her bottom lip, inwardly debating her problem.

'You don't look it. Are you unwell? You haven't seemed yourself recently.'

'And you noticed. Wow. Aren't I honoured?'

He pulled out a chair on the opposite side of the table and sat down. 'What's going on? I'd never have pegged you for making facetious comments for the sake of it. You know I hate that sort of thing.'

Decision made. He needn't think he could get the better of her by acting like she was the one doing something wrong.

'I went for a drink the other night with DCI Walker.'

'I didn't think you liked her. And now you're hanging out together. Why?'

'It doesn't matter why. It matters where we went.' She stared directly at him, searching for any tell-tale signs of his guilt. And there were plenty of little ticks. 'Don't you want to know where the pub was?'

'Tell me if you want.' He acted like he couldn't care, but she could see he did.

'I do want. It was the Black Swan in Hollowton. Do you know it? Of course, you do.'

His face paled. 'It's not what you think,' he said quietly.

'And what do I think, exactly?'

'You saw me there with a woman, and you think I'm cheating on you.'

'Ten out of ten,' she retorted.

'It doesn't mean anything.'

George gave a hollow laugh. Could he have come up with anything more clichéd?

'And that's supposed to make me feel better, is it? Because let me tell you, it doesn't. I'm having a quiet drink with a colleague, and suddenly I see my boyfriend. My live-in boyfriend, with his arm around another woman. And you were so wrapped up in each other you didn't even realise I was there.'

'I'm sorry.'

Was he? His relaxed shoulders and casual expression didn't support the words coming from his lips.

'Sorry for what? Your seeing another woman? Or I found out?' Her body tensed. She was in danger of losing control, and no way would she let that happen.

'Does it matter?' he asked, suddenly appearing less contrite.

'Yes, it does.'

'You haven't even asked why I started seeing someone else.'

'I don't need to. You always put it about in the past. Foolish me, I assumed once we got serious and started living together, it would stop. Clearly I was mistaken.'

Nausea coursed through her. He'd made a total fool out of her. She wondered how many of their colleagues knew.

'I'm not the only person in the wrong here,' he stated.

Was he now planning to put the blame on her? It beggared belief.

'What's that meant to mean? I haven't been seeing anyone else behind your back.'

'No. You were doing it in front of me. All the time.'

'What the fuck are you talking about?' she demanded. He was making no sense at all.

'I'm fed up of coming second to your work. It's all work, work, work with you.'

She flinched, her stomach in knots. 'I've never hidden how important my career is. It always has been. So why are you suddenly using it as an excuse for your infidelity? I don't believe it. There's something more.'

'Okay, there is more.' He paused. 'You're predictable and boring.'

Her shoulders slumped, as she held onto the table to steady herself. He certainly knew how to hit below the belt.

'Thanks. That's good to know. Anything else about me you don't like?' she asked, immediately regretting it, because she could tell from the expression on his face she'd given him carte blanche to say whatever he wanted.

'Yes. You're cold and unfeeling. It's like you've had an emotion bypass. Do you ever cry?'

He was wrong. She got emotional just like the next person, but she kept it to herself. She hated people seeing her cry. Tears were threatening to spill now, but she'd be damned if he was going to see. Luckily, she was wearing her glasses, and she blinked them away without him realising.

'So, because I don't cry, I'm cold and unfeeling?'

How could he be so cruel? She'd never dream of being so vindictive. Most people had annoying tendencies, but that didn't mean you had to destroy their confidence by pointing them out.

What an idiot she'd been to think they had some sort of future together.

'I'm sorry. I didn't mean to tell you these things.'

She glanced at him, the look on his face unreadable. Why the sudden backtrack? It didn't make sense.

'Don't be. These are your opinions. I'm sure you have others you'd love to share.'

She could've kicked herself for yet again giving him free rein for further insults.

'I don't want us to fall out. It's just sometimes everything is too predictable. Even down to your jigsaws.' He nodded in the direction of the one she was currently doing.

She loved her jigsaws. So what? Some people do crosswords. Some do Sudoku. They were her relaxation of choice.

'And they make me predictable, how exactly?'

'It's your behaviour when you're doing them. You won't let anyone touch a single piece because you have it *just so*.'

He was right. She had a thing about people not touching them. But was that really so bad? She could think of far worse ways to be.

'I take it this woman you're seeing isn't boring or predictable.'

Did she really want to know about the woman? It wouldn't serve any purpose.

'I'm not serious about her. But you're right, she isn't like you. She's passionate. Has a thirst for living. Is spontaneous.'

'All things I'm not.'

'You said it.' He shrugged.

'Could you insult me anymore?' She clenched her fists in her lap and looked away before she totally lost it and punched him in the face.

'You asked.'

He was right. She did ask, and she had her answer. But now she knew exactly what to do about the situation.

'I'm so sorry I've been so unbearable to live with. But that stops right now. Pack your belongings. I want you out of my house. Today.'

'Bu—' Shock washed over his face, like he honestly expected she wouldn't be giving him his marching orders.

He walked over to where she was sitting and placed his hand on her arm. Her skin crawled and she brushed him away, swallowing back the nausea from his touch. She stood up and faced him.

'No buts. Go upstairs and pack.' She stepped to the side, giving him a path to the dining-room door.

'I have nowhere to go,' he pleaded.

'I don't care. Ask your new girlfriend.'

'I can't. She's married.'

George stared at him, full of disgust. And now she knew why he'd tried to apologise earlier. He didn't want to be out on his ear.

'You really are a piece of work. Not only do you ruin our relationship, you're trying to ruin someone else's too. You make me sick.' She looked at her watch. 'I'll give you an hour to pack. Anything you leave I'll put in the garage for you to collect.'

'What will we tell people?'

'I couldn't care less what you say. It's not important enough for me to worry about. Now, if you'd please leave me alone, I have some boring and predictable work to get on with.'

Chapter Thirty-One

George stared into space, unable to concentrate. Stephen had taken a car full of things and left in a huff twenty minutes ago after throwing his keys on the table. His words haunted her. She thought she knew him. Really knew him. And yet he'd been so mean, it was quite obvious she didn't know him at all. Was she really all those things he'd said?

She liked her routine. What was wrong with that? Not everyone could be spontaneous. But he knew what she was like before he'd moved in. What had hurt most, was being called cold and emotionless.

The doorbell went. Should she ignore it? It was probably Stephen because he'd forgotten something. He could wait and come back for it another time. She had no desire to see him again. Ever.

The bell went again, accompanied by three loud knocks. Giving an exasperated sigh, she went to the front door and opened it, surprised to see Whitney standing there.

'Hello. I didn't expect to see you,' she said.

Whitney rushed past her into the house and promptly burst into tears.

She quickly closed the door. Should she hug her? No. It didn't feel right.

'Come into the kitchen. I'll make some coffee.'

Whitney nodded as she sniffed and pulled out a tissue from her pocket, which she used to wipe her eyes and nose.

She put on the kettle and took out two mugs from the cupboard. Whitney stood beside the table, moving from foot to foot and sniffing loudly.

'Sorry,' Whitney said between sniffs. 'I'd held it together until you answered the door, then it all came pouring out.'

'Don't worry, no need to apologise.' What on earth had happened to cause such a reaction? 'Tell me what's upset you.'

'There's been another murder. Lydia Parker, the twins' flatmate.'

What? But how? It made no sense. There couldn't be another dead girl. They'd got the murderer. Hadn't they?

'What about Kevin Vaughan?'

'It wasn't him. He was in custody. No way could he have broken out of his cell, committed the crime, and then got back in again.'

'It's my fault,' she said.

'Don't be stupid. Of course it's not,' Whitney replied.

'I was the one who told you Vaughan was hiding something. If I hadn't screwed up, Lydia might still be alive. She—'

'Stop. It's not you. I'm the lead detective on the case. I made the call to arrest Vaughan. It's down to me.'

'Competing with each other for the blame isn't going to help.'

She still couldn't grasp she'd got it all wrong. Her

assessment of Vaughan had been accurate. He was definitely hiding something.

'You're right,' Whitney said.

'Even if Vaughan isn't the murderer, there was something there. Maybe it was all the images you found on his computer. They would've been enough for him to be dismissed from his job.'

'Yes. It's probably that.'

They would need to check over all the evidence again. They now had four bodies. The more they had, the easier it would be to find something.

'We still have a lot to go on. My profile still stands. We'll catch him.'

'Not going to happen.' Whitney pulled out a chair from under the table and sat down.

'Okay. I understand if you no longer want my help. But I'm here if you change your mind.'

'That's not what I'm saying.'

'I don't understand.' She paused. 'By the way, how did you know I was at home?'

'I went to your office first. They said you were working from home today. That wasn't why I came. I wanted to let you know about the murder and also to tell you I've been kicked off the case.'

'What? That's crazy. Why? And by whom?' she asked.

'Jamieson decided I'm not competent, and he's ordered me off the case. He'd been on my back since the drug bust went wrong. Looking for a reason to dump me, and now he has it.' Whitney hung her head.

'Who's running the case now? Because whoever it is, they won't have your in-depth knowledge.'

'According to Jamieson it doesn't matter. He's given me forty-eight hours to get everything in order to hand over to one of his cronies. DCI Masters, who's on holiday at the moment.'

'Do you want me to help?' she offered.

'With what?'

'You have forty-eight hours to turn the investigation around and solve it. Then there'll be no need for this Masters guy.'

'There's no point. If we haven't been able to do it by now, how will another two days make any difference? Anyway, I've been ordered to do nothing other than *advise*, write a report, and pull what we have so far together.'

George stared at her. Whitney was on a real downer. She'd never seen her like that before. It was unsettling.

'You should listen to yourself.' She let out a sigh.

'What's that meant to mean?'

'Since I've known you, which I accept hasn't been for very long, you've never shied away from anything. You always face things head on. Doing what you want to do, on your terms. You've never been afraid to say what you think. And I should know, you haven't been exactly nice and friendly with me. Not counting the other night when we were out drinking.' She hoped she hadn't come across as too strong. She liked to be measured in her dealings with people.

Did that make her boring and predictable?

Shut up.

One thing she wouldn't do was give Stephen and his arsewipe comments headspace.

'This is different. I can't do anything about being pushed off the case,' Whitney said.

'Yes, you can. Your boss gave you two days. You don't have to tell him you're following up leads and still working it. Let him think you're doing as he ordered. He needn't know anything.' She heard her words but couldn't believe they'd come out of her mouth. Since when had she advocated breaking the rules? Answer: never.

Whitney stared at her, clearly mulling over her words. 'I suppose we could. But we can't operate out of the incident room because Jamieson would find out.'

'We can work from here, then,' she offered. 'I'll help you.'

'What about your job?' Whitney asked.

'Fuck my job.'

Did she just say that? What the hell was going on in her head? She'd broken more of her tacit rules in the last half an hour than she had in her entire life.

'Bloody hell. What's got into you? I thought your work was the holy grail.'

So did she.

But this was different. She couldn't sit back and watch.

'I'll take two days leave and tell my Head of Department something personal has come up. The next couple of days aren't too heavy, anyway. And it's not like I regularly take time off.'

'Okay. Thanks. But I can't ask the whole team to put their jobs on the line. We'll take a select few with us, those I know won't blab to Jamieson. Unless they don't want to be part of it, of course. What about your boyfriend? Won't he mind us being here, taking over your house?'

'Don't worry about him. We've broken up.' It sounded like she didn't care. And actually, it dawned on her she wasn't too bothered. She'd never been one to dwell on things, and this was clearly one of those times. It told her a lot. Mainly, she hadn't cared about him as much as she'd thought. So, he could take his belittling comments and shove them where the sun don't shine.

'I'm sorry.'

'Don't be. It's for the best.'

'When did it happen?' Whitney asked.

'Just before you arrived. But it's okay. I'm okay. And helping you on the case is just what I need to take my mind off it.' Just saying it lightened her mood.

'Then we're in business. We need to start straight away. Where shall we set up the operation?'

'See what you think of the dining room.' It was the largest room in the cottage, and there was plenty of space to use the mobile board she had.

As they walked through, she remembered at the end of the large oak table was the jigsaw. She hoped they could work around it, as she didn't want to put it away, seeing as she'd already done over half of it.

'This room's great.' Whitney wandered over to the table and stared at her jigsaw. 'I don't know how you have the patience. It's hard for me to sit still for longer than ten minutes.'

'It's therapeutic. Especially when I'm writing up my research. If I get stuck on finding the right words, I'll take a break and do some of the puzzle. It helps clear my mind.'

'Oh look. I've found a piece that fits,' Whitney said excitedly, as she placed it into the body of the puzzle.

George stared at her. Why wasn't she annoyed?

'Come on. We don't have time to waste. What shall we do first?' she asked.

'I'll contact Matt and ask him to meet us here in a couple of hours and to bring Frank and Ellie. In the meantime, we'll go to Lydia Parker's house to speak to her flatmates. The twins. Hopefully, they'll have information which will help us.'

Chapter Thirty-Two

There wasn't much traffic as they drove to Lydia's house. Next to her, George was staring out of the car window. She had said she wasn't bothered by her relationship ending, but Whitney wasn't so sure. George was hard to read because she always seemed so calm and in control. But surely, even if there had been problems, she'd have felt some emotion over the break-up.

'Are you okay?' she asked.

'Yes. Why?' George replied, frowning.

'Just asking. You seemed distant, and I wondered if you were thinking about what happened earlier with your boyfriend.'

'I'm fine,' George said quickly. 'I was just going through what we know about the killer to see if there's anything I've missed.'

She took that to mean she should mind her own business. She got it. Why would George want to confide in someone like her? She was hardly an expert on relationships. The last date she went on was months ago, and it hadn't exactly been a great success. As in, he didn't ask to see her again.

Anyway, George clearly wasn't going to let the break-up impact on the job they had to do, which was all Whitney could ask for.

'And have you thought of anything?'

'Nothing stands out yet. Once we're back at my house, we'll put everything up on the board and look together. Scrutinise each murder with fresh eyes.'

'Good idea.'

She'd told Matt in confidence about being removed from the case, and asked him not to tell Ellie and Frank, but just to say they were meeting at George's house. She trusted him not to betray her confidence. She'd helped him through his sergeant's exams and wanted him to consider applying for inspector next year. He was certainly ready for it. She instructed him on the tasks to give the rest of the team, so they wouldn't be suspicious of her absence.

She pulled up alongside the house and turned to George. 'Leave the talking to me.'

'I always do.' George gave one of her trademark condescending looks, but rather than wanting to sling a retort in her direction, she ignored it. Accepting it as being one of George's infuriating mannerisms. It didn't actually mean anything, and possibly George wasn't even aware she did it. Actually, she didn't even find it as infuriating as she used to.

After knocking on the door several times, Henry Spencer answered, his left arm in plaster.

'Hello, Henry. What have you done?' she nodded at his arm.

'Playing football during the week. I got tackled and fell awkwardly. It's fractured.'

'May we come in? We'd like to speak to you,' she asked.

'Sure. We're all in the sitting room.'

They followed Henry, and as they entered the room Whitney's heart sank. Seated on the sofa next to Harriet was Tiffany. How the hell was she going to cope once she found out what had happened?

'Mum, what are you doing here?' Tiffany jumped up.

'DCI Walker is your mum?' Henry asked, looking from Whitney to Tiffany, his brow furrowed.

'Yes.' Tiffany bit down on her bottom lip, looking at him from under her eyelashes.

Why had she kept secret her mum was in the police? They'd discuss it later; it wasn't important at the moment. She debated asking her daughter to leave the room, but it wouldn't achieve anything. She'd find out about Lydia soon enough. It was better they were told together.

'I've come to see Henry and Harriet. Please, sit down, all of you.'

She waited until everyone was seated before sitting herself. George remained standing by the door.

'What is it?' Harriet asked, her voice shaky.

'We have some bad news about Lydia. I'm sorry to have to tell you we found her body this morning.'

Tiffany and Harriet burst into tears, and Henry stood up and went over to the window. Whitney had to fight the urge not to scoop Tiffany up in a big hug, but it wasn't appropriate. It killed her to watch her daughter so upset. After a few minutes, when the crying began to subside, Henry turned to them.

'What happened?' he asked, his voice strained.

'We believe it's the work of the person who killed the other students.'

'But you said the Campus Killer had been caught. You

had him in custody,' Tiffany blurted out, her face tearstained.

'We'd got the wrong person,' she replied, shaking her head. 'I'd like to ask you all some questions. I'm sorry if it seems insensitive, but we need to get as much information as we can to help us catch him.'

'Of course,' Harriet said, grabbing a tissue from the box on the coffee table and wiping her eyes.

'When was the last time you saw Lydia?' she asked.

Henry walked back to the chair he'd just left and sat down. He traded glances with Harriet. 'Was Lydia here at the weekend?' he asked.

'I saw her on Saturday afternoon. She popped in to collect some clothes. She said she was staying with Sean, her boyfriend.'

'Do you have contact details for Sean?' Whitney took out her notepad and pen from her bag.

'No. Sorry. It will be on Lydia's phone, if you have that.' Harriet said.

'Do you have them, Henry?' she asked.

'No.'

'It's no use asking him,' Harriet said. 'He uses my phone most of the time. You'll find no one in his contacts apart from me. And Tiffany.'

She thought that was strange. She'd never met anyone of their age who wasn't on their phone all the time. Though he could still use his phone constantly, even if he didn't collect contacts.

'How did Lydia seem when you last saw her?' she asked.

'Same as usual,' Harriet said. Her eyes filled with tears. 'I can't believe she's gone. We've been friends ever since we started our course over four years ago. She was a year above us.'

Whitney stole a glance at Tiffany, who was sitting back in the sofa looking totally shell shocked. At least she was with Henry and Harriet, so they could comfort each other.

'How long had Lydia been seeing Sean?' she asked.

'Maybe two years,' Henry said. 'I'm not sure exactly. They were definitely seeing each other when we moved into this house, because he helped shift our furniture. This is our second year here.'

'What about boyfriends before Sean?' she asked.

'Sean was Lydia's first boyfriend at uni,' Harriet replied.

'Can you think of anyone who might have had a grudge against Lydia?'

'I thought her killer was the same as the other students. So why would he have a grudge against Lydia?' Henry asked.

'We investigate all angles. We're still waiting confirmation it was the same killer and not a copycat.'

'Oh. I see,' Henry replied.

'We'd like to take a look at Lydia's bedroom, please,' she said.

'It's upstairs, the second door on the left. Would you like me to take you?' Harriet said.

'No, you stay here. We'll find our own way.'

They left the twins and Tiffany in the sitting room and went upstairs to Lydia's bedroom. George pushed open the door and scanned the large square room, her eyes drawn to the exquisite ceiling rose and coving which ran along the walls.

Several pairs of jeans and some jumpers were strewn over the bed as if Lydia had only just popped out. Her wardrobe door was open, and Whitney slipped on some disposable gloves and started flicking through the clothes.

'Do you have another pair?' George asked as she stared at the bedside drawers.

Whitney pulled a pair from her bag and threw them over. 'Here.'

After catching the gloves, she pulled them on and opened the top drawer. Under a pile of receipts and other pieces of paper, she found a diary. It was nice to see a youngster still using a more old-fashioned method of writing a journal. She read some of the entries. Lydia mainly recorded class times, assignment deadlines, and other appointments. On some days she'd written a little more. One entry caught George's eye: *I caught him staring at me again. He creeps me out.*

'Look at this.'

'What?' Whitney headed over.

She showed her the entry.

'Hmm. Interesting. When did she write that?'

'October the fourteenth. Not long ago.' She flicked through, looking for similar entries. 'Here's another: *He makes my skin crawl. I want to tell Sean, but he won't believe me. It's his best friend, after all.*'

'We need to speak to Sean and his best friend,' Whitney said as she pulled out her phone and keyed in a number. 'Matt, it's me. Ask Ellie to look in Lydia's phone for her boyfriend Sean's number. You need to speak to him. Find out if he has an alibi. He might not know about Lydia, unless her family have been in touch, so you'll need to tell him. We also want to know the name and number of his best friend. Take Ellie and Frank, and then go straight to George's house.' Whitney ended the call.

'Don't you think it's a bit of a long shot?' she asked.

'Not at all. If he's a student at the uni, then he could

know all the girls. Even if it is, I can't begin to tell you how many long shots have ended up in me solving cases. Is there anything else of note in the room?'

George frowned. It was a typical student bedroom. Messy. Photos around the mirror. She peered in closer. Some were with Harriet and Henry. Some with a guy she assumed must be Sean. Others wearing silly hats. There was a photo in a frame on her dressing table of Lydia wearing riding gear, standing next to a horse.

'Nothing strikes me as out of the ordinary. Anything you can see?'

'No. I'm finding it hard to concentrate. I keep thinking about Tiffany. How's she going to cope? I'd told her everything was okay.'

'It was a shock to all of them, but she's in good hands with Henry and Harriet. I'm sure they'll take care of her,' she said, trying to placate her. Not being a mother herself, she'd no idea whether she'd been successful.

It was times like these when she was glad she didn't have children to worry about. She couldn't begin to imagine how the dead girls' parents coped.

'Yes. You're right. I'll see her tonight. Come on. We need to get back to your place and get cracking before the day gets away from us.'

Chapter Thirty-Three

The best of Whitney's team sat around George's dining table. Matt, Ellie, and Frank. Yes. Even Frank. They'd given her nothing but loyalty her whole career. Even when the drug debacle blew up in her face, they stood by her. Okay, they might have given her stick for it, but it was good natured, and nothing she didn't deserve or couldn't take. She was dreading breaking it to them Masters was taking over. She'd no idea how he was going to use their skills, if he was going to use them at all.

'Thanks for meeting here,' she said. 'I know you're wondering what's going on, and rightly so. There's no easy way to say this. The Super has taken me off the campus murders.'

'It makes no sense,' Matt said, shaking his head.

'Just what I was thinking,' Ellie added.

'Fucking idiot,' Frank said.

'He doesn't think I'm up to it. Not helped by the other case I fucked up.'

'You haven't fucked this one up,' Matt said. 'We're making progress.'

'Thanks, Matt. But we haven't got very far. We took our eye off the ball by arresting Vaughan and then letting it be known we're not looking for anyone else.'

'Who's taking over?' Frank asked.

'DCI Masters,' she replied.

'You're shitting me,' Frank said. 'That arse-licking wanker. My two-year-old granddaughter would do a better job.'

They all laughed at Frank's description, which was so apt.

'At the moment he's on holiday. Jamieson gave me forty-eight hours to get things in order for a handover. But as far as I'm concerned, we use the time to solve the case. That's why we're working out of Dr Cavendish's house, so we're not spotted working on it. Questions?'

As one by one, her team shook their heads, determination glittering their gazes, her eyes began to well up, and she hurriedly blinked the tears away. She couldn't let them see how emotional their reactions made her.

'We'll nail him, guv.' Matt said.

She flashed him a grin. 'Too right we will. Did you speak to Sean, Lydia's boyfriend?'

'Yes. He'd been away at a research conference, in Manchester, and had only just got back. I confirmed with the conference organisers he was there. I asked him about his best friend. His name's Hamish. He dropped out of university a few weeks ago and is currently somewhere in Bali.'

Her heart sank. Another lead bit the dust.

'Thanks. That rules him out. Have you gone through the phone contacts in Poppy's phone?'

'Yes. Kevin Vaughan's number is in there. But we know Poppy is part of Godwin, so that explains it.'

'His number would be given to new students during

Fresher's week,' George said. 'But even though he's excluded, it doesn't stop him from being sleazy. Those images on his PC should be sufficient for him to lose his job.'

She couldn't agree more. But at the moment that was the least of her worries.

'Unfortunately, we can't pass them on to the university,' she said.

She went over to the board. 'Let's think about the common themes between the four murders.'

'His cooling off period between each killing is getting shorter,' George said. 'That means the high he's on from each murder isn't lasting as long. It's a classic symptom of many serial killers.'

Whitney drew up a time line on the board. 'Okay. Millie Carter was first, on the third. Two weeks later, Olivia Griffin. One week after that, he murdered Poppy Brooks, and only four days later, we now have Lydia Parker. The time is decreasing drastically.'

'It could go in our favour. The less time between murders, means less time planning. And that's when mistakes are made,' George said.

'So he could be out there now with his next victim,' she said.

'It's a possibility,' George replied. 'More. A probability.'

'Then we don't have time to debate this. Let's get back to the common themes. Water being one of them,' she said.

'Yes, water features in every place the bodies are left. Millie Carter beside the river. Olivia Griffin next to the water feature. Poppy Brooks alongside the lake. Lydia Parker under the bridge going over the stream,' George said.

'What does that tell us?' she asked.

'The murderer's a fish,' Frank said, laughing.

The others joined in and she shot them a glare, then thought better of it and gave a small laugh.

'You might be closer to the truth than you think,' George said, looking thoughtful.

'I hope this isn't one of your crazy academic theories,' she quipped.

'No. Hear me out. What if the killer is like the anglerfish?'

'What the fuck's an anglerfish?' She shook her head.

'The anglerfish has a small luminous lure, which resembles a juicy worm. The other fish come over and then it pounces. What if our killer is a charismatic man, who lures his victims in, and when they let down their defences and are least expecting it, he strikes?'

'How do you know this stuff?' she asked.

'My father's a fisherman. I picked it up from him.'

'I've never been able to go fishing. Seeing those poor fish with the hooks in their mouths. Even when people throw them back in, it's still creeps me out,' she said.

'We're getting distracted,' George replied. 'I don't go fishing myself, but many in my family do. It's just how it is. Back to the water. As I've previously mentioned, water is definitely significant to our killer. My guess is it's related to something in his past.'

'Do you think the way he poses the bodies is also to do with the water?' she asked.

'Everything is connected; we just don't know exactly how at the moment,' George replied.

'We need something concrete. Time's running out.' She tried to hide her frustration.

'Don't get hung up on it,' George said. 'We'll get there. Let's get the other themes up on the board.'

'Stomach contents are interesting. He fed them all different things,' Matt said.

'True,' she replied as she wrote on the board. 'According to Dr Dexter, Millie had jelly and ice cream with sprinkles. Olivia had pizza. Poppy had sushi, and Lydia … we don't know yet. Why all different things? What does it mean?'

'What if the foods he fed them were their favourite? Or, alternatively, food they hated,' George said.

'How would he know?' Frank asked.

'The killer knows what he's doing. Everything is planned and controlled. He could have found out in his research. Especially if he already had a connection to the victims,' George replied.

'Ellie, get in touch with the victims' friends or family, and find out if the choice of food means anything,' she ordered.

'Yes, guv. I'll go into the kitchen, if that's okay.' Ellie looked at George, who nodded, and then took her laptop and left the room.

'Next theme,' she said.

'The phone in the lap, with photos of the victims. It's all part of his signature,' Matt replied.

She wrote up *phone*. 'They're all in Godwin College,' she added. 'So we have: water, food, rape, posed like they're begging, and a photo of them tied up on the bed.'

'It's all to do with control,' George said. 'The killer has the urge to be in control because he either lacks control in his life presently, or at some impressionable time in his past. Especially the rape. It could be he has sexual problems, and his libido can only be satisfied by having control over the person he's having sex with.'

'But how is that going to help us catch him?' she asked, unable to hide the exasperation in her voice.

'It helps us eliminate suspects,' George replied.

'Great, if we actually had any suspects. Because right now we have jack shit.'

'Don't forget the party they were all at,' Frank said.

'We don't know if Poppy went,' Matt said.

'Why not?' George asked.

'We didn't ask Poppy's friends because we'd already got Vaughan in custody.' She wrote *party* on the board.

'That's what we should focus on. We need to go back to Poppy's friends and find out.' George insisted.

'If they all went to Henry and Harriet's party, it means our killer might be a student. Is that likely?' Matt asked.

'Anything is likely. Though it could be the killer staked out the party, checking on who came and went,' George replied.

'Wouldn't someone have seen a strange man hanging outside the party?' Frank asked.

'There were so many people there, they might not have noticed,' she said.

'Depending on the age of the man, he could've blended in. The other students might have thought he was a mature student,' George said.

'What about Henry Spencer? It was his party. Lydia was his flatmate. He's central to everything,' Matt asked.

'I don't see how it could be him, as his arm's in plaster. He injured it in a football match last week.' She wrote his name on the board but immediately wanted to erase it. How could she think her daughter's boyfriend would be a suspect? She'd get the team to investigate him, anyway. Just to put her mind at ease.

'Guv, I've got something,' Ellie said as she walked back into the dining room.

'What?'

'Pizza was Olivia's favourite food, according to

Hannah. And Nathan Harris said jelly, ice cream, and sprinkles was Millie's. Dr Cavendish was right about their last meals being their favourite.'

'Good work. We need to confirm with Poppy and Lydia's friends or family.' She added the word *favourite* next to *food* on the board. 'Matt, you get onto that.'

'If you think he might strike again, should we hang around the campus and look for anything suspicious? Especially near water?' Frank asked.

'That would work, if we want to be too late to stop him from murdering his next victim. Frank, pop back to the incident room and note any information the rest of the team have. Meet us back here later. Ellie, I want a background check into Henry Spencer. See what you can dig up. George and I will go to see Poppy Brooks' friends.'

Chapter Thirty-Four

'I hate to say this, but I can't see us having a break on the case in time. I'll be letting everyone down,' Whitney said as she parked her car outside the block of student flats where Poppy Brooks lived. She couldn't remember the last time she'd felt so down about everything. It wasn't just her career going down the toilet. She had a responsibility to those who worked for her. Knowing Masters, he'd bring in his own team and relegate hers to the most menial duties he could find. Just to get one up on her.

'If you think like that, it will become a self-fulfilling prophecy,' George said as she looked at her. 'We still have time.'

'Is that one of your fancy academic things that has no bearing at all to real life? Because if so, I don't buy it.'

'Pull your head in, Whitney. You need to stop being so emotional, or you won't be able to do your work.'

Whitney scowled at her. Except she knew George was speaking the truth. Why couldn't she be rational and clear headed like George, never allowing her emotions to get in the way? She blew hot and cold, depending on what was happening. The thing was, part of her success in cracking cases in the past was because of her gut. Aka, her emotions.

'You're right. I need to be calm and rational. Come on, let's go. Her flat is on the sixth floor, number 611. She shared with three others.'

They got out of the car and went into the recently built student accommodation. Everything was modern and sleek. She was impressed. They took the lift up to the sixth floor and went to the flat. She knocked on the door.

'Leave the talking to me,' she said.

'I think you've told me enough times in the past for me to take it as read,' George replied, arching an eyebrow.

The door was opened by a young woman. 'Yes?'

'DCI Walker and Dr Cavendish. We'd like to talk to you about Poppy.'

The girl's face dropped at the mention of Poppy's name and her eyes welled up.

'Come in,' she said, sniffing. 'We were wondering if you'd want to talk to us. We haven't been to college since it happened. We couldn't face it.'

They walked into the flat and followed the student into the living room.

'I'm sorry for your loss,' she said. 'What's your name?'

'I'm Rachel. I'll fetch the others. They're in their bedrooms.'

She glanced around the room, her fingers itching to tidy up. There were dirty plates on the dining table in the corner of the room. Books were lying on the floor. Clothes strewn over the furniture.

'The state of this place,' she muttered.

'I've seen much worse.'

'I don't know how they could live like that. I'm not a tidy person, but this.' She waved her arm around. 'It's disgusting. I swear there's mould growing on those dishes. Were you the same as a student?'

She'd bet a month's wages on the answer.

'Not exactly.'

'You mean, not at all. Maybe I should be a forensic psychologist, because I've got you pegged. I think you were born with a list in your hand. You—' She paused as she noticed the expression on George's face. 'Sorry. I was only joking. I didn't mean anything by it.'

George shrugged. 'No offence taken. I like things planned and organised. But some people think my lack of spontaneity makes me boring and predictable.'

She didn't know what to say. She sort of agreed, but on the other hand George wasn't so boring she didn't enjoy being in her company. They hadn't exactly spent a lot of time together, but George was interesting and different from the usual people she hung out with.

She smothered a laugh. Tiffany was mixing with posh people, like the twins, and Whitney now knew George. They were certainly moving up in the world.

Her thoughts were distracted by voices coming down the stairs.

The three girls walked into the living room and stood in front of them.

'Please sit down,' she said gently.

The three of them sat on a dark green sofa, and she sat opposite on a matching easy chair. George walked over to the dining table and drew out one of the chairs, sitting away from the rest of them. Whitney assumed it was so she could watch the body language and make a better assessment of the situation.

'Please tell me your names,' she asked the two she hadn't met.

'I'm Becky,' the one with curly red hair said.

'And I'm Gemma.'

'I'm DCI Whitney Walker. I'm leading the investigation into the campus murders. I'd like to ask you a few questions about Poppy, if you're up to it.' She wanted to take it steady, as not one of them appeared strong.

She glanced over at George, who nodded.

'We've talked about it non-stop but can't think of anything,' Rachel said.

'That's okay. My questions might prompt something you hadn't thought of.'

'Okay,' Rachel said.

Clearly, she was going to speak on the others' behalf.

'There was a party a few weeks ago at the house belonging to Henry and Harriet Spencer. It was their birthday. Do you know if Poppy went?' she asked.

The girls looked at each other. Hmm. What was that about?

'Yes. We all went. Why?' Rachel asked.

She debated whether to mention all the other victims had been there. It wasn't something they'd publicised, but she was on such a short time frame she had no choice.

'We've discovered the other victims were there. Who else were you with at the party?'

'I was with my boyfriend,' Rachel said.

'Me, too,' Gemma added.

She looked at Becky. 'You?'

'No. Poppy and I spent most of the time together.'

'Did Poppy have a boyfriend?' She cringed internally, knowing that she'd totally fucked up by not even covering all of this earlier, at the time of the death. But rehashing her mistakes wasn't going to help them now.

'Not really,' Rachel said.

'Not really? What does that mean?' Whitney asked.

'She had the hots for Henry.'

'Henry Spencer?'

'Yes. But most of the time he wasn't interested.'

'Most of the time?' She frowned.

'One night she went out with him, but it didn't go well,' Rachel said.

'In what way?' she asked, her senses on full alert, and her heart pumping.

'They went back to his house, and they were—you know—kissing and stuff. Then he suddenly told her to leave. Said he didn't want to take things further,' Rachel said.

'Did he say why?'

'He said he couldn't do it because he had feelings for someone else,' Rachel said.

She shifted awkwardly in her seat. This was her daughter's boyfriend they were talking about. She flashed a glance at George, who was sitting on the edge of her chair, no doubt having similar thoughts to hers.

'What happened then?' she asked.

'Nothing. He was still nice to Poppy. Like he is to everyone.'

'Becky, did you notice anyone paying particular attention to Poppy? Did anyone proposition her? Anything you can think of that might help us,' Whitney asked.

Becky was quiet for a few seconds. 'Not really,' she finally said. 'Although she did say something about Henry and the way he couldn't keep his eyes off a girl who was there. I don't know her name. She's in the engineering department, I think.'

Did she mean Tiffany? She pulled out her phone, calling up a recent photo of her. 'Is this the girl?'

'Yes, that's her,' Becky said.

'Can you think of anything else?' she asked as she popped the phone back into her pocket.

'Actually, now you ask. I do remember Poppy commenting on a guy who was sitting on one of the sofas in the corner of the lounge. He was on his own. I didn't see him, though.'

'Can you remember her exact words? Did she say anything at all about him? His name. What he looked like. Anything?' This could be the lead they were searching for.

'She said to me there was this guy, who was sitting holding a can of beer, and he kept looking at her. She said he was kind of cute but seemed out of it. Like he was drunk or high. That's all. I got the impression she didn't know him. She'd have mentioned his name if she did. Do you think he's the killer?' Becky's hand flew up to her chest.

'We don't know. But we'll investigate further. Thank you. I appreciate your cooperation.' She pulled out a card from her pocket. 'Give me a call if you remember anything. However inconsequential you think it might be.'

'Okay,' Becky said as she took it from her.

'Before we go. What was Poppy's favourite food?'

'Sushi,' Rachel replied. 'Why?'

'We just need it for our records. We'll see ourselves out. Thanks for your help.'

They had very little time left, so it was important for them to speak to Henry and Harriet straight away to see if they could remember the guy Becky mentioned. As they left the flat and walked to the lift, she turned to George.

'We need to find this young man. Let's go back to the twins' house.'

Chapter Thirty-Five

George leaned back in the car seat while Whitney put her foot to the floor and flicked the switch on the siren. She'd never been in a police car with the siren blaring, and despite the situation, adrenaline spiked at her pulse points.

'Enjoying yourself?' Whitney grinned at her.

'Why do you ask?'

'The look on your face. Everyone has it the first time they're speeding in a police car.'

'It is sort of exciting,' she said, feeling stupid for having such a juvenile reaction.

'I still love it, after all these years. Even though most of the time I'm heading into an unknown situation which could be potentially dangerous,' Whitney admitted in a confiding voice.

It was the friendliest Whitney had been the whole time since they'd met. Had working together to such a tight deadline brought them closer? What she liked most about Whitney was she had none of the academic pretensions that existed at the university. Most of the time it didn't bother her, but occasionally she wished her colleagues stop trying to outdo each other. Especially when it came to research. A research conference, where academics tried their utmost to discredit other presenters, had to be seen to be believed.

'How long have you been a DCI?'

'Less than a year. It still hasn't sunk in, especially as it wasn't an easy journey.'

That piqued George's interest even more. 'In what way?'

'I made it to sergeant without any problems, then the wheels started to come off.'

'What do you mean?'

'In case you haven't noticed, I do have a tendency to do things my way and worry about the consequences later.'

'Yes, I've seen the way you work.' George laughed.

'Well, the trouble with the police is they expect you to do everything by the book. I agree. But sometimes the book, or should I say *the way some of my superiors view things*, isn't always the best way to proceed. Especially the likes of Jamieson, who has zero idea about the real nature of the work.'

'But I thought he was new?'

'He is. I was just using him as an example. When I was thinking about applying for DI, I was involved in a case which took me in direct opposition to my DCI, and he blocked my promotion.'

'But you proved him wrong by solving the case?' George asked.

'It didn't matter to him.'

'That must have hurt.'

'It wasn't just that. He didn't like I was a single parent with a young daughter. Though he didn't actually say so, I know it went against me.'

'What about Tiffany's father?' she asked.

'Tiffany's dad was a little shit who I hooked up with one night after too many vodkas. I didn't even tell him I was pregnant. His name isn't on the birth certificate.'

'That can't have been easy.'

'It wasn't. I dropped out of my A-levels to have her and applied for the police when I was eighteen. I couldn't have done it without the help of Mum and Dad.'

'How does Tiffany feel about everything?'

'She's never been interested in finding out about him. I told her it was a one-night stand, and she accepted it. Do you think I was wrong?' Whitney glanced at her, as if expecting to be judged.

'Not at all. It was your decision. Nothing to do with me, or anyone, other than you and Tiffany.'

'Agreed. I don't even know if he still lives in the area.'

'But you could find out.'

'We're not allowed to use the system for our own gains,' Whitney said.

'Like that would stop you,' she said, laughing.

'You know me well.'

'Getting to. Have you ever been married?'

'No. I've never been interested. My job takes up most of my time. Plus, looking after Tiffany and spending more time with Mum and Rob. It's hard for Mum now she's getting older.' Whitney's voice tailed off.

'Is there something wrong?' she asked.

'Not wrong exactly. Mum's memory seems to be going. She's started to repeat things and occasionally gets confused. I'm sure she's fine; she's probably just tired. It's tough having to look after Rob at her age. I help where I can. She's not well off financially, so I give her money each week.'

'Maybe you should ask her to go to the doctor and

mention what's been happening,' she suggested. It could be early signs of dementia.

'I doubt she'll listen to me. But once the case is over, I'll see. Do you think it could be serious?'

'I don't know. But any change in behaviour should be investigated, to put your mind at ease.'

'Okay. Will do. Now it's your turn.' Whitney flashed a smile in her direction.

'For what?'

'You know all about me, and now I want to hear about you. You said you'd broken up with your boyfriend. Why? Were you together for long?'

She bristled. Talking about herself was something she went to great lengths to avoid. Especially to someone she didn't know very well. It looked like she wasn't in charge of her own life. Then again, Whitney had just confided a lot, so perhaps she owed her.

'We'd been together for about fifteen months. Six of which he lived with me.' She made it sound all matter of fact.

'Did you find it hard?'

'Why?' Was Whitney pointing out how difficult she could be? Stuck in her ways and resistant to change.

'I'm curious. I haven't lived with anyone before, but I'm sure it would drive me crazy.'

Okay. So, she'd totally misinterpreted the question.

'Well, yes it was hard. I have my routines and he had his. But they often didn't coincide.'

'Is that why you finished it?'

'No. He was seeing someone else.' The words struggled to come out, but once they had, it was like a weight was lifted.

'What a bastard. How did you find out?'

'Remember the other night at the Black Swan?'

'Yes.'

'I saw him leave with her. They'd been in the dining room having a meal. He didn't even notice me. I confronted him about it earlier today.'

'What did he say?'

'He tried to put the blame on me. Told me I was boring and predictable, and he wanted someone more passionate.' The words stuck in her throat.

It seemed like a dream. A bad dream. But one she was glad she'd had. It had only been a short time, but she didn't miss him. *Stephen who?* And it wasn't like she'd be bumping into him all the time at work. Not if the previous few months were anything to go by. Sometime soon, everyone in the department would find out, and then she'd sit back and watch the students and staff start making a play for him.

'Take no notice of him. He just said it to make himself feel better. He's not worth the shit on your shoes. You're much better off without him.' Whitney banged the steering wheel for emphasis.

She laughed. Whitney had him nailed, and she wasn't even the one who'd studied psychology.

'You're right. I'm better off without him, the prick.'

'You know what? He didn't deserve you. So what if you like routine and predictability? I'd kill to be like that sometimes. All I manage to do is lurch from one situation to another. I go off on one when I should keep quiet and think things through. It's like there's something missing between my brain and my mouth. It's got me in trouble on so many occasions. Whereas you. You always seem so in control. Calm and controlled. I envy you.'

'I like being in control,' she admitted. 'Most of the time. Sometimes, though, I wonder what it would be like to take each day as it comes. To do things on the spur of the moment, instead of planning to the nth degree. But I can't change who I am.' She shrugged, trying to make light of it.

'Seriously? I'd have thought being a psychologist you would assume people could change who they are. Don't you work with people to help them get over their problems?'

Whitney's insight surprised her. She'd definitely misjudged her. Assuming because of the way she talked, and the job she did, she couldn't put forward a rational argument. How could she have been so narrow-minded and judgemental?

'You're right. Sorry. I'm not thinking straight.'

'That's got to be a first. You've been hanging around with me for too long.' Whitney chuckled. 'Don't say I didn't warn you. Before long you'll be getting all hot headed and emotional.'

'At least you recognise your traits and how they manifest. I hadn't realised how boring and predictable mine make me.'

'You're not boring or predictable.' Whitney paused. 'Well, most of the time you're not.' She grinned. 'Don't let the arsewipe get under your skin.'

She stared out of the window. This was all too much for her brain to process. She watched the trees flash by as they turned into the street where the twins lived. 'I won't. I assume nothing's changed and we're operating as before, when we get to the twins' house. You talk. I'll listen and watch.'

'You really needed to ask?' Whitney replied.

Chapter Thirty-Six

George stepped out of the car and shivered, wrapping her arms tightly around her. It had been dark for a while now and the icy wind whistled past. She cursed herself for not bringing any gloves. While Whitney was finishing the call she was on, she stared at the house the twins lived in. A typical end terrace in Lloyd Road, dating back to the nine-teen thirties. Solid brick with a single bay window over-looking the street.

'Let's go.' Whitney's voice distracted her from her thoughts.

They walked down the short concrete path, and Whitney knocked on the door. After waiting a while, she knocked again. Finally, Harriet answered, her eyes red and swollen.

'Hello, Harriet. Do you mind if we come in? We'd like to talk to you again,' Whitney asked.

'I'm the only one here. Hal has taken Tiffany home. She was very upset. We all are.' She sniffed, standing back from the door to let them walk through, and closing the door behind them.

They walked into the sitting room and sat down.

'When did Henry and Tiffany leave?' Whitney asked.

George glanced at Whitney. It was obvious from her anxious tone she was worried.

'Not long ago.' Harriet looked at her watch. 'Maybe ten minutes. Hal said he'd come straight back, once Tiffany was okay.'

'Thanks. I'll call her after we leave. It's a lot for all of you to absorb.'

'Do you want to wait for Henry to come back?'

'No. We can talk to you.'

'Okay.' Harriet leaned forward in her chair, looking directly at Whitney.

It was a good chance to see the twins separately. When together, they were so close, it was like they knew exactly what the other one was thinking. But, without Henry, Harriet lost some of her charisma. Though that could have been down to her being so upset about Lydia.

'I'd like to ask about your party,' Whitney said.

'Didn't we discuss it before?'

'Yes. But we've now discovered every girl who was murdered did attend.'

Harriet's hand shot up to her mouth. 'That's awful. Was the murderer here, too?'

'Not necessarily. But we do have to consider it.'

'But we don't know everyone who was there, so how can we possibly work out who he is?'

'Do you remember a guy sitting on his own, in here on the sofa?' Whitney asked. 'Maybe drunk or high.'

Harriet frowned. 'Not really. No.'

'Think hard,' Whitney pushed.

'I'm trying.' Harriet was silent for a few seconds. 'I need the loo. I'll be back in a minute.'

As Harriet left the room, Whitney turned to her. 'What do you think? Are we wasting our time here?'

'Too early to say. Give her time. Remember, she's in shock.' She wandered over to the shelf over the fireplace and looked at the ornaments, which she recognised as being from the Middle East and South America.

'We got those on our travels overseas.' She started at the sound of Harriet's voice from behind her.

'You've travelled a lot?' George asked.

'You could say. Not many continents we haven't been to.' Harriet went over to the sofa and sat down. She appeared calmer now. 'I've been thinking about this guy. Do you know what he looks like?'

'Cute. That's the only description I have,' Whitney replied.

'Let me think. The sofa was moved over there into the corner.' Harriet pointed over by the window. 'Whenever I was in here, there were usually people sitting on it. Or on cushions on the floor. Or just standing around. But I can't remember a cute guy sitting there alone. Unless—unless—' Harriet paused.

'What?'

She became on full alert, praying Harriet would come up with something they could use.

'I can't be sure, and I'll have to ask Hal. When it got to midnight, they sang happy birthday to us. We were in here, and everyone was on their feet except one guy who sat on the sofa. I've only just remembered. I'd had quite a lot to drink.'

'Do you have a name?'

'No. Sorry.'

'Can you describe him to me?' Whitney took out her notebook and pen from her pocket.

'Not really. It wasn't very light as we only had a couple

of small lamps. Hang on. I do remember. Someone turned on the main lights and got shouted at, so they turned them off almost immediately. Yes. He was sitting in the middle of the sofa, holding a drink. A bottle of something, but I don't know what. He had longish dark hair. Well, just to his shoulders, and it was falling in front of his face.'

'What was he wearing?'

'Jeans and shirt. I can't remember the colour.'

'And you've no idea of his name?'

'I've already told you, I don't know the names of half the people who came.'

'Do you remember him arriving at the party?'

'Around ten-thirty, loads of people turned up together. He could've been one of them. Before then, I remember seeing most people arrive, as Hal and I hovered close to the door to say hello.'

'Did you see this guy talking to anyone?'

She sensed the frustration in Whitney's voice. The only lead they had, and Harriet couldn't help her nail him down.

'No. Bu—' Harriet stopped at the sound of the front door banging. 'It must be Hal. We're in here,' she called out.

The lounge door opened, and Henry walked in. She noted how drawn he looked. His eyes weren't red like Harriet's, but he still looked distraught. She could only imagine what they were going through.

'Hello.' Henry glanced at each of them and sat on the sofa next to Harriet. He took hold of her hand.

'How's Tiffany?' Whitney asked.

'She's still in shock over Lydia. I made her a cup of tea and offered to stay, but she said she'd be fine and you'd be home soon.'

'Thank you for looking after her. I'll see if she wants to

stay with her granny tonight, in case I have to work late.'

'A good idea. It's not advisable to be on your own at a time like this,' he replied.

'They think the killer was at our party, Hal,' Harriet said.

Henry's eyes widened. 'What? Impossible. We'd have noticed anyone who wasn't a student.'

'We don't know the killer isn't a student,' Whitney said. 'We were talking to Harriet about a guy who sat on his own on the sofa. Do you remember him at all?'

'I noticed him when the lights were switched on briefly, just before they sang happy birthday to us,' Harriet said.

'I'm not sure. There were so many people there. What did he look like?' Henry asked.

'That's what we want to find out from you,' Whitney replied.

'All I could remember was his hair an—'

'Please don't prompt Henry. We need him to try to remember himself,' Whitney interrupted.

An annoyed expression fleetingly crossed Harriet's face, but it disappeared so quickly George doubted anyone else would have noticed it. She clearly didn't like being told off.

'Sorry,' Harriet said.

'Henry?' Whitney asked.

'Thinking about it, I don't remember the lights being turned on, but obviously they did or Harriet wouldn't have mentioned it. But I do vaguely recall seeing a guy on his own on the sofa. Holding a can of beer,' Henry said.

'Was it a can? I thought it was a bottle,' Harriet said.

'If we saw him at different times, then it could have been both. He could have started with one and then gone into the kitchen for another.' Henry gave Harriet a tiny nudge with his elbow. There was something going on between them. He definitely took the lead in their relationship and was prompting her to agree with him.

'Then someone would've seen him in the kitchen. I don't remember him being there,' Harriet said, shaking her head.

'Did you spend a lot of time in the kitchen?' Whitney asked.

'Yes. So did Hal. We were hanging out with our friends.'

'And you definitely don't remember this guy in the kitchen?'

'Not early on. No. I'm sure of it,' Harriet said.

The questioning was leading nowhere fast. Whatever the pair of them remembered, it wasn't much. And certainly nothing that was going to assist. It was almost like they were pretending to want to help. But she had nothing to base her opinion on. Other than her gut. Not exactly scientific.

'I agree. He wasn't in the kitchen when we were, which was early on, before the party really got going,' Henry said.

'Could you go through the photos of the party again and see if he's in any of them?' Whitney suggested.

'Yes. We'll do it straight away,' Henry said.

Whitney stood, and she followed. 'Thank you. And if you do see him in a photo or remember anything else, please let me know. Can you think of anyone else we can question, who might know this guy?' Whitney asked.

'Lydia might have known him,' Henry said.

'Yes.' Harriet nodded, and started to cry again. Henry leaned in and put his arm across her shoulders.

'We'll go now. Remember, anything you think might help us, please phone. Any time, day or night. It doesn't matter.'

Whitney and George left and didn't speak until they got to the car.

'Not very helpful,' she said as she plugged in her seat belt. 'Now what?'

'Back to the beginning. Did you get the feeling they were holding out on us?'

'Definitely.'

'We're missing something. Surely they wouldn't be covering for this anonymous guy? Not if we believe he could be connected to the murder.' Whitney turned on the engine and pulled out into the road. This time minus the siren.

'I didn't get that exactly. But I agree, something was slightly off. Judging by the body language, it could be something totally unconnected to the investigation.'

'Like what?'

'Harriet might be jealous. Henry left her alone to be with Tiffany. When you factor in they do everything together, an outsider coming in might make a difference.'

'Tiffany hasn't mentioned there being any tension between her and Harriet.'

'If Harriet was clever, then she wouldn't overtly show her feelings in case she pushed Henry away. Then again, we might be making something out of nothing. We have to remember they're only young and have been surrounded by all these murders. It's hard for anyone to deal with, let alone kids in their twenties.'

'True. Do you want to call it a night? I'll drop you back at your house. We can start again first thing.'

'Are you sure you don't want to go over everything one more time?' She was conscious of time slipping away from them and was prepared to work through the night if that was what Whitney wanted.

'No. We'll be better with fresh heads. I want to see Tiffany and make sure she's okay.'

'Of course,' she said quickly. She'd forgotten about her.

Going home would give her a chance to grab something to eat, as they'd missed lunch, and then sort out the rest of Stephen's belongings and put them in the garage. If he didn't collect them within the week, she'd drop them off at the local charity shop.

Chapter Thirty-Seven

After dropping George off at her house, Whitney drove home, pushing aside the frustration at their lack of progress. They had twenty-four hours to solve the crime. Yes, it was a big ask, but she'd work her arse off to do it. Giving up wasn't on the agenda. The killer might be clever. But so were they. Her team was the best. They'd find out who the guy at the party was, and if that didn't work out, they'd find something else.

As for Jamieson. Whatever he had in store for her, she'd deal with. And make a comeback. Okay, she'd be an outcast for a while, but eventually she'd return.

Would she see George again after tomorrow? Probably not, as she'd go back to her academic tower, with her long words and cleverness. She hadn't liked to say anything earlier, seeing as George seemed upset, but what an idiot her ex was. George wasn't boring. Intimidating maybe, but that was just her way. She was glad they'd got to know each other better. She liked her. Admired her.

Turning into her street, her thoughts went back to Tiffany. How was she going to cope with the deaths? She'd need her support. After parking the car on the road outside of her house, she ran down the path leading to the front door and hurried in.

'Tiff. I'm back. Where are you?' She dropped her bag beside the hall table and headed towards the kitchen. 'Tiff,' she called again when there was no answer.

She rushed into the kitchen, but it was empty. She went into the living room, but that was empty, too. Where the hell was she? Surely she wouldn't have gone out without telling her. Henry said he left her here.

She charged up the stairs, two at a time, her heart thumping in her chest. She headed towards Tiffany's bedroom. The door was shut, so she turned the handle and pushed it open.

Tiffany was sitting on the bed, wearing headphones. Why had she suddenly got all stupid about it? Henry had brought Tiffany home and settled her down. She knew that.

'Hello, Mum.' Tiffany glanced up from the book she was reading.

She rushed over and sat next to her on the bed. 'I couldn't find you. I was worried. Are you okay?' Tiffany's eyes were still red and sore.

'I thought reading would take my mind off of everything. But it hasn't. I can't believe this is happening.'

Tiffany closed the book and placed it beside her on the bed as tears started to run down her cheeks. Whitney pulled her close into a hug, stroking the top of her head.

'I know, love. We're doing what we can to catch him. We'll get him. I promise we will.'

'You think he was at the party.' Tiffany pulled out of the hug and sat up.

'How do you know?'

'Harriet texted Henry while he was here with me. It

was while you were there. That's why he left. He said you'd want to speak to him, too. Did you?'

She frowned. Why hadn't the twins said anything? Unless they didn't think it was important. Except Henry acted all surprised when he was told. 'I did get to see Henry, yes. Unfortunately, they couldn't be much help as they didn't know the guy I'd been asking about.'

'I was at the party. Can I help?'

'Maybe. He was sitting on the sofa on his own, holding either a can or a bottle and looked out of it. Either drunk or high. He had longish dark hair which fell forward over his face. Ring any bells?'

Her daughter thought for a moment and nodded. 'I know who you mean. It's Felix Browne. I remember trying to speak to him, but he was so drunk I could hardly understand what he was saying. He was upset because his girlfriend, Jess, dumped him about six weeks ago, after three years of being together.'

Her chest tightened. The murders started after the break-up. Was he trying to get his own back? 'Tell me about him.' She grabbed her phone from her pocket and keyed in Matt's number.

'He can't be the killer. He just can't be.' Tiffany held her hands up to her chest. 'He's on my course. He's been here to the house. We've worked together on an assignment. You've met him.'

The killer had been in her house?

'Hang on,' Whitney said to Tiffany as Matt answered. 'Matt, get over here. We've got a lead.' She ended the call and turned back. 'Tell me everything you know about this Felix.'

'You think he's the killer just because he was at the party on his own and drunk?'

She realised the link was tenuous, but it was her only

lead, and she had to follow it through. 'I'm not saying he's the one, but we need to question him, if only to eliminate him from our enquires.'

'He's a nice guy. He's in most of my classes and we often hang out together.'

'And what about his ex-girlfriend? Jess. What happened?'

'She's also on our course. They were seeing each other before uni. They both come from Birmingham and knew each other from school.'

'Where does she live? We'll need to speak to her, too. What's his behaviour like now, since the break-up?'

'He seems like he's always been. They're still friends and live together.'

'They live together?' she repeated, frowning.

'They have a student flat. The only difference is now they have separate bedrooms.'

'And is Felix okay with that?'

'I think he hopes they'll get back together. I also think he'd rather be friends than have no contact at all with her.'

'What about Jess?'

'She's cool with it. And it's not like either of them are seeing other people. I believe they'll get back together. I think the pressure of the course got to her, and Felix can be quite intense. But not in a horrible way. It's just how he is.'

Whitney's initial excitement dwindled. He could be their guy and had to be checked out, but they needed to be careful. She didn't want to arrest him without concrete evidence because then what she was doing would become public knowledge, and the Super would find out she'd gone against his orders.

'Do you have their address?'

'Yes.' Tiffany went into her phone and read it out to her.

'I don't know how long I'm going to be. Shall I drop you at Granny's, and you can stay there tonight?'

'No. I'll stay home. I've got work to do, and it's easier to do it here.'

'Okay. Until we've caught the murderer, I'll be taking you to uni and picking you up to bring you home when you've finished for the day.'

'You don't have to. I'll be okay. I can ask Henry.'

'I want to. What time is your class tomorrow?'

'It's early. Eight-thirty.'

'Okay. I'll take you.' The doorbell interrupted her. 'That's Matt. I'll see you later.' She leaned in and kissed Tiffany on the top of the head.

Running down the stairs, Whitney grabbed her coat from the banister. She opened the door. 'Matt. We'll go in your car.'

'Guv.'

While they were driving, she told Matt what Tiffany had said about Felix Browne. 'He fits the profile. Sort of.' She'd wondered about calling George but decided against it. She couldn't call her every time there was the slightest lead, and she didn't want Matt to feel excluded.

The journey to the block of flats took around twenty minutes. Felix lived in one of the older blocks of student accommodation, which were situated close to the university grounds. They took the stairs to the first-floor flat and knocked on the door.

There was no answer. She knocked again, only louder. Still no answer, but the door to the next door flat opened.

'I'm looking for Felix Browne,' she said to the young man standing there.

'He's in here,' the guy said. 'Felix. It's for you.'

A skinny guy came to the door, not very tall. How would he be able to lift the victims and take them to their resting places? Especially Millie Carter, who would have been at least eight inches taller than him and easily a couple of stones heavier.

'Felix Browne?' she asked, holding out her warrant card. 'I'm DCI Walker and this is DS Price. We'd like to ask you a few questions.'

'Sure. What do you want to know?' he asked, looking puzzled.

'We'd rather talk in your flat,' Matt said.

'Okay.' Browne pulled out a key from his pocket and opened the door.

They followed him in and stood in the entrance hall.

'You were at the party of Henry and Harriet Spencer on the twenty-sixth of October.'

'Yes.'

'We have eye-witness accounts saying you sat on your own drinking. Not talking with anyone.'

'I got wasted. I don't remember much. Why?'

'We're investigating the campus murders. All the young women who have been murdered went to the party. What were you doing on the third of November, the eighteenth, the twenty-fourth, and last Thursday?'

'Why? Do you think I have something to do with the murders?' The shock in Felix's voice was evident.

'We'd like to eliminate you from our enquiries. Those dates?' Matt asked.

'I'm not sure.' He paused for a moment. 'On the third, I was here at the flat.'

'Can anyone vouch for you?' Whitney asked.

'Jess, I think. Oh no. She was out that evening. On the eighteenth I was at home for the weekend. My dad was rushed into hospital, and I went to see him. My parents can vouch for me.'

'What about the twenty-fourth and last Thursday?' she

asked, already mentally crossing him off the list of suspects. List being an exaggeration, as there was no list.

'I was here. Jess was with me.'

'Thank you for your time,' she said. 'We might need to speak to you again.'

They left the flat and she turned to Matt. 'Another lead gone.' She shook her head. 'We've got one more day to find him. We just have to hope there isn't another murder.'

Chapter Thirty-Eight

George rose early and had showered and breakfasted by seven. She'd no idea what time the rest of the team would be arriving, but it had to be early to give them the best chance of cracking the case. At seven thirty, she switched on the kettle, got out the mugs for coffee, and put out some croissants. Just as the kettle had boiled, the doorbell went and when she answered, everyone was standing there.

'Come in,' she ushered, not sure how they'd managed to coordinate their arrivals.

They sat around the table, and everyone except her grabbed a croissant from the plate.

'We found our mystery man last night,' Whitney said.

'I didn't think you were going to do any more work.' She frowned. Why was she only just being told? She could've helped.

'Tiffany knew who he was, so Matt and I went to interview him.'

'And?'

'He's not our man.'

'Are you sure?'

'He has an iron-clad alibi for one of the dates. He was home with his parents because his father was in hospital. I checked it out.'

'So, this means we're back where we started.' She tried to fight back the dejection, but it wasn't easy.

'No, it doesn't. With every person who's excluded, we're one step closer to finding our man.'

She stared at Whitney, encouraged by her determination. 'True. Let's look at the patterns of behaviour again. See if there's something we've missed.'

She stood up, but before she reached the board, Whitney's phone went.

'Walker.' She paused while listening. 'Right. We'll be over straight away.' She ended the call. 'Dr Dexter. She's found something interesting and wants to show us. George, we'll go.' She looked at her watch. 'Damn. Matt, would you mind going to my house to pick up Tiff and take her to uni? Her class starts at eight-thirty.'

'No problem, guv.'

'Thanks. Ellie and Frank, go to the station and start compiling what we've got so we can hand it over. It will look suspicious if none of us are there. We'll meet you in the incident room later. I still have my report to write up. We'll take my car,' she said to George. 'I'll drop you back here later.'

They picked up their files and belongings and headed out of the door. George locked up behind them and followed Whitney to her car, which was parked on the opposite side of the road.

'No siren, then?' she asked as they took off down the road.

'Not today. I like to pick my moments. You never know who's taking note.'

'You know, even if we don't find the murderer, it's not

from lack of trying. We've done what we can. Maybe this other DCI will be able to come up with something. Do you think he'll want my help?'

'Seriously, you're going to work for him?' Whitney's hands gripped the steering wheel so tightly her knuckles were white.

'I want to find the murderer.'

Whitney's eyes stayed focused firmly on the street ahead. 'And you think I don't?'

'I didn't say that. All I meant was I'm prepared to offer my help to anyone who needs it. Surely you don't begrudge that?' She was conscious of all the good feelings between them slipping away.

'Forget what I said. If Masters wants you to help, then do it. Anything to stop these murders.' Whitney's voice cracked, and she wanted to comfort her but didn't know what to do. If she gave a reassuring touch, she was sure Whitney would pull away. So she sat there in silence for the rest of the journey. And Whitney didn't offer any conversation either.

As they arrived at the morgue and were about to go in, Whitney's phone rang.

'Walker.'

'It's Matt. I'm at your house, but there's no one here.'

'What? Are you sure?' She frowned. Where the hell could Tiffany be?

'I rang the bell several times and peered through the window, but the place seems deserted.'

'Thanks, Matt. Leave it with me.' She ended the call. 'Damn.'

'What's wrong?'

'It's Tiffany. She wasn't at home when Matt went. Give me a second. I'm going to call her.'

'No problem.'

She keyed in the shortcut, shifting from foot to foot, unable to keep still.

'Mum?' Tiffany replied after several rings.

'Where are you? Matt Price has just been home to take you to uni.' She tried to hide her annoyance but wasn't very successful.

'I'm with Henry. We're going out for breakfast.'

'What about your class?'

'I didn't feel like going. Not after everything that's happened. Henry didn't want to go in either, so we're just going to hang out. Do you mind?'

'I wished you'd called me. You knew I was going to take you.' She glanced at George and rolled her eyes. 'It's up to you. Are you going in later?'

'I don't think so. I'll ask Henry to take me home, to save you.'

'Okay. As long as you're not going home on your own. I'll see you later.' She ended the call and shook her head.

'Is everything okay?'

'Tiffany decided not to go to uni today. She's with Henry. They're all still upset over Lydia, obviously. I understand; I just wished she'd phoned me, so I didn't worry after Matt found her missing.'

'The main thing is you know where she is.'

'True. Come on. Let's see Claire.'

She pushed open the double doors, and they went into the lab, heading to the back. Lydia Parker's body was on the table, and Claire was standing next to her, her hands on her hips.

'What have you got for us?' she asked, walking up to her.

'And good morning to you, too,' Claire said.

'Good morning.' George grinned.

'Having good manners never hurt anyone.' Claire arched an eyebrow.

'Point taken,' she said. 'What's this interesting evidence?'

'I've looked at all the evidence on the bodies and compared them. The rape. The ligature marks on the wrists and ankles. The drugging. The washing. Etc. Etc. But when we get to the strangulation, this body is different.'

Whitney and George peered at Lydia's body. 'What's different?' she asked.

'The bruising's the same,' George added.

'Is it?' Claire asked.

They looked intently again, and then exchanged a glance.

'Yes,' George said. 'Four finger marks on one side, and the thumb mark on the other.'

'Look again,' Claire persisted.

'Claire, stop with the playing around. We don't have time. Just tell us.' She shook her head in frustration.

'The bruising is reversed. This strangulation was carried out by a right-hander.'

They both stared at Claire.

'How can everything else be identical and this different?' she asked.

'Could the killer have hurt his hand and used his other one?' George suggested.

'Doubtful. Most people don't have the power in their non-dominant hand. Strangulation with a single hand requires considerable strength,' Claire replied.

'So where does that leave us?' she asked. 'We're looking

for a very strong, ambidextrous man. It's not doing it for me.'

They were losing valuable time.

She paced the floor, staring at the body as she walked past. What was it telling her? 'Do you think there were two men?'

'There's no evidence of a second person being involved,' Claire said. 'If there was, I'd expect to see slight differences. Like the vaginal bruising, for example, is the same. The ties have been put on in exactly the same way.'

'What if they both had their roles, only this time the man who usually did the strangulation couldn't, so the other person had to? Then everything else would still be the same,' George said.

'And if there were two of them, carrying the bodies wouldn't have been an issue.' Whitney nodded in agreement.

'Then again, if we had two men abducting a young woman, surely there would've been more of a struggle? We've assumed the victims knew their attacker because there was no indication of a struggle. But even so. Two guys with one girl. It should've rung warning bells. Especially after the first murder and the police warnings to women,' George said.

'Unless the second man came after the first had drugged them,' Whitney said.

'True,' Claire agreed.

'Shit,' George muttered.

Whitney came to an abrupt halt and stared at George. 'What?'

'Shit. No,' George repeated, her face drained of colour.

'What the fuck are you talking about?' Whitney demanded.

'What if the two people aren't both male? What if one is female? No warning bells, then.'

'How likely is that?' she asked.

'You'd be surprised. There are many instances of husbands and wives who murder together. But that's not what I'm thinking. One man. One woman. Both closer than husband and wife even. Both loved and trusted by everyone who knows them—'

Whitney's hand slapped across her mouth as the realisation hit. 'The twins. No, it can't be. Tiffany's with Henry now. I've just spoken to her.' She grabbed her phone from her pocket, her fingers trembling as she called. 'Answer, damn you. Answer.' She let out a relieved sigh when it clicked. 'Tiffany, it's Mu—'

'Can't speak. Leave a message,' Tiffany's voice sung out.

'Tiffany, it's Mum. Call me.' She ended the call and immediately tried again. But it went straight to voicemail.

Were they jumping to conclusions? It seemed a bit of a leap to go from possibly two people to it being the twins. Except it all fitted. The party. The victims knowing their abductor. Giving each other alibis.

Fuck.

This couldn't be happening. It had to be a mistake. Henry could be the murderer, and he'd got Tiffany.

She started as George tapped her on the arm. 'Come on. Let's go to the twins' house. We'll get there before they can do anything to Tiffany. We've got a head start. They're totally unaware we've made the connection. Trust me. It will be okay.'

Chapter Thirty-Nine

Whitney put her foot down and got to the twins' house in record time. She was lucky they hadn't crashed. There had been a couple of near misses. George had been continually calling Tiffany on Whitney's phone, but every time it went to voicemail.

Why hadn't she known Tiffany was in danger?

She was her mother.

Mothers are meant to sense those things.

Her stomach cramped. She'd die if anything happened to Tiffany. She'd never forgive herself. She'd … Tears welled in her eyes, and she brushed them away with the back of her hand. How could they all have been taken in by the twins? She usually had a nose for bullshit, but not this time. They'd conned everyone. No one had a bad word to say about them. They were fun to be with, great friends to everyone, and popular.

She brought the car to a screeching halt outside the house, and they both leapt out. She got to the front door first and banged hard.

'Answer the fucking door,' she yelled.

George peered into the front window. 'No one in the living room. Shall I go around the back? There's probably an alley in Billington Road.'

'We'll stay together. I'll come with you.'

They raced around the corner and into the alleyway. When they got to the twins' house, she opened the gate, and they ran through the overgrown garden to the kitchen door.

She tried the door and it was locked. Grabbing a stone, she went to break the glass.

'Wait. There might be a key out here somewhere.' George moved a couple of the flower pots, but there was nothing there.

Crap. George was right. The broken glass would warn them. She had to get it together. It was Tiffany in there, and she could be hurting. But she couldn't save her unless she acted rationally. She scanned her surroundings and spotted a garden gnome about three feet away. Underneath was the key. 'Got it.' She hastily put it into the lock and turned it. As the door opened, she ran in. It was silent downstairs. She put her fingers to her lips and stealthily crept up the stairs with George behind.

The first door they came to was Lydia's bedroom. Whitney pushed it open, but it was empty. The bathroom came next and that was empty, too. As were the other two rooms.

'They're not here,' George said.

Whitney sat on the end of the bed, her head in her hands. Where was Tiffany? Why wasn't she answering? She mentally shook herself. This wasn't helping. 'This looks like Henry's bedroom. We need to search it.'

'Did Tiffany say they were going to come back here?'

'No. All she said was they were going out for breakfast.' Was she overreacting? Had they got it wrong?

Could Tiffany be perfectly okay, just out in a café somewhere?

She looked through some of Henry's possessions. 'You know, this doesn't look like the bed used in the photos. This is a slat bed with no headboard, but in the photos the bed had one. The victims were on the same bed. We could've got this all wrong.'

'Maybe.'

Her attention was diverted by a small notebook beside the bed. She opened it and read. *Millie Carter. Jelly, ice cream, sprinkles. Drinks cider. Likes small men. Party girl. Olivia Griffin. Pizza. Whore.* She scanned the rest, and bile shot into her mouth as she read Tiffany's name. 'No.' The notebook fell from her hand, banging on the wooden floor.

'What is it?' George rushed over.

She took hold of the notebook, and shoved it in front of George. 'Look.'

George's eyes widened as she read down the list of entries.

'Fuck. That's confirmed it.'

She gasped for breath, and her legs gave way. George caught her. She needed air. She had to get out of there. But she couldn't give in. Tiffany's life depended on it. She pulled out an evidence bag from her pocket and held it out for George to drop the notebook in.

'What now?' George asked.

'Back to the incident room. We need to find out where they could be. Where the actual murders took place. I'll place some officers close by, in case they come back here first.'

She forced to the back of her mind any thoughts about what was happening to Tiffany. For the first time in her life, she needed to park her emotions and allow logic to help. She could breakdown after they'd found Tiffany. Because they'd find her alive. They had to. Anything else was out of the question.

~

'Listen up, everyone,' Whitney shouted once they were back in the incident room. 'We have our man. Actually, it's a team. The twins, Henry and Harriet Spencer. They have their fifth victim, but we don't know where they are. We have to find them. And find them fast.'

'Do we know who the fifth victim is?' one of the team called out.

Whitney glanced at George, her face falling.

'It's Tiffany Walker,' George said.

Silence fell over the whole room, the collective shock palpable.

'But remember, we have the advantage here. They have no idea we suspect them. The last time Whitney spoke to Tiffany, they were going out for breakfast,' she added.

'Thanks, George. I'm okay to continue,' Whitney said with determination.

'Sure.'

'We've been to their house and it's empty. I've found some evidence linking Henry to the murders, so he's definitely our man. And his sister, Harriet, is his accomplice.'

'What evidence, guv?' Matt asked.

'A notebook detailing the young women and information about each of them. Millie's love of jelly and ice cream. Olivia being an escort. Tiffany …' Whitney's voice cracked, and George rushed to her side.

'It was mainly their likes and dislikes. What they wear. Where they go,' she said, finishing off.

Whitney flashed her a thankful look.

'What do you want us to do?' Frank asked.

Whitney visibly pulled herself together, drawing in a long breath. 'We need officers out of sight, close to the house, in case they go back there. We don't believe the murders took place there, as all the beds are different from the one in the photos.'

'I'll take lookout on the house and get someone from uniform to come with me. In plain clothes, so we won't be spotted. We'll get the fuckers. I promise.'

'Thanks, Frank.'

'Ellie. I want you to run background checks on the twins. Anything you can find out about them, going right back to them as children. There must be a clue in there somewhere. We're going to find the bastards before they can lay a finger on my daughter.' Her voice cracked again, and she coughed to hide it.

'I'll go over everything we have so far, and look for anything that might help,' George said.

'Good idea. I'm going to see the DSI. Fill him in on where we are. We'll need more officers on-board.'

'I don't think it's a good idea, guv,' Matt said.

'Why?' Whitney asked.

'As soon as he knows the killer has Tiffany, he'll make you to stand down. You know that.'

Whitney shook her head. 'You're right. I didn't think it through. Matt, you liaise with uniform. We need officers on the lookout everywhere.'

'I'm onto it.'

'Okay. Everyone go. Check in regularly.'

The team left the incident room, leaving Whitney, George, and Ellie. Ellie sat at her computer, and Whitney and George stared at the board.

'What if we can't find Tiffany until it's too late?' Whitney asked.

'Not going to happen. We'll find her. We're not some amateur sleuths. We have the knowledge and experience.'

'You're right. Thanks.'

'Okay. First, we need to go through the board together. It's going to make a big difference now we know who the killers are,' she said.

She peered at the board, chewing on her bottom lip. 'Okay. Come on tell me something.' The faces of five girls stared back at her. Aside from all being students, there was no similarity in terms of looks or subjects they took. They were all in Godwin College. The same as the twins. Why? What was significant about Godwin?

'Ellie, in your research into the twins, please will you look to see if Godwin College figures somewhere.'

'No problem,' Ellie replied.

'You think Godwin has something to do with it?' Whitney asked.

'I'm not sure. It's interesting all the victims were from there. The twins, too. It's not like they didn't have friends outside of Godwin. So, why only choose victims from there? It might tell us something.'

'Okay.'

'Guv,' Ellie called out. 'I've found something on Henry Spencer you'll want to know.'

Whitney and George hurried over to Ellie.

'What is it?' Whitney said.

'Ten years ago, he was admitted into St Peter's mental institution. His parents had him committed. He had a breakdown. He was in there for six months before being allowed home.'

'Do we know what caused the breakdown?' she asked.

'I can't get into his records.'

'Do you have the name of the doctor who signed him off?' Whitney asked.

'Yes. A psychiatrist called Joel Martin. I've got his number. Shall I contact him?'

'No. I'll do it. It's better coming from one professional to another,' she said.

'Agreed. You carry on with your research into Godwin,' Whitney said.

George phoned Martin, but he was out of the office, so she left a message with his assistant.

As Whitney was engrossed in a conversation with Ellie, she went back to scrutinising the board.

Four photos of four girls tied up on the bed. All identical. Except—she got up close to the one of Lydia. It was taken from a slightly different angle. They hadn't noticed it before, mainly because it hadn't appeared different, and they hadn't looked in such detail. She leaned in. The bottom of the window was on show. In the corner was a tiny sticker.

'Ellie. Do you have copies of the photos from the victims' phones?'

'Yes.'

'Do me a favour and pull up the one of Lydia Parker and enlarge it, please. There's something I want to check out.'

She headed over to Ellie's desk and looked at the screen at the enlarged photo.

'What do you want to look at?' Ellie asked.

'See here.' She pointed to the sticker in the corner of the window. 'This photo was taken at a different angle from the others. We can see the corner of the window and this sticker. What does it say? Can you enlarge it a little more?'

'Yes.' Ellie magnified it.

They both peered at it. It was a no smoking sticker and below it said Lenchester University.

'This was taken in university accommodation.' She glanced over to Whitney, who'd just ended her call. 'Whitney, quick. Over here.'

Whitney ran over. 'What?'

'Look.' She pointed at the photo. 'See that sticker in the corner? It's from the university. They're keeping their victims in a house or flat belonging to the uni.'

Whitney stared open-mouthed at her and then enveloped her in a huge hug. 'Thank you. Thank you. Ellie, get into the university accommodation database and find out if any of their flats or houses are rented out to one of the twins.'

'Sorry, guv. I don't have access to it. It's separate from the student database we had access to when we had Kevin Vaughan in custody.'

'Give me a second, and I'll see what I can do,' George said, remembering one of her mature students worked part-time in the accommodation office.

She phoned the university.

'Please may I speak to Mary Goff?'

'It's Mary speaking.'

'It's George. Dr Cavendish.'

'Hello, Dr Cavendish. How can I help?'

'I don't want to get you into trouble, but I'm working with the police on an important investigation, and we urgently need some information.'

'Is it the campus murder case?'

She glanced at Whitney, who was moving from foot to foot, her hands twitching. Strictly speaking, she shouldn't say anything, but this was different. 'Confidentially, yes.'

'I won't say anything,' Mary said. 'What information do you need?'

'Please can you tell me if either Henry or Harriet Spencer rent any university accommodation?'

'No problem. It won't take long.'

'She's looking,' George mouthed to Whitney.

'Thanks,' Whitney replied.

They stood in silence, waiting for Mary to complete her search. It seemed like forever, but it was probably only a few minutes.

'Got it,' Mary said. 'There's a house in Harriet Spencer's name in Dorchester Street. Number sixty-six.'

'Thanks, Mary. I owe you one,' George said.

'Glad to be of help. See you next week in class.'

George ended the call.

'Right,' Whitney said. 'George, come with me. Ellie, call Matt and Frank. Tell them the address. We'll meet them there. No sirens. We can't afford to warn them.'

'Yes, guv. Do you want me there, too?' Ellie said.

'No. I want you to call Jamieson and explain the killers have Tiffany and ask for back-up.'

'Me?' Ellie grimaced.

'I know it should be me, but I have to get to Tiffany. Please do this,' Whitney implored, tears in her eyes, which she brushed away.

George's eyes prickled, too, and she blinked until they were gone.

'No problem. I'm onto it. Good luck, guv,' Ellie said.

'Come on, Whitney,' George said. 'We've got them. Tiffany will be back with you in no time.'

Chapter Forty

This is going to be our last murder. For now. And we're planning to go out with a bang. A huge bang. What better than to take the most treasured possession from the women trying to ruin our lives? DCI Walker will never be the same again after her daughter draws her last breath. The pain from her loss will stay with her for the rest of her life. Not only that, Walker will remember us for ever.

Infamy can never be overrated.

Sadly, we won't be playing around with Tiffany for as long as we'd like. As long as we did with the others. Making them think we were all having fun together. And the less fun it was for them, the more it was for us.

But not this time. We can't afford the risk. We did take Tiffany out for breakfast, though, and insist she had her favourite. Eggs Benedict. See, we're not all bad. We make sure our victims have something good to remember. And what better than food? The staff of life, as the Bible says.

We're having fun listening to all the messages Walker's leaving for her daughter. I thought about texting as Tiffany, so Walker thinks she's okay. But where's the fun in that? I'd rather the pain started now and not when the body's found.

Right now, we've brought Tiffany to our house. Not the one the police know about. We're not that stupid. This bolthole is our little secret. Tiffany's in the living room at the moment, totally unaware of what's about to happen to her. She's feeling honoured we trusted her with our secret. Because we don't tell anyone. You should've seen her excitement at the thought she was so special. For all I know, she's already seeing us having a long-term relationship.

Of course, that's never going to happen. I don't even like her. She's way too immature and giggles all the time. But I like her enough to murder. As I've already told you, there's a reason behind every murder, mostly to do with the girls themselves. I say mostly, because this one is about her bitch of a mother.

In an ideal world, we should've gone for the mother. But it really wasn't practical. Not to mention the others were all students, and I like things ordered. A police officer among several students wouldn't work. It's much better knowing she'll be blaming herself for her daughter's death. And we'll make sure she knows it's totally her fault.

After we're done with Tiffany, we're planning to go overseas for a while. We'll disappear to somewhere remote, where we'll never be found. We'll set ourselves up as vets. We've just got to get away before the body's found, because they'll close the airports and stations. The plan is to head for France on the train, and from there take a flight somewhere.

Anyway, I don't have time to sit ruminating over the future. I've a job to do. At least we have the whole day. Tiffany isn't expected home until later this afternoon. That gives us enough time. It's frustrating it's not me actually strangling because of my arm. But that's the only thing I can't do. The sex will be great.

Chapter Forty-One

'Get out the fucking way,' Whitney shouted, glaring angrily out of the windscreen. 'Look at the idiots in front of us. Can't they hear the siren? Or see the blue light?' Her hands tightened over the steering wheel. 'About fucking time,' she yelled as she skirted around the red Mini which had finally pulled to the side to let them past.

'Take some deep breaths. You can't let this get to you.'

George was sitting next to her, acting all calm and relaxed. How could she be like that, when so much was at stake?

'Of course it's getting to me. This is my daughter we're talking about. We have to get there before …' Her voice faded as bruised, strangled bodies of the other victims flashed across her eyes. Thoughts of what could be happening to Tiffany penetrated her brain. Was she already tied up? Had they stripped her? She shook her head to shut down her thoughts. She had to keep it together.

'Look. They have no idea we're on to them. We know

from the other victims they don't murder them instantly. We will get to Tiffany before they can do anything to her.'

'What about the rape? What if we're too late to stop that from happening?'

She'd fucking kill the bastard if he laid one finger on her. And his bitch of a sister. Whatever the consequences.

'Think logically. Tiffany told you they were going out for breakfast. That would have taken a while, so even if they're already back at the twins' house they wouldn't have had time to rape her. They have a ritual to follow—it's how this works. Beginning with giving Tiffany her favourite food. They build up to the restraining and then the sexual assault. We'll be there in time.'

Her jaw lost a little of its tension. 'I hope you're right.'

'I am.' George gave a sharp nod of her head. 'Does Tiffany usually eat breakfast?'

'Yes. It's her favourite meal. I don't know how she does it. All I can bear first thing in the morning is coffee. If she's got an early start at uni, she'll have cereal and toast. At weekends, she loves a fry up.' And usually she left the pans for Whitney to do. But at that precise moment, she'd kill for Tiffany to leave a sink full of pots and pans.

'There's every chance she's not even back at Harriet's house yet, in which case we can wait for them.'

Her breathing slowed down as George's calm words soothed her. The doctor was right. There was a good chance they'd beat them back there. She gave her a grateful nod and tightened her fingers around the steering wheel.

'Dorchester Road is second on the left,' she said, looking at the GPS. 'Sixty-six is halfway up on the right.'

She switched off the siren and turned into the street, driving past sixty-six and parking on the left. The street was deserted, and there was no discernible movement at Harriet's place.

'Come on.' She released her seatbelt. 'Let's go.'

'Shouldn't we wait for the others?'

She glanced towards the house and then at George. She was right. It wasn't wise for the two of them to go alone. Not to mention, taking in a civilian went against all the regulations. And even if she did let George come with, it would be two against two. The twins weren't small and could easily fight back. She looked at her watch. 'We'll give them five, and then we're going in. I can't leave Tiffany any longer.'

'We need more of us to take them down. I know we have the element of surprise, but that might not be enough. Especially as I don't know what to do in these situations.' George's jaw was tense.

'You're forgetting I have this.' She patted her Taser. And if she got within spitting distance of either of the twins, she'd fry their fucking brains.

'What if they try to escape? What help will I be, other than being able to use my height and body weight?'

'That will be enough. We'll be fine going in there together.' She was unable to push aside the thoughts it wasn't right. She shouldn't be putting George at risk. That wasn't part of her job.

She'd go in alone.

'Okay, bu—' George paused, and she saw Matt's car had pulled up on the opposite side of the road.

She pressed her radio. 'Walker here. Who's with you?'

'I'm with Frank,' Matt replied.

'They know me, so I don't want to be seen before we enter the premises. I want you to go around the back. There's bound to be an alley leading to their house. Check it's all clear and leave Frank on guard. Then come back and we'll go in together.' She turned to George. 'You can stay in the car.'

'No. I'm going in with you. You and Matt can deal with Henry and Harriet, and I'll take care of Tiffany.'

All she wanted to do was gather Tiffany in her arms and take her away from there. But she had her job to do. She had to trust George.

'Okay. But make sure you keep well back. Leave the heavy stuff to us.'

Matt and Frank got out of their car and walked briskly to the turning off Dorchester Road and then down to where the alley ran behind the row of houses. They stayed put. After a couple of minutes, Matt reappeared. He looked across at them and nodded.

'Right. Let's go.' She jumped out of the car.

They hurried across the road, careful to keep out of sight. Matt was waiting for them outside number sixty.

'How do you want to play this?' he asked.

'If the door's locked, we'll break in. Then we'll search the house room by room.'

They ran along the pavement and up the short path leading to the door of the terraced house. When they got there, she pushed the door, but it was locked. She used her elbow to break the pane of glass in the door and then put her hand in and opened it. She held her finger up to her lips while they listened.

They crept in. The place was silent. Stealthily, they went into the living room. She let out a small gasp and pointed to the sofa. 'Tiffany's bag,' she whispered. 'They're here somewhere.'

After finding the kitchen empty, they headed up the stairs. They could hear low voices coming from the room at the far end of the hall. She took out her Taser and led, with Matt going second and George behind.

She swallowed hard as she pressed down on the handle and pushed open the door. 'Police. Stop what you're doing. Hands up,' she shouted as they all piled into the room.

Oh, God. She was going to be sick.

The room was chaos. Tiffany was stripped to her underwear, spread-eagled, her wrists and ankles tied to the bed. Her head lolled to one side and her eyes were glazed. Henry was holding up his phone, videoing, and Harriet stood over Tiffany, a beer bottle in her hand. Horror gave way to rage. She could only imagine what was going to be done with the bottle, if they hadn't got there in time.

Henry turned his phone towards Whitney, his top lip turned up in a sneer. 'Smile for the camera.'

'One more warning,' she snarled. 'Hands up.' She turned as George rushed over to Tiffany.

Henry shrugged and raised his hands. She holstered the Taser and twisted the arm without the plaster cast behind his back, taking hold of the other and cuffing him.

'You too,' Matt said to Harriet, swiftly taking the bottle and handcuffing her. He pulled out his radio. 'Assistance required at sixty-six Dorchester Road. Two suspects in custody. Ambulance required.'

'They're already on their way,' an officer replied.

'Frank, in here,' Matt said into his radio.

'Coming,' he replied.

'It's okay,' George said softly, but loud enough for Whitney to hear. 'It's over.'

She wasn't sure if Tiffany understood.

'Scissors. I need scissors,' George shouted, pulling on the ties around Tiffany's wrists and ankles.

Matt passed her his Swiss army knife, and George cut through the ties, sweeping Tiffany into her arms. She took off her coat and put it around her. 'Where the hell are her clothes?'

Tiffany didn't speak. She was just lying all floppy in George's arms.

Nausea caught in Whitney's throat. She swallowed hard and turned back to the twins, her voice like iron.

'Henry Spencer and Harriet Spencer, I'm arresting you both on suspicion of the murders of Millie Carter, Olivia Griffin, Polly Brooks, and Lydia Parker. Also, the abduction and sexual assault on Tiffany Walker. You do not have to say anything, but it may harm your defence if you do not mention something which you later rely on in court. Anything you do say may be given in evidence. Do you understand?'

Henry looked at her. 'You spoiled my game. If only you'd arrived ten minutes later, it would have been so much more fun.'

Before she could stop herself, she slapped him hard across the face, leaving finger mark indentations in his cheeks and her palm stinging. He reeled backwards.

'Guv,' Matt warned.

'I know.'

'You'll regret that,' Henry snarled.

'Do your worst,' she said, finally able to run to the bed and scoop up Tiffany in her arms. Her daughter's body was limp, but her eyes fluttered, and she let out a soft groan of recognition as her arm snaked around Whitney's neck.

'I'll find her clothes.' George stood up and looked around the bedroom, which was bare, apart from the bed.

Frank came bounding up the stairs and into the bedroom.

'Keep your eyes on her,' Whitney said, nodding at Harriet. 'Matt, keep hold of him.'

'Guv.'

As George left the room, she heard the sound of officers coming up the stairs.

'In here,' she yelled.

The officers burst in.

'Take them away.'

She released a sigh of relief as they escorted the twins out of there.

George came back through the door. 'Are these Tiffany's?'

She nodded and took them from George. They should've gone into an evidence bag. Proper police procedure. But she didn't care. Being a parent came first.

She removed the coat George had rested over Tiffany and carefully dressed her daughter, like she'd done so many times over the years. Her hands shook.

Just as she'd finished, two paramedics came into the room. 'We'll take it from here,' one of them said to her. 'We need to get her to hospital.'

She glanced down at her daughter, who had her eyes closed and was breathing deeply. 'I'm coming with you.'

'Before you go, I'd like you to take a look at the other bedroom. It won't take a minute,' George said.

'Okay.' She followed her into the bedroom down the hall.

As she stepped in, an agonising groan escaped her lips. On one of the walls was a huge mural of photos. She moved closer. It comprised all the victims.

Millie.

Olivia.

Poppy.

Lydia.

A pictorial view of their crimes. The three of them together, eating, smiling, and having fun. Then, the victim passed out. Next, Harriet stripping them and shots of her tying them up. The rape followed. Then the strangulation. Henry's hands around the first three, and Harriet's around the last. All the time smiling for the camera. Finally, shots of each girl lying where they'd dumped the body.

The nausea threated to rise again. What sort of monsters could do that?

'What the fuck?' She shuddered at the grotesqueness of it all.

'I know,' George said.

George rested her arm around her shoulders. 'We've got them. It's over. They can't harm anyone else. Tiffany's going to be okay. We got to her before they could do their worst.'

She looked at George. 'Thanks to you.'

She'd be indebted to George for the rest of her life. And if there was any way she could repay her for what she'd done, she would. No questions asked.

'You'd have worked it out.'

Would she? Maybe. But what if she hadn't worked it out in time?

'But I didn't. You did. I'll never forget. Never.'

George squeezed her shoulders. 'I'm glad it all worked out.' The paramedics walked past the door with Tiffany on a stretcher. 'Off you go. We'll catch up later.'

Chapter Forty-Two

'We're pleased to announce we have charged two people with the murders of Millie Carter, Olivia Griffin, Poppy Brooks, and Lydia Parker. They are also charged with the abduction and attempted murder of a fifth female.' Detective Superintendent Jamieson beamed at the reporters.

'Who are the people under arrest?' a reporter asked.

'Their names aren't being released at the moment. All I can say is they're related to each other, and we're not looking for anyone else in respect of the crimes.'

'Do they come from Lenchester?' another reporter asked.

'No, they don't. They're students at the university.'

A collective gasp came from the audience, and Whitney shook her head. What was it with people they thought serial killers couldn't be educated? Had they totally forgotten about Dr Harold Shipman, the worst serial killer the UK had ever known? Or was it because they were young? But there have been younger.

'What's the name of the fifth female, and how did she escape?' shouted a voice from the crowd.

She nudged Jamieson, shaking her head. She didn't think he'd actually name Tiffany, but she wanted to make sure.

'We're not releasing the name of the fifth female. She was rescued thanks to the excellent work of DCI Walker and her team.' He turned to her and smiled.

She almost started to warm towards him, until realising it was all for show. They hadn't actually sat down and talked through her behaviour, and she expected that wouldn't be so friendly.

'Superintendent—' came another voice.

'That's all. Thank you for coming. We'll update you once we have anything further to say.'

Jamieson stood and gestured for Whitney to do the same. She followed him out of the room.

'Let's go to my office,' he said.

Her heart sank. Traffic duty? A desk job? What was he going to find for her to do? Or maybe he'd let her stay with her team, seeing as she'd actually solved the crime. But he was such a stickler to the rules, he'd be more concerned with her going directly against his orders than any outcome.

They walked in silence until reaching his office. Once inside, he gestured for her to sit down.

'Sir. I know what you're going to say. That I kept on investigating, but I couldn't sit by and let those monste—'

Jamieson held up his hand to silence her. 'Walker. Whitney. You disobeyed my orders and continued investigating. Under normal circumstances it would warrant disciplinary action. But I understand. You also continued working the case when it was discovered your daughter had been abducted by the killers, whereas you should have come to me. I suspect you didn't because you knew I'd immediately take you off it.'

'Yes, bu—'

'Please let me finish. You have this infuriating habit of jumping in with two feet. Just let me say what I have to say. I will then give you the opportunity to reply. Understood?'

'Sir.' She clenched her teeth together to stop from saying anything else.

Talk about prolonging the inevitable. She was sure he was enjoying every minute of what he was doing to her.

'As I was saying. You should have come to me. But I accept you acted on the spur of the moment, and any delay could have resulted in something more disastrous.'

'Tiffany's murder,' she said, unable to stop herself from saying it.

'Agreed. So, under the circumstances, the incident rests here. I won't be taking it any further.'

Her jaw dropped. 'Thank you, sir.'

'And now we've got that out the way, I want to congratulate you for a job well done. We've not only got the killers in custody, our public profile has increased a hundredfold.'

'Thank you, sir. We wouldn't have cracked the case so soon if it hadn't been for Dr Cavendish, the forensic psychologist from Lenchester University. She was the one who made the connection after we'd received evidence from pathology.'

'It's good of you to give Dr Cavendish the credit.'

'I always give credit where it's due.' *Unlike you.* She immediately regretted the thought. He was being nice, so she should return the favour. 'Dr Cavendish worked with us for free. But I was wondering whether you could put some money in the budget for us to use her in the future, when we have cases needing her input?'

It was ironic. Before the murders, she'd have rather walked over hot coals than have someone like George involved. But now … well …

'I don't see why not. Yes. We'll budget for outside help, when required. I'd like to meet her.'

'Thank you.' She refrained from punching the air. She'd gone into his office believing her career would be taking a nose dive, and this was the outcome.

He hadn't even mentioned the missing informant, who she'd now got her team looking for. She hoped they'd find him soon, so she could go back to Jamieson before he remembered about it and hauled her over the coals again.

'Congratulate your team for me. Good work.' He looked down at some papers on his desk, which Whitney took to mean she'd been dismissed.

Chapter Forty-Three

The pub was busy when George arrived. Out the corner of her eye, she saw an arm waving. It was Whitney, and she pushed her way through the crowd of people to where she was sitting at a round table near the open fire. It was the first time they'd met since two weeks ago when they'd rescued Tiffany. She hadn't wanted to get in touch, in case Whitney was busy. She also had work to catch up on.

'Hello.' Whitney stood as she got to the table.

'Hi.' It was really awkward. Should they shake hands, hug, or do nothing? She always struggled with these sorts of social interactions.

But she needn't have worried, because Whitney pulled her into a big hug.

'I got you a beer,' Whitney said once she'd let her go. 'Is that okay?'

'Perfect,' she replied as she sat down. 'How's Tiffany? I wanted to call but know how busy you are finishing off the case.' It sounded a lame excuse. She should have made the first move.

'She's doing well, thanks. I've arranged for her to see a

counsellor, and she's not going back to uni until next term. She's been given extensions on all her assignments.'

'With you there to support her, I'm sure she'll make a full recovery.'

'I hope you're right.' An uneasy expression crossed Whitney's face.

'It'll take time. But she'll be fine.' She realised reassurance was exactly what Whitney needed at the moment.

'I still can't thank you enough for what you've done.'

'It was a team effort.'

'Maybe, but you sussed out the link with the twins.'

'A classic folie à deux situation,' she mused.

'What the fuck's that?'

'It means madness of two. It's where two people share the same psychosis. They're both deluded. Often these delusions are harmless. Unfortunately, in the twins' case they were damaging. Think Fred and Rose West, from years ago. A classic case.'

'But what made the twins like that?'

'No one can be one hundred per cent certain, but it likely stemmed from their early childhood. What have you found out about it?'

'Their father's a captain in the navy, and they both went to boarding school. About ten years ago, there was a complaint against the father for beating up his wife, but the charges were dropped. It was around the time Henry had a breakdown. We also found out their mother had been to Lenchester University and was in Godwin College.'

'Hmmm. So, there's our link to Godwin. And also, the water link. Interesting. My guess is if the father abused their mother, he might have abused them, too. Or possibly they'd tried to stop him but couldn't. They felt helpless because they had no control over the situation. Hence their need to control the victims.'

'Why Godwin, if it was the college their mum went to?' Whitney frowned.

'Obviously we can't know for sure, but they might have felt resentment towards their mum, too, for not being able to stand up for herself or them. Parents are there to protect, and from the twins' standpoint neither parent lived up to that expectation. We might never understand their true motivation. What have they said during the interviews?'

'Nothing. Literally nothing. They don't even say "no comment" when we ask them questions. They've both totally switched off. We've kept them apart, but it's like there's some sort of mental telepathy between them because they're acting identically.'

'It's not uncommon for twins to have that link. Though usually it's identical twins. Not fraternal twins, which they are.'

'I'm concerned their lawyer will claim diminished responsibility. The CPS is seeking a psychiatric evaluation, so let's hope it comes back in our favour,' Whitney said.

'Don't worry. They'll get to the truth.' She took a sip of her beer.

She should find out the name of the psychiatrist and give her take on the twins. They knew exactly what they were doing and deserved to be incarcerated in a prison, not a mental institution. She'd also be interested in finding out who took which role in the abductions and murders. On the face of it, it appeared Henry took the lead, including the strangulation. Until he broke his arm, then they swapped.

'Yes. I'll have to trust they know what they're doing. I'm getting good at that.' Whitney laughed.

'What do you mean?'

'I trust you now, and in case you didn't notice, I didn't initially.'

She remembered Whitney's manner when they'd first met. But things had changed so much she hardly thought about it now.

'Yes, I noticed. You were infuriating. But it's all forgotten.'

Whitney was totally different from any friends she'd had in the past. She was way too emotionally driven, which made her uncomfortable. But maybe she'd be good for her. If Stephen was right about her being cold, which she wasn't admitting he was, then hanging out with someone like Whitney, who didn't pull back on showing her feelings, might be a good thing. Then again, when would they be together? Their careers were all consuming, not leaving a lot of time for a social life. Plus, Whitney had Tiffany and the rest of her family to consider. Envy washed over her.

'I've got something to ask you.' Whitney cut across her thoughts.

'Yes?'

'My Super has agreed to budget for a forensic psychologist to work with us on future cases. What do you say? Will you?'

She'd been thinking something was missing from her life. At first, she'd wondered if it was Stephen, but seeing him at uni made her realise it wasn't. They were speaking now, just about civilly, and he'd already found himself another girlfriend. She, on the other hand, had no desire to become involved in another relationship. Involvement in further criminal cases, however, appealed greatly.

'I'd love to.'

'The Super wants to meet you. Are you free tomorrow?'

'Sure, I can come in. Will we meet him together?'

'Yes, but let me do all the talking.'

Would you like to find out what happened to the twins and see how Tiffany and Whitney are coping after their ordeal? I have written an epilogue which is set 18 months later when they go to court.
You can read this for free by signing up for my newsletter here

Book 2 - George and Whitney return in ***Fatal Justice***, to face a string of mutilated bodies. But will they be able to save the next victim from a gruesome death?
Tap here to get book 2 now

DEADLY GAMES - Cavendish & Walker Book 1

A killer is playing cat and mouse....... and winning.

DCI Whitney Walker wants to save her career. Forensic psychologist, Dr Georgina Cavendish, wants to avenge the death of her student.

Sparks fly when real world policing meets academic theory, and it's not a pretty sight.

When two more bodies are discovered, Walker and Cavendish form an uneasy alliance. But are they in time to save the next victim?

Deadly Games is the first book in the Cavendish and Walker crime fiction series. If you like serial killer thrillers and psychological intrigue, then you'll love Sally Rigby's page-turning book.

Pick up *Deadly Games* today to read Cavendish & Walker's first case.

FATAL JUSTICE - Cavendish & Walker Book 2

A vigilante's on the loose, dishing out their kind of justice...

A string of mutilated bodies sees Detective Chief Inspector Whitney Walker back in action. But when she discovers the victims have all been grooming young girls, she fears a vigilante is on the loose. And while she understands the motive, no one is above the law.

Once again, she turns to forensic psychologist, Dr Georgina Cavendish, to unravel the cryptic clues. But will they be able to save the next victim from a gruesome death?

Fatal Justice is the second book in the Cavendish & Walker crime fiction series. If you like your mysteries dark, and with a twist, pick up a copy of Sally Rigby's book today.

DEATH TRACK - Cavendish & Walker Book 3

Catch the train if you dare...

After a teenage boy is found dead on a Lenchester train, Detective Chief Inspector Whitney Walker believes they're being targeted by the notorious Carriage Killer, who chooses a local rail network, commits four murders, and moves on.

Against her wishes, Walker's boss brings in officers from another force to help the investigation and prevent more deaths, but she's forced to defend her team against this outside interference.

Forensic psychologist, Dr Georgina Cavendish, is by her side in an attempt to bring to an end this killing spree. But how can they get into the mind of a killer who has already killed twelve times in two years without leaving a single clue behind?

For fans of Rachel Abbott, L J Ross and Angela Marsons, *Death Track* is the third in the Cavendish & Walker series. A gripping serial killer thriller that will have you hooked.

~

LETHAL SECRET - Cavendish & Walker Book 4

Someone has a secret. A secret worth killing for....

When a series of suicides, linked to the Wellness Spirit Centre, turn out to be murder, it brings together DCI Whitney Walker and forensic psychologist Dr Georgina Cavendish for another investigation. But as they delve deeper, they come across a tangle of secrets and the very real risk that the killer will strike again.

As the clock ticks down, the only way forward is to infiltrate the centre. But the outcome is disastrous, in more ways than one.

For fans of Angela Marsons, Rachel Abbott and M A Comley, *Lethal Secret* is the fourth book in the Cavendish & Walker crime fiction series.

~

LAST BREATH - Cavendish & Walker Book 5

Has the Lenchester Strangler returned?

When a murderer leaves a familiar pink scarf as his calling card, Detective Chief Inspector Whitney Walker is forced to dig into a cold case, not sure if she's looking for a killer or a copycat.

With a growing pile of bodies, and no clues, she turns to forensic psychologist, Dr Georgina Cavendish, despite their relationship being at an all-time low.

Can they overcome the bad blood between them to solve the

unsolvable?

For fans of Rachel Abbott, Angela Marsons and M A Comley, *Last Breath* is the fifth book in the Cavendish & Walker crime fiction series.

FINAL VERDICT - Cavendish & Walker Book 6

The judge has spoken......everyone must die.

When a killer starts murdering lawyers in a prestigious law firm, and every lead takes them to a dead end, DCI Whitney Walker finds herself grappling for a motive.

What links these deaths, and why use a lethal injection?

Alongside forensic psychologist, Dr Georgina Cavendish, they close in on the killer, while all the time trying to not let their personal lives get in the way of the investigation.

For fans of Rachel Abbott, Mark Dawson and M A Comley, Final Verdict is the sixth in the Cavendish & Walker series. A fast paced murder mystery which will keep you guessing.

RITUAL DEMISE - Cavendish & Walker Book 7

Someone is watching.... No one is safe

The once tranquil woods in a picturesque part of Lenchester have become the bloody stage to a series of ritualistic murders. With no suspects, Detective Chief Inspector Whitney Walker is once again forced to call on the services of forensic psychologist Dr Georgina Cavendish.

But this murderer isn't like any they've faced before. The murders are highly elaborate, but different in their own way and, with the clock ticking, they need to get inside the killer's head before it's too late.

For fans of Angela Marsons, Rachel Abbott and L J Ross. Ritual Demise is the seventh book in the Cavendish & Walker crime fiction series.

~

MORTAL REMAINS - Cavendish & Walker Book 8

Someone's playing with fire.... There's no escape.

A serial arsonist is on the loose and as the death toll continues to mount DCI Whitney Walker calls on forensic psychologist Dr Georgina Cavendish for help.

But Lenchester isn't the only thing burning. There are monumental changes taking place within the police force and there's a chance Whitney might lose the job she loves. She has to find the killer before that happens. Before any more lives are lost.

Mortal Remains is the eighth book in the acclaimed Cavendish & Walker series. Perfect for fans of Angela Marsons, Rachel Abbot and L J Ross.

~

SILENT GRAVES - Cavendish & Walker Book 9

Nothing remains buried forever...

When the bodies of two teenage girls are discovered on a building site, DCI Whitney Walker knows she's on the hunt for a killer. The problem is the murders happened in 1980 and this is her first case with the new team. What makes it even tougher is that with budgetary restrictions in place, she only has two weeks to solve it.

Once again, she enlists the help of forensic psychologist Dr Georgina Cavendish, but as she digs deeper into the past, she uncovers hidden truths that reverberate through the decades and into the present.

Silent Graves is the ninth book in the acclaimed Cavendish & Walker series. Perfect for fans of L J Ross, J M Dalgleish and Rachel Abbott.

∽

KILL SHOT - Cavendish & Walker Book 10

The game is over.....there's nowhere to hide.

When Lenchester's most famous sportsman is shot dead, DCI Whitney Walker and her team are thrown into the world of snooker.

She calls on forensic psychologist Dr Georgina Cavendish to assist, but the investigation takes them in a direction which has far-reaching, international ramifications.

Much to Whitney's annoyance, an officer from one of the Met's special squads is sent to assist.

But as everyone knows…three's a crowd.

Kill Shot is the tenth book in the acclaimed Cavendish & Walker series. Perfect for fans of Simon McCleave, J M Dalgleish, J R Ellis and Faith Martin.

～

DARK SECRETS - Cavendish & Walker Book 11

An uninvited guest…a deadly secret….and a terrible crime.

When a well-loved family of five are found dead sitting around their dining table with an untouched meal in front of them, it sends shockwaves throughout the community.

Was it a murder suicide, or was someone else involved?

It's one of DCI Whitney Walker's most baffling cases, and even with the help of forensic psychologist Dr Georgina Cavendish, they struggle to find any clues or motives to help them catch the killer.

But with a community in mourning and growing pressure to get answers, Cavendish and Walker are forced to go deeper into a murderer's mind than they've ever gone before.

Dark Secrets is the eleventh book in the Cavendish & Walker series. Perfect for fans of Angela Marsons, Joy Ellis and Rachel McLean.

～

BROKEN SCREAMS - Cavendish & Walker Book 12

Scream all you want, no one can hear you….

When an attempted murder is linked to a string of unsolved sexual attacks, Detective Chief Inspector Whitney Walker is incensed. All those women who still have sleepless nights because the man who terrorises their dreams is still on the loose.

Calling on forensic psychologist Dr Georgina Cavendish to help, they follow the clues and are alarmed to discover the victims all had one thing in common. Their birthdays were on the 29th February. The same date as a female officer on Whitney's team.

As the clock ticks down and they're no nearer to finding the truth, can they stop the villain before he makes sure his next victim will never scream again.

Broken Screams is the twelfth book in the acclaimed Cavendish & Walker series and is perfect for fans of Angela Marsons, Helen H Durrant and Rachel McClean.

Other books by Sally Rigby

WEB OF LIES: A Midlands Crime Thriller (Detective Sebastian Clifford - Book 1)

A trail of secrets. A dangerous discovery. A deadly turn.

Police officer Sebastian Clifford never planned on becoming a private investigator. But when a scandal leads to the disbandment of his London based special squad, he finds himself out of a job. That is, until his cousin calls on him to investigate her husband's high-profile death, and prove that it wasn't a suicide.

Clifford's reluctant to get involved, but the more he digs, the more evidence he finds. With his ability to remember everything he's ever seen, he's the perfect person to untangle the layers of deceit.

He meets Detective Constable Bird, an underutilised detective at Market Harborough's police force, who refuses to give him access to the records he's requested unless he allows her to help with the investigation. Clifford isn't thrilled. The last time he worked as part of a team it ended his career.

But with time running out, Clifford is out of options. Together they must wade through the web of lies in the hope that they'll find the truth before it kills them.

Web of Lies is the first in the new Detective Sebastian Clifford series. Perfect for readers of Joy Ellis, Robert Galbraith and Mark Dawson.

SPEAK NO EVIL: A Midlands Crime Thriller (Detective Sebastian Clifford - Book 2)

What happens when someone's too scared to speak?

Ex-police officer Sebastian Clifford had decided to limit his work as a private investigator, until Detective Constable Bird, aka Birdie, asks for his help.

Twelve months ago a young girl was abandoned on the streets of Market Harborough in shocking circumstances. Since then the child has barely spoken and with the police unable to trace her identity, they've given up.

The social services team in charge of the case worry that the child has an intellectual disability but Birdie and her aunt, who's fostering the little girl, disagree and believe she's gifted and intelligent, but something bad happened and she's living in constant fear.

Clifford trusts Birdie's instinct and together they work to find out who the girl is, so she can be freed from the past. But as secrets are uncovered, the pair realise it's not just the child who's in danger.

Speak No Evil is the second in the Detective Sebastian Clifford series. Perfect for readers of Faith Martin, Matt Brolly and Joy Ellis.

NEVER TOO LATE: A Midlands Crime Thriller (Detective Sebastian Clifford - Book 3)

A vicious attack. A dirty secret. And a chance for justice

Ex-police officer Sebastian Clifford is quickly finding that life as a private investigator is never quiet. His doors have only been open a few weeks when DCI Whitney Walker approaches him to investigate the brutal attack that left her older brother, Rob, with irreversible brain damage.

For twenty years Rob had no memory of that night, but lately things are coming back to him, and Whitney's worried that her brother might, once again, be in danger.

Clifford knows only too well what it's like be haunted by the past, and so he agrees to help. But the deeper he digs, the more secrets he uncovers, and soon he discovers that Rob's not the only one in danger.

Never Too Late is the third in the Detective Sebastian Clifford series, perfect for readers who love gripping crime fiction.

Writing as Amanda Rigby

Sally also writes psychological thrillers as **Amanda Rigby**, in collaboration with another author.

REMEMBER ME?: A brand new addictive psychological thriller that you won't be able to put down in 2021

A perfect life…

Paul Henderson leads a normal life. A deputy headteacher at a good school, a loving relationship with girlfriend Jenna, and a baby on the way. Everything *seems* perfect.

A shocking message…

Until Paul receives a message from his ex-fiance Nicole. Beautiful, ambitious and fierce, Nicole is everything Jenna is not. And now it seems Nicole is back, and she has a score to settle with Paul…

A deadly secret.

But Paul can't understand how Nicole is back. Because he's pretty sure he killed her with his own bare hands….

Which means, someone else knows the truth about what happened that night. And they'll stop at nothing to make Paul pay…

A brand new psychological thriller that will keep you guessing till the end! Perfect for fans of Sue Watson, Nina Manning, Shalini Boland

Acknowledgments

Thanks to my critique partners, Amanda Ashby and Christina Phillips, for your continued support and encouragement. Despite your cajoling, it took a long time for me to move into writing crime fiction, I wish I'd done it sooner.

I would also like to thank Emma Mitchell for being such an amazing editor, and continuing to help me with all the procedural stuff. I couldn't do it without you! Thanks, too, Amy Hart, for your brilliant and insightful proofreading.

Also, thanks to Stuart Bache for the incredible cover. You're a creative genius!

To my family: Garry, Alicia, and Marcus, thanks for all your support and contributions.

About the Author

Sally Rigby was born in Northampton, in the UK. She has always had the travel bug, and after living in both Manchester and London, eventually moved overseas. From 2001 she has lived with her family in New Zealand, which she considers to be the most beautiful place in the world. During this time she also lived for five years in Australia.

Sally has always loved crime fiction books, films and TV programmes, and has a particular fascination with the psychology of serial killers.

Sally loves to hear from her readers, so do feel free to get in touch via her website.

Printed in Great Britain
by Amazon